OBLIVION'S REACH

THE
BATTLE FOR
HUMANKIND
IS ON

MICHAEL STAFFORD
DON GLADDEN

Carpenter's Son Publishing

Copyright © 2021
by Michael Stafford
and Don Gladden

Published by Carpenter's Son Publishing,
Franklin, TN

First Edition

ISBN 978-1-952025-52-5

Produced and designed by
Koechel Peterson & Associates, Inc.
Minneapolis, MN.

Manufactured in the United States of America

Before the Earth's last days,
before there would be
a population left behind . . .

1

THE FALLEN
ANGELS
DESCENDED
INTO A
DARKNESS WITH
NO BOTTOM.
THERE WAS NO
GOING BACK.
GOD HAD BEEN
QUITE SPECIFIC
ABOUT THAT.

I WONDER WHY THEY CALL THIS THE GOLD COAST? Sonta was perplexed. He had never been to this part of America, wasn't from here, and never could be called a history buff. The high-rise condos lining Lake Shore Drive along the Chicago skyline were undoubtedly impressive. Hailing a limousine at Grand Central Station, he headed to his destination with his entourage.

Sonta could have flown, but the train was more conducive for his activities while traveling. The accommodations of the two compartments on the City of New Orleans allowed him to continue the party with his companions. He was unwilling to give up the enjoyment and attention his entourage showered on him.

Sonta was a Fallen Angel and possessed powers far beyond those of earthlings. In his demonic state, he towered over the tallest mortals. His wings spanned nearly twenty feet tip to tip. Sonta answered only to a few.

When Lucifer and his followers went tumbling out of Heaven's confines, Sonta was among them. The castoffs had eventually gathered in a place called the Second Heaven, from whence they dispersed, bringing their wrath to all civilizations.

Like his brethren, Sonta was a changeling, capable of altering his appearance. The importance of this capability could not be overstated, since there were many races on Earth where Christianity flourished. Here, he presented as a tall European gentleman with somewhat aristocratic roots.

Arriving at the address given to him, Sonta and his attendants waited impatiently for the private elevator to whisk them up to the penthouse. Luxury fairly oozed from the marble floors, the window treatments, and the reception area. The lavish surroundings fit his persona. There was no reason why he should not be enjoying more of these moments, but it had not happened yet.

Boarding the elevator, Sonta daydreamed about being able to enjoy all the creature comforts available in this world he now temporarily called home. Being one of the Fallen Angels God cast out of Heaven eons ago had resulted in an always fluid algorithm of changing conditions. Assignments with no end and battles with no resolution had led him to this place in a land called Earth where all was available.

Sonta couldn't help think that his master, Koal, Jeremiah Koal to the locals, was collecting chits that carried his imprint. *I have been as successful in battle as he has, yet here he is, summoning me.*

Jeremiah Koal was just a name chosen because its prefix had biblical standing. A Christian name in the mortal community seemed necessary for an Overlord of the demonic Kingdom whose direct responsibility was the heartland of America.

Koal was a handsome man in his earthly presence, but an object of fear and loathing in his demonic form. There was no measuring the evil that resided within him. He had blood-red eyes sunken beneath a misty haze, foulness oozing from his pores. When thoroughly demonized, he was nearly twelve feet tall, with a twenty-five-foot wingspan and yellow-hued complexion.

He had fallen slightly behind Lucifer.

Koal engendered such fear that his adversaries, with good reason, always wanted to run, but couldn't, being frozen with fear's massive adrenaline shooting through their veins.

The elevator stopped one floor below the penthouse. Sonta cautioned his companions to behave as they stepped out into a reception area. People scurried everywhere. It was a busy place, a typical American corporate office setting. Computer screens received data and routed it away. Phones rang. Quiet conversations were taking place.

Two security personnel, handguns holstered at their waists, approached Sonta from a rear stairway area that was hidden by beautiful palm trees.

"Are you Alexander Sonta, sir?" one asked.

"Well, yes, I am Sonta," he replied. "I don't know where Alexander came from, but I am Sonta, and I am expected."

It was apparent to Sonta that Master Koal had given him a first name, an earthling name, entirely without his permission.

"Sir," said the other guard, "please walk up to the next floor where Gozan will meet you. We will keep your companions here in the lounge area," he added, with no hint of emotion.

Sonta didn't want to leave his "traveling party." Nevertheless, he had to comply.

Gozan was Koal's chief of staff, his right-hand man, who held down the position that should have been his, a position Sonta had rightfully earned on the battlefield.

Perhaps if I were more accommodating, thought Sonta, *things would change.* He brushed the thought aside. Whatever the role he had played, the lives he had taken certainly merited a promotion. One day soon, he would become a member of the high council presided over by the great master Satan himself.

"Sonta, so good to see you," said Gozan, forcing a smile. He had never liked Sonta, whom he considered too full of himself. Sonta wanted his job, and Gozan knew it. Fat chance of that happening.

"Sure, good to see you, too," Sonta mumbled as he scanned

the surroundings, barely hiding his contempt for a lackey who was most obviously not a warrior.

"What's up with the names? I was just told I am Alexander."

"First names only exist when humans are present. We can't be bothered with them here. How was your trip?"

"Other than having to board the City of New Orleans at 3 a.m., it was just fine. It passed the smell test."

"I don't understand those words," said Gozan.

Sonta looked at the man with a condescending stare. "None of my associates had any complaints, so all's well that ends well."

"Associates?" Gozan seemed taken aback.

"Yeah. We had a good party going on at departure time so I brought everyone with me," replied Sonta, almost laughing out loud at what he perceived as embarrassment on Gozan's face.

"Well, what you do is your business unless it's mine," replied Gozan, looking at him evenly with no hint of inferiority.

"Well said," replied Sonta, thinking that he might need to reassess his situation. On display were Koal's and Gozan's new lives, not his.

"What is on the agenda?"

"That depends on Master Koal," said Gozan. "He doesn't clear his schedule with me."

"That's quite an admission, Gozan, coming from his chief of staff. I was summoned, had to leave in the middle of the night to get here, endure an hour and a half cab ride in rush hour, and still have to wait on his supremeness. To top it all off, you don't know the agenda!"

"I don't know why I'm giving you this heads-up, Sonta," Gozan said, "but our master has read your recent report, and I observed some discomfort on his face when he was through."

"How so?" asked Sonta, seeing a smirk on Gozan's face.

"Not for me to say," replied Gozan, walking toward a door

on the right and motioning for Sonta to follow.

Opening the door, they entered a large suite. The usual complement of office equipment was scattered neatly around. A large mahogany desk flanked by chairs and a small conference table occupied the center of the room. On the east wall, several large picture windows looked out over Lake Michigan.

Gozan pressed a button and the wall to the west began to fold on itself, exposing as it did an expanded version of the present room. The Chicago skyline was in full view.

"Settle in, Sonta," advised Gozan. "It's a little after one. I'll have lunch brought in. Hard to say how long you'll be here before Master Koal makes himself available."

"I doubt it will make any difference," said Sonta, "but I do have an eight o'clock train reservation."

"You're right again," replied Gozan, leaving the room. "It doesn't matter."

Arrogant jerk! thought Sonta, quickly dismissing the speculation, knowing full well the powers of Koal, one of which was advanced telepathy. It allowed him to monitor thoughts as a way of controlling the demons around him. He could have been listening to this entire preamble.

Lunch arrived, but Sonta ate fitfully, still not knowing why he had been summoned. Eventually, he settled into a comfortable chair and dozed off. Awaking, he checked his watch. It was three thirty.

Looking around the vacant room, his gaze meandered to the east windows that revealed several sailboats bouncing on the lake's small waves. The beachfront up and down Lake Shore Drive was also in view, which attracted sunbathers and windsurfers. It was a hot day, and through the binoculars lying on an adjacent table, he spotted a stunning blonde sunbather roll slowly to her back, attracting the attention of several men in her proximity.

Sonta breathed hard as he observed the dynamics of the scene, so caught up in the grand design that he completely missed Koal's entrance.

"If you are that interested in her," Koal said, snapping Sonta's head around at the sound of his voice, "I can have her brought up later."

"Master Koal, I didn't hear you enter," Sonta sputtered.

"I've reviewed your report on southern Illinois. As is, it appears in alignment with our master plan but looks a little skimpy. Did you leave anything out? Anything that affects our chances of success?"

Sonta felt as though he was caught totally off guard. The distraction of the blond down on the beach had carried his thought processes to a different time zone. But Koal was here now, and he needed to pay attention. The demon's mortal appearance had changed since Sonta's last visit. More aristocratic-looking, probably to help push his "Jeremiah" agenda.

"The report is factual, Master Koal," Sonta replied as he wiped sweat from the binoculars and dabbed his brow with the back of his hand. He hadn't realized how disturbed he had become with the beach activity.

"According to your two-year timetable," Koal continued, "our takeover will be complete. We will have determined who is faithful and who is not and turned the hearts and minds of the masses to our agenda. The population will be controlled or eliminated. Your confidence rides high, Sonta, does it not? But what about the opposition? In the past, you have not always been effective in that arena. There have been mistakes. What's your strategy?" Koal's Earth form began to melt at the utterance of these words.

Sonta read the shapeshift as a danger signal. Tensing, he said, "I remind you, Master, earthlings are a poorly evolved species. They are simple people, and our plan has already yielded promising results. Land acquisitions have largely gone unnoticed. Those who became aware of even small portions of our plan have been neutralized. Possible adversaries have been identified. People who pose a potential problem, well, let's just say they are on the watch list. We have aligned with past partners and are bringing them into the area. Let me assure you. . ."

The setting sun had suddenly dipped below a roof overhang, causing Koal and Sonta to shield their faces as the sun's rays momentarily blinded them. Koal turned and groped for a panel on his desk. At the press of a button, the blinds lowered, obscuring the panoramic view of the Chicago skyline. Too much sunlight was dangerous.

"Let me assure you," Sonta continued, "that this plan will be the gold standard for similar takeovers elsewhere."

"Much depends on it. Much," Koal said, his eyes framed with fire boring a hole through Sonta. "Let me assure you that your existence depends on it as well."

Sonta understood. Koal did not make veiled threats.

"As you know, our region is one of four. We are the test quadrant bringing the battle for humankind to the entire nation. Your plan will be a blueprint for the conquest of Earth. I have three counterparts, as do you. Our Grand Master Satan has chosen America because of its decadence. In my opinion, we could not have selected a better environment. Our Master has one worry that he voices regularly. He fears our takeover will not be completed before the Rapture sends all of us who follow him to the fiery pit, from which there is no escape. This event the Christians call the Rapture means we must be busy fulfilling our mission."

The message was understood.

"Master Koal, do you remember how early last century you maneuvered the Ottoman Empire to eliminate the Armenians?

"At your direction during World War I, I was able to infiltrate the Turkish leadership and harden their hearts and minds against the Armenians. We convinced the government that the Armenians were a dangerous foreign element. Today history calls it the Armenian Genocide. You were bloody and ruthless in your elimination of this Christian element. As I recall, this campaign won you your seat on the high council."

"Yes, I remember the assignment, Sonta. Be careful in your analysis; these are entirely different operations. Here we are seeking to break the faith of those who would disappear should the Rapture occur. They are our priority. The nonbelievers are easily taken. There is no shortage of targets. Concern yourself with the righteous. Lord Satan himself has picked this land for us as a test case." Koal had softened his voice somewhat, which Sonta took as a positive.

"I understand you have a train to catch. Gozan made sure your companions were accommodated while relaxing in the lounge. They should be fresh for your return trip. My limousine is waiting for you."

2

-◆◆◆◆-

"AND YOU WILL HEAR OF WARS AND RUMORS OF WARS. SEE THAT YOU ARE NOT TROUBLED; FOR ALL THESE THINGS MUST COME TO PASS, BUT THE END IS NOT YET."

MATTHEW 24:6

JONES O'BRIAN STOPPED READING HIS BIBLE AND looked across the kitchen table into his wife's big brown eyes. She still captured his attention after all these years.

"Ominous, isn't it?" she said, brushing back a wisp of auburn hair while straightening in her chair.

"What?" said Jones.

"All these wars, murders, drugs, evil acts without end. Everywhere you look. It can't be a coincidence. Besides, you don't believe in coincidences," she said tauntingly.

Her voice trended country, a product of growing up and working on Kazenski Acres, her parents' farm. Although her given name was Connie, somewhere along the line, Kaz took over.

"Don't start bringing blowing up the world again, Kaz. Not everything is falling apart," Jones replied. "And don't get started on Washington either," he added, knowing full well it was her favorite destination.

"Calm down, honey. I'm just saying the political world is wild out there and shows no signs of going away."

He had walked away after one of her interruptions a few nights ago, and right now, she was trying to atone.

"Well, thanks for the input," he said with a scowl.

"Anytime," she had replied.

"What do you have spinning inside that head of yours?" she asked.

"I'm thinking about the men who built the roadmap, especially John. The man was centuries ahead of his time."

"Explain," said Kaz.

"He was laying out the path that men would walk in the final days, before the Rapture. His vision was one of wars and rumors of wars, horrible events without end."

Jones' favorite biblical subject was prophecy. It was easy for him to go there.

"Everyone has an opinion," he said, "but my feeling is there is too much upheaval for all this conflict to be random. These events are not mere happenstance. Your observations about our government seem right on, though it's hard to make sense of the mess. It does hurt sometimes having to agree with you."

"You'll get over the hump," said Kaz, flashing him a big smile.

"Anyway," Jones continued, "the government's confusion and lies represent not just us but our times. We are all God's creatures, flawed and in need of salvation. Many of us long to see a great leader emerge, but that may not happen until humanity evolves and sheds its penchant for money, power, and territorial control. We have no real say in who we elect; they are chosen for us by the ruling tribes. If our thousands of churches in this land would only vet these candidates and do what Jesus would do, there would be no uncertainty. I am convinced Satan has infiltrated our churches with nonbelievers posing as Christians, whose tasks are to sow discord and doubt among the faithful. It is the hand of The Most Evil come to bear upon us all, and I pray the righteous can and will overcome it through the intervention of our Lord and the power of prayer.

"Somedays I feel abandoned in the field," he added, thinking back to his horrific days of combat in Afghanistan. Death, blood, and destruction were all around, and some wanted more. "Who wants that world, Kaz?" he asked.

"Lucifer and his fallen angels. . ." she replied, "they help to install the hate, the corruption, the misery that men bring upon themselves. Over time, the demonic forces take ownership and further damage the people and society."

"That's what I think John envisioned and wrote about, Kaz," said Jones.

"I wouldn't presume to guess at that," she answered.

"Sure makes me think that the end-times are closer than we realize," said Jones.

"It makes me almost glad we can't have children," Kaz blurted out.

Reality bit hard as Jones witnessed her pained expression, one that had existed just below the surface for years. The topic had vanished from their conversations despite countless attempts at coming to peace with her barrenness.

Refocusing, Jones said, "It's all okay, Kaz. It's all okay."

Kaz looked expressionless, still a prisoner of her thoughts.

"Sure, honey, I know."

No one was convinced.

Jones had spent untold hours studying the Bible, a book he treasured over all others. The words there had convinced him to be vigilant and keep watch for signs of world conflict. He was doing just that.

"The good news, Kaz, is that the Bible is clear about angels in our midst, present and active in the affairs of men, just as they were with the Israelites in the olden days. How else could we have survived without angels and prayer?"

"True," said Kaz. "I believe that."

Jones and Kaz had been down this road before. Both, in their own way, wanted to believe so very badly. Kaz had prayed her heart out for a baby and gotten no for an answer. Jones had not stopped questioning how you could write that off to "God's Will."

It was murky water at best; even Jones conceded that fact. The details of divine intervention had many interpreters and interpretations. How the Heavenly Host interacted with mortals was tough to figure out sometimes. Try as he might, he couldn't dismiss Raphael, and the other Grand Masters' images of mighty Joshua led into battle by a flock of precious, winged cherubs.

"So, Kaz," he asked hesitantly, "you think the angels have kept the struggle between light and darkness at a stalemate all these years? There is a war going on between God and Satan. I'm just not clear on what part we play in the overall scheme." He had to get off the baby thing.

"I'm just saying; there's no reason to think there's something so special about our time." She began to cough.

"I've never felt caught up in a world invaded by monsters. Of course, Jesus did say the end would come when we least. . ." She succumbed to a fit of shivering and hacking.

Dear Lord, not again, Jones thought. Kaz was manifesting a deep-down kind of sickness that was growing within her. The coughing spells had been happening for several months. Jones continually prayed for healing, sending his prayers into the void. The silence was deafening.

"Are you okay, Kaz? Should we go to the ER?"

She just shook her head. "Get me some water. I'll be fine."

After Kaz took a few sips of water, they finished their study time without further discussion and closed with a prayer. Jones noticed the coughing spell had taken some of the fight out of her. Moving around the table, Jones gently helped Kaz to her feet. Moments later, he tucked her into bed and lumbered back to the kitchen.

Pushing his hand through his short-cropped black hair, he grabbed a chair and a bag of chocolate chip cookies. He had been a pretty good athlete once, but those days were long since passed. Still yet, he tried to keep active and in some semblance of shape. Just a few more cookies, he reasoned.

Sitting at the table, he went back in time to figure when Kaz's coughing spells started. The sickness had been infrequent at first, presenting no real effect on her daily routine. But earlier this year, shortly after their thirteenth wedding anniversary, Kaz's symptoms worsened. Something wasn't right with her body. The coughing would double her over, grinding any activity to a halt. Some attacks came on so quickly there was no safety net. Everything went boom and shuddered to a stop. Everything.

The shivers came first, causing her body to shake almost uncontrollably. Her fever rose, and nothing stayed down. Sometimes an electric blanket would help, sometimes not. But going to the doctor—no it wasn't going to happen. He couldn't convince her, no matter how hard he tried. Kaz insisted her fate was in God's hands. *What kind of logic was that,* Jones wondered. *How could all this be God's will?* He was confused.

While washing down his fifth cookie, the solution came to him. Kaz needed a doctor. God helped those who helped themselves.

Abby Soloman, he reasoned, Kaz's best friend growing up, should be able to convince her to go to the doctor. At least it was worth a try. Knowing Abby was a deputy sheriff possibly on duty at this hour, he dug into Kaz's tote, found her phone, located the number, and gave her a call.

"It's getting a little late, isn't it, Kaz?" Abby sounded asleep.

"Abby, it's Jones. I've already put Kaz to bed."

"Well, I haven't heard your voice in a while, Jones, although I do hear about you regularly. What's up?"

"Has Kaz mentioned her health issues lately?"

"No, she hasn't. What's she been keeping from me?"

"She's been having coughing spells for some time, and they are getting worse. She coughs, shivers, gets fevers, and it's downhill from there. She has to use an electric blanket to get warm."

"Not good, Jones. What's the doctor say?"

"That's just it, Abby. She won't go. I don't think she realizes how bad this may be. Do you think you could get her to go see the doc?"

"Of course I'll get her to go, Jones. I won't give her any choice. She'll probably be upset that you've told me."

"Then don't tell her," Jones interjected, violating principles that didn't seem too important right now.

"Right. . ." said Abby. "If she does find out she'll just have to get over it. I'll get right on it, Jones. I'd do anything for you guys."

A more accurate statement had seldom been voiced. The O'Brians, Jones and Kaz, would not exist without Abby. She had realized way back in high school that love was in the air, their air, considerably before the two lovers did.

Early the next morning, Abby was on the move. She called and made an appointment for Kaz, and then she showed up at the front door with appointment slip in hand. The anger on Kaz's face was evident when she found out about the collaboration.

The visit didn't go well. Kaz had a coughing fit in the exam room. All the usual tests took place. Blood work, MRI, and myriad other investigations into Kaz's health began. However, in the end, there was no resolution, no definitive conclusion that pointed to a starting point for treatment.

The small-town hospital was not equipped to diagnose her symptoms. Referrals were their only answer, so appointments were made, and eventually, several specialists in the city examined Kaz stem to stern. Videoconferences with other specialists across the U.S. cost thousands while Kaz continued to wither as the hand of man and science yielded no definitive diagnosis.

The life that Jones and Kaz had forged came apart. Their daily routines of times together disappeared. She was too weak for Bible study to be a cooperative venture. Her accommodations became the sole priority of the Jones household.

Kaz was the executive director of Hope House, a local home for unwed mothers. Unable to have a child of her own, she dedicated her life to helping others bring new life into the world. Despite her true passion for the services that Hope House provided, she began coming home early almost daily.

Jones' life changed in sync. He started taking time off from his position as operations manager for Southern Distributing to tend to Kaz, whose condition continued to worsen. Time seemed to be in slow motion as Kaz deteriorated. Several prayer groups in the community prayed daily for her recovery, but there was no change.

Early one Sunday at 2 a.m., when no good is afoot, Jones stepped out of the house. Some lady friends were tending to Kaz as he fired up his truck and headed to Lake Murphysboro, an old "out of the way" fishing hole with darn near as many cottonmouths as fish. It had been one of two favorite parking spots with Kaz in high-school days. It was quiet there, the right place to ponder the future.

Parking his truck in the empty lot, Jones walked toward

the rundown boat dock that occupied the east side of the lake. The water was deeper there, which meant more fish and fewer snakes. As was his habit, he stopped to scoop a handful of flat rocks for skipping across the water.

It was a cloudless, pleasant night; the warm, humid southern Illinois spring was in full bloom. The moon was in waning gibbous status. The air stood still. As he threw each rock across the water, rings rippled out and finally disappeared in the darkness.

"Kaz," he whispered into the nothingness, "I'm so sorry."

His confusion mounted.

Was God listening?

He wanted to believe that God heard his prayers, but why wasn't He answering?

Jones felt helpless. He cried. There was nothing anyone had been able to do to spare her pain. *I would gladly take the illness on myself. Just spare Kaz*, he forwarded to the universe. As he stood in the faint moonlight examining the smooth rocks in his hand, the wind started to blow gently. The humidity shrank.

Not sure what was happening, Jones felt a great calm come over him. The breeze stopped. Thinking he heard someone calling his name, he turned toward the parking lot to acknowledge the call. No one was there. Instead, all the light in the sky seemed concentrated at the end of the dock.

As he looked, dozens of figures seemed to materialize. They were large.

"No. No way. Angels?" came from his lips.

There they were. No other explanation. Angels. No little, small cherubs. They were all over the end of the dock, and they covered the rough terrain that led to the walkway.

They appeared to have a leader, who, although not the biggest, had an aura of authority and responsibility that declared, "I am in charge here."

He was not earthly, of that Jones was certain. What was it about him? His eyes radiated a look of peace. Jones could feel it. Taking a step toward Jones, he spoke, "Jones, I knew we would meet someday. I do wish the circumstances could be better."

Jones was overwhelmed by his presence. The voice sounded familiar, but there was no basis for that assumption. They had never met. It was more of a "knowing" deep inside of him. Like something that was just around the corner, invisible but there nonetheless, keeping him protected, making way for him. His voice sounded familiar. *Who. . .?*

The answer came before he could form the question.

"I am Arrow, and yes, I've been just around the corner many times for you, and will continue to be."

Jones processed the greeting. Knowing that angels were often used to bring messages in stories he read in his Bible, he stammered, "Kaz isn't going to make it, is she?"

"The Master is pleased with your Kaz," Arrow replied. "She has saved many lives at her home for unwed mothers. Multitudes more will be spared in the years to come because of her stand for righteousness and life. The Darkness that has attacked her body has not gone unnoticed. More defenders are coming, even at this moment. Now, go be with Kaz. She needs you," the angel said.

There was a stirring in the air, and Jones was alone.

The moon seemed to shine more brightly. Frogs and crickets continued their music.

Got to go, he thought, simultaneously running for his truck. *I've got to get to Kaz now.*

As he drove, Arrow's words kept ringing in his head, "The Master is pleased with your Kaz."

3

AND WE KNOW
THAT IN ALL
THINGS GOD
WORKS FOR THE
GOOD OF THOSE
THAT LOVE HIM,
WHO HAVE
BEEN CALLED
ACCORDING TO
HIS PURPOSE.

ROMANS 8:28

ENTERING THE FRONT DOOR, JONES SAW THE Night Owls, church women whose husbands were third-shift miners, kneeling on the floor in the living room with their Bibles open, arms lifted toward the Heavens. Tears were streaming down their faces.

Closing the door, Jones headed toward the bedroom, thanking them for being there as he went. Pausing for a deep breath, Jones relived the scene at the dock. The conversation with Arrow played through his mind. Kaz had always been adamant about angels and their active role in the affairs of men.

Could she have been prophesying, forthtelling, about his conversation at the lake?

He spoke softly in her direction as he entered the bedroom, "Kaz, I'm here."

Her eyes opened, and in her old southern drawl, the one he fell in love with from days gone by, said, "How did your boat dock visit go, big boy?"

Jones shuddered but said, "Good Kaz, and oh yeah, the Master is pleased with you."

She smiled, just as she had when he asked her out for their first date.

Their eyes met.

Together since birth when they shared a crib as babies at

their old church, they had walked this world for thirty-five years, the last fifteen as man and wife.

Kaz closed her eyes and was gone, but the smile lingered on her face.

An inexplicable illness had consumed her life. It was all too complex for reasoning. What a price to pay.

"A future and a hope," a verse from the book of Jeremiah came to mind.

What is a future without Kaz, and how could there be any hope?

How could a benevolent God allow such loss? Their lives were ahead of them. Not over. Not done.

Stop being so selfish, Jones thought. *Kaz is with Jesus. She wouldn't want to return.*

Maybe she was his test. That would be too cruel, but then there was the biblical story of Abraham and Isaac, a boy whose father was asked to sacrifice him.

To say Jones' belief was shaken would be an understatement. Where should he draw the line between faith and fact? Prayers had not saved his beloved, and Jones believed in prayer. His wife had died way before her time in spite of all the prayers. Kaz was a life helper whose founding of Hope House would save multitudes more in the years to come. Why her?

Jones was about to start life on a "one day at a time" basis.

4

IN THE LAST
DAYS, BEFORE
THE RAPTURE,
ALL HELL
DESCENDED,
TRYING TO
TURN AS MANY
BELIEVERS AS
POSSIBLE, THOSE
WHO WOULD
BE GONE.

"SO, YOU'RE CONFIDENT THE FIRES ARE WORKING?"
Sonta quizzed his chief underling, Zorah.

Mustering the most assuring voice he could, while concealing his irritation at being asked this question yet again, Zorah replied, "Yes! The fires are causing uncertainty, sowing discontent with the authorities."

Zorah's connection in the Jackson County Sheriff's Department was adamant about the distraction the fires were causing. They had popped up out of nowhere with no seeming origin and were causing a sense of unease throughout the community of humans. The sheriff and his deputies had not been able to solve the unsolvable and were facing a barrage of criticism for their lack of progress. It was, in fact, a regional strategy that, if successful, would have national implications. Their counterparts in the other three quadrants were watching, evaluating.

Zorah's eyes followed Sonta as he moved across the spacious room, transforming as he went from his demonic persona into a mortal. As with all demonic morphs, there was a smell associated with the changing that had not yet been eliminated or duplicated. It was the stench of death that clung tenaciously to the demon and disappeared as he gained mortal status.

Sonta's particular signature was intertwined with his extermination of over a million Armenian Christians back in the early twentieth century. It had been a bloody slaughter, including untold numbers of dismemberments. Men, women, and children were all murdered and left to rot in town after town as the Ottomans tried to rid themselves of what they had been led to believe was a threat. Master Koal had manipulated the carnage, but Sonta was the front man who carried out the attacks. His demonic personality would always remember with a smile the smell of rotting flesh. It was an exquisite perfume that never failed to recall and celebrate the victory he had led.

"Master, we are bringing in supplies to finish construction of our Wondren headquarters and ready it for the battles to come," said Zorah.

"Recruiting the nonbelievers has been less demanding than I ever thought possible. Their counterparts are more tenacious but are showing signs of vulnerability. Your methods have proved legendary."

Sonta nodded in acceptance of the praise. This coming battle carried his signature; no one else need apply. It was also true that his tactics predated these events by centuries. The hordes had proven that populations drowning in drugs, sex, and violence were ripe fodder for influence. The launch point centered around creating a sense of unease in the community regarding their leaders and their ability to govern. *People are Lemmings*, thought Sonta, recalling the mass suicides of the little creatures known in children's fiction for following one another to their deaths. *Doubt leads the way in the minds of the mortals; they are famous for it*, he thought.

His human form now complete, Sonta said, "We create problems that only we can solve, promises none but us can keep. As confusion creeps in, doubt creates a fog in the human thought process. At some point, darkness captures the minds and hearts of the faithful as they become disoriented and unsure of their god. Their small, weak, throbbing little pink hearts are seared and ripe for manipulation. Without knowing, they begin to live lives contrary to the moral upbringing of their culture. How good is that?" Sonta said, lifting his arms in celebration.

"Your genius elevates this recruiting methodology," Zorah finished, hoping his flattery would score some points and divert Sonta's attention elsewhere.

Sonta sat down in a regal, high-backed chair. It was his throne for the moment. He raised an eyebrow on hearing the tribute, but only momentarily; realizing he invented the speech for Koal. He would be more attuned in the future.

"I just want to be sure you understand the importance of your assignment in this scheme," Sonta said, his voice taking a hard edge, his eyes boring into Zorah's. "When I am successful in taking over control of this quadrant, my next promotion will be assured. Our Supreme Leader will notice the template we are creating for others to follow as we continue to conquer this nation called America. My success will elevate my position. I will have status in the command hierarchy. Others, less capable, will bow.

"Stay on schedule, Zorah. Koal has been alerted about our plans and may present himself unexpectedly, as he is known to do. Be ready for anything."

Zorah understood the stakes were high, for everyone.

"Yes, Master," he replied, "your wish is my command. Rest assured my contact is embedded and close to the sheriff. He's aware of every nuance. Thanks to his intervention, our shipments of supplies and recruits are moving through the region without interference. We are on schedule."

Zorah turned to leave Sonta, pleased with his performance.

Nothing he could say would stop this delusion. Disguising his contempt, he closed the door behind him, confident that although he could outperform Sonta, there was life to consider, his life. It would be prudent to follow orders regardless of his perceived outcomes.

5

‑✦✦✦✦✦‑

AFTER KAZ'S DEATH, JONES WAS FULL OF DOUBT ABOUT GOD'S ABILITY TO INTERVENE WHEN PRAYERS WERE OFFERED. IT WEIGHED ON HIM MIGHTILY. PERHAPS HIS PRAYERS LACKED SUBSTANCE. THEY SURELY LACKED SOMETHING.

HIS APPRECIATION OF THE ROUTINE AND THE application of that discipline were the distraction he needed. No good would come of rehashing how it all went down. Besides, there was work to do, and the food distribution business waited for no one.

Jones was working up his daily schedule when Ma Hale's restaurant in Grand Tower called in a late request for more kitchen supplies. It was late afternoon, and being down a deliveryman, Jones decided to fill the order personally.

Ma Hale's sat less than two hundred yards from the Mississippi River levee and had been there since the '40s. They were thrilled to see him.

As Jones drove back towards Murphysboro on Town Creek Road, he began to make out a glow, visible from one curve to another. The road straightened as it hit bottomland, revealing a large cornfield sandwiched between a creek bed and the right of way.

Jones was aware of the mysterious fires that were being reported around the county with no explanation for their causes. Maybe this was one of them. Probably some farmers are burning stumps.

Jones pulled up across the field from the fire and parked his truck on the side of the dusty gravel road. He ran toward the blaze, pushing his way through corn stalks that were brown from ripening, taking constant hits from ears that were dry and ready to harvest.

As he closed on the burn, he called out, hoping to get a response from someone, anyone, tending the fire. There was none. All he heard was the crackling of the flames. *If the wind picks up, we'll have an event*, he thought, reaching for his phone. *This brush fire will light up those corn stalks and go right into the woods close to the field's west end.* Jones called 911.

"What's your emergency," came the response from Judy Gage at the Jackson County Sheriff's office.

"Judy, this is Jones O'Brian. I've come on one of those strange fires we've been having lately. This time it's next to a cornfield."

"What's your location, Jones?"

"I'm on Town Creek Road, about four miles west of 20th Street Bridge. There's a cornfield here bounded by a woods. I'm afraid the whole thing is going to catch fire."

"Wait one."

"Okay, I've got City on the way. The Township Department is already out on a call. What's that noise I hear in the background?"

"It's just a cedar tree burning," Jones confirmed.

"Good to hear your voice, Jones. Take care." She signed off.

While waiting for the firemen, Jones inspected the area around the fire. Darkness was settling in, and the flames were creating eerie shadows across the landscape. Jones did a quick survey of the surroundings. There was no substitute for good intel. He had learned that lesson in Afghanistan doing night recon with his pathfinder squad. His instincts said to pay attention. The present would soon become the past.

In the military, most field exercises, mock or real, were refined processes culminating from years of trial and error, most of which had a sufficient bounty of lost lives. The brush fire was no different, he told himself, slipping seamlessly into the routine.

There were no tire tracks in the weeds, no footprints, but when he saw a slight movement at the edge of his line of sight, he edged forward. There was nothing. Must have been a shadow from the flames. The whole scene felt off. He could sense a presence but saw only burning brush.

The fire was still manageable when a siren sounded in the distance, and Jones started back across the field to his truck when he ran headlong into Lozen and her bloodhound Hunter. Lozen was an Apache woman who ran with the Mountain Men. Rumor had it that she was prescient.

"What are you doing here?" he asked.

"I sensed evil in this area and moved toward it. The fire was fueled by dark spirits who have entered our dimension. As I approached and was recognized, they disappeared."

Jones was distracted by a loud popping sound. When he turned to Lozen, she and the dog were gone.

The fire truck that arrived was specially equipped to attack a field fire. Two men jumped out, grabbed some equipment, and headed into the cornfield.

Jones recognized the lead fireman.

"Jack, I didn't know you worked the night shift."

The two men had grown up in the same neighborhood, and Jack Wilson, lucky sucker that he was, had married the homecoming queen from Jones' class.

"Well, I've started hanging out at the station at night since all these fires started happening," he said. "Marsha's not too happy, but she'll have to get over it. Have you seen anyone?" he asked.

"I covered the entire area down to the tree line," said Jones, waving his arm around to encompass the perimeter. "Nothing. I thought I saw something, but it was probably just a shadow blowing in the wind. No indication of any human activity," he said.

"Hold on a sec."

Jack spoke into his pack radio, "Dispatch, this is the Chief. Let County know there's no need to send a deputy out to 20th Street. Out."

A response crackled back, "Copy, Chief. Out."

Jack pulled out his smartphone and made some notes.

"Just another clueless report to turn in. We've had a lot of them lately. Interesting though, no one has ever been injured, at least physically, by any of these events. Folks are getting unsettled and will be seeing alien invaders before long."

"I ran into Lozen, an Apache friend of the Mountain Men before you arrived. She was here," said Jones.

"Doing what, exactly?" said Jack.

"I don't think you want to know," replied Jones, not sure how to interpret what Lozen had said.

He watched as the two men quickly snuffed out the fire and loaded their equipment and rumbled off. Firing up his truck, Jones followed close behind, mulling over the Chief's statement and coming to the same conclusion. Every day people were getting edgy about the strange fires. Fires that hurt no one and burnt nothing important made it challenging to connect the dots. Something was going on, but what? Why would anyone want to mess with a place this unimportant?

Thinking back, he tried to remember when these fire events had crossed his radar. Hard to say. Southern Illinois was changing. So was his town. A steady influx of new families was growing the tax base.

Some undoubtedly were coming to work at the University, since the school was by far the county's biggest employer. Other than that, there was little here to attract them—nothing overt, anyway. A few more lawyers for the courthouse or maybe a new factory could be a reason, but not a solution. He was aware that some hiring was going on in Jonesboro, another county seat south of Murphysboro. Still, it just didn't make sense. Maybe they were having fires there too. He'd find out.

Jones latched on to the thought and decided to ask Sheriff Cable when he had a chance. Yeah, Sheriff Cable. They'd been friends from high school days when he was one of Jones' coaches. He might be able to provide some answers.

6

---◆◆◆◆◆---

BOB CABLE WAS A SHORT MAN WITH A BROAD SMILE. A HOMETOWN GUY, HE HAD PLAYED HALFBACK FOR THE UNIVERSITY OF ILLINOIS FIGHTING ILLINI.

THE TEAM ROSTER LISTED HIM AT 5'9", BUT THEY MUST have put him on a stretcher to get that figure. He joined the army after college graduation, as many young men at the time were doing, and was a certified combat vet with a purple heart for his efforts when he reentered civilian life. Sergeant Cable put his degree to work coaching football and dabbling in school administration. Retiring early he entered the political arena and got himself elected County Sheriff.

Cable, as most everyone called him, sat behind a large oak desk, chin in hand, deep in thought. If he'd known his second term as sheriff would be this puzzling, he might not have considered reelection.

Fires. More fires. No explanations. A mountain of resources was being spent investigating, with no results worth mentioning to show for the effort. County Board Members had become so frustrated over the cost of chasing this madness they had demanded an accounting of expended funds.

The only thing Cable could come up with was possibly rounding up the Mountain Men and turning them loose out there in the great beyond.

The Mountain Men were known to hang out at The Kitchen, a local restaurant, almost every morning. They were all combat vets of varying ages who lived in the deep countryside yet seemed always to be together. Putting the Mountain Men in the field would be like inserting a force recon unit throughout the fire zone. Whatever was there they would see. No telling what the Board members would say if they knew the Mountain Men were involved. There would be no hourly wages coming into play, which was a plus, and the board wanted answers to these mysterious events that bordered on the unexplainable.

The Mountain Men's name was somewhat deceiving. One of their members was a woman who answered to the name Lozen. Jones had run headlong into her at the field fire. She was a full-blooded Apache who lived alone with her big red bloodhound Hunter. The two were inseparable. Lozen was prescient, and the dog could smell a fart in the Sahara.

The sum of the parts was a group that could hunt, trap, and track a man better than any of the sheriff's staff. The Crew, as they liked to call themselves, including the dog, wore CIB badges, which pretty well said it all. They made one for the dog.

The Mountain Men didn't live in the mountains. Southern Illinois doesn't have any. That didn't stop them from looking and dressing like Jeremiah Johnson. Lozen, tall for an Indian squaw, as she referred to herself, was unmarried and proud of it. Hunter was her man. Mostly she wore a fine wolfskin jacket with beaded turquoise trim and a Bald Eagle talon necklace. Rumor had it the eagle wintered at The Garden of The Gods, high up in the hill country near the tiny town of Herod. Occasionally, her friend Dani, an old Cherokee woman who lived in the Garden, was known to summon the giant bird, whose Cherokee name was Myoconda, which meant "he who flies high." Lozen told the Mountain Men of her ancestors' move to this part of Illinois from the west many years ago. The Apache called her spirit woman. All in all, this formidable crew would be a tremendous asset if they chose to come onboard.

Cable reasoned there were ways to get a yes vote. His blind eye to their off-season hunting habits had undoubtedly earned some chits. The Crew wasn't known for shying away from trouble. The fires were an inconvenience, some of them burning valuable food and cover. A little extracurricular activity might be in order.

Sheriff Cable stood up from his desk, picked up his hat, and headed toward The Kitchen, one short block away. Founded by a former sheriff to keep him and his family busy during his retirement, the restaurant's primary source of business was feeding juries when the circuit court was in session. The midmorning regulars were filing out as he walked in, and he spotted the Crew sitting in their favorite northeast corner, talking among themselves.

Eight men clustered around a trio of square tables shoved together into a makeshift ten-seater. Cable noticed an empty chair and looked for the woman who was nowhere to be seen. That did not mean, however, that she was not there.

As Cable approached, chair legs screeched against the floor and gazes rose.

Dick Arnold, the group's unofficial leader at the moment, spoke for them all. "Bob, is this a social visit or sumthin' else?"

One of the Mikes chimed in, "Whatever it is, I didn't do it."

Cable ignored the claim of innocence.

"I'm sure you all are aware of the unexplained fires that have been going on all over the region for the last several weeks."

The men nodded their heads.

"Anybody got ideas on what's going on?"

John tipped his chair back. "Why're you coming to us?

Hasn't anyone from your stable of crack investigators figured this out yet?"

Cable locked eyes with John.

"Look, I want to know what you think. These fires have nothing to do with you not passing the deputy's exam, John. You can retake it. Right now, I need your help."

Dale spoke up, "Lozen says it is evil and comes from the spirit world. The force is otherworldly and not human. She and Hunter went to one of the fire locations close to my house at the bottom of Cemetery Hill. I had scouted the area for a couple of hours with nothing to show for it. Right away, her eyes quickened, jumped, twitched, you know what I mean?"

Cable nodded, but really didn't grasp what was said.

"The dog, Hunter, walked around the fire circle and howled. Lozen caught him up, and they left."

"Whatever this is, it's bad medicine. Count on it," said John.

"Been to any of the other sites?" Cable asked the group.

"Went out to the McLaughlin place on the Ava blacktop a few nights ago," said one of the Mikes.

"It turned out one of the kids had been messing around in the fire zone. The only evidence was a bunch of trampled, burnt cornstalks. It had rained, but there were no footprints or tire tracks. After a couple of hours, we gave up and headed out."

There was an open spot at the table so Cable pulled up a chair.

As the server brought his coffee, Cable turned in his chair to say thanks. At that very moment, a strange feeling came over him. He looked around the room. No one was arguing or shouting. The room wasn't burning. What then?

Over in the opposite corner a man sat alone, apparently finishing a meal. No alarm there, still his antennae were up and he wasn't sure why.

In a quiet voice, he asked the guys if any of them knew who

the man was. The Crew shrugged almost in unison and shook their heads. *Strange. These boys know everyone in town.*

Cable glanced over at the outsider again, and as he did the hairs on the nape of his neck rose as, at that very moment, Lozen and the big bloodhound entered straight through the door. A cooling sensation laced the air.

Facing the stranger as he stood, her dog not moving so much as a muscle, Lozen asked in clear English, "Who are you? What is your name? What is your purpose?"

The big dog had lain down, his jowls and head completely one with the floor. Cable knew from watching his old friend Cyrus Kohler's Plott hound, Scout, take down a red weasel that this was clear intent. He had watched him settle down the same way Hunter did before exploding into the weasel's throat.

The stranger's face seemed to cloud in a fine mist, covering his facial features. He moved. Hunter jumped to his feet, a low growl emanating from a deep recess. Lozen moved like the wind; so fast that in the next moment, she was standing inches from the stranger.

The stranger pivoted around her and just like that was between her and the exit. He dropped money on the counter as he disappeared out the front door.

"I'll be back in a second," Cable said as he got up and sprinted toward the door. Stepping out on the sidewalk, he scanned the surroundings. There was nothing. The stranger had vanished into thin air.

Cable walked back inside and asked the cashier if she'd seen the customer before. She hadn't.

Cable sat down and spooned his coffee. Lozen motioned her dog to the front door and walked over. In a very subdued voice, she said, "Sheriff, you have just seen a dark messenger. They are among us." She walked to the door, summoned her dog, and left. *Incredible*, thought Cable, along with everyone else at the table. *Has our Indian just seen the devil?*

Dan exhaled and said, "If Lozen says we have trouble, you can bet we do. We've been aware of this crap taking place for several weeks but never thought it could be anything, shall we say, extraordinary.

"Lozen has picked a fight, and we need to protect our sister. Let's develop a plan we can execute. No one is as agile as they used to be, but we're very well armed and ready to put our old Pathfinder skills to good use. Since you're asking for help, we're ready. We were already talking about how we could help track down whatever is causing this trouble. We'll let the rest of the Crew know you need help. We'll get to the bottom of this."

7

-◆◆◆◆-

SHERIFF CABLE WORKED
LATE INTO THE NIGHT.

AFTER THE SITUATION WITH LOZEN, THE STRANGER
who vanished in plain sight, and his conversation with
the Mountain Men, he appreciated the silence night could
bring. Maybe putting the guys on the case would do it. Maybe
whatever it was had run its course. No matter what he did,
though, the mist-faced stranger continued to haunt him.

The phone's ring jolted him from his concentration. Caller
ID showed it was dispatch.

"Sheriff, you need to take this call. It looks like another fire
has sprung up at the Reiman place off the Ava blacktop."

Cable took a deep breath of relief or apprehension, he wasn't
sure which, and accepted the call.

"Sheriff Cable here. How can I help?"

"Sheriff, this is Jeanie Reiman. We got 480 acres plowed
under just west of the house. Nothing out there to burn, but it
is. Same as what happened at the McLaughlin place west of us
a couple of weeks ago."

"I'll have a deputy there shortly, Jeanie. Stay in the house, but
keep watch to see if you can see any people or cars on the road."

Cable holstered his phone and marched straight down the
hall to the radio room. As he approached the door, he could see
that both operators were taking information on additional fire

locations. He told them to call in more deputies if needed and headed for the Reiman homestead.

As he drove west out to the Ava blacktop, traffic was virtually nonexistent. Twenty minutes later, the Reiman household came into view. As he pulled into the drive, he saw smoke about a quarter mile out behind the house. As he approached the front door, Jeanie opened it quickly. She had been waiting for him while watching the fire burn itself out.

Cable went back to his car and got his high-beam spotlight, checked his Sig 26, and started toward the fire. In a plowed field, with no undergrowth or fallen timber of any kind whatsoever, burned a bonfire composed of neatly stacked logs. Strange. It was a handmade hot dog pit. Someone went to a lot of trouble to set this fire. These logs had been cut and hauled out here, he reasoned. Cable walked around the fire in decreasing concentric circles, checking the ground for footprints, tire tracks or other evidence. He circled the blaze four times and then widened his search. Nothing, just logs in the middle of nowhere. His report was going to look like all the others making up the growing stack on his desk.

Cable didn't get it. What was the purpose of all this? What kind of a fool did it take to build a fire in an open field? Maybe it was a Stonehenge sort of play. Who did it, and where did they go? No sightings to confirm the slightest activity. He packed up and headed back to town.

Pulling up to his office, Cable went directly to dispatch. Three hours had passed since the first call came in. The dispatcher on duty told him there had been fifteen calls so far. Fifteen fires. Things had quieted down in the last half-hour, but still, fifteen was a number that could not be ignored. It was a mini-invasion.

Tomorrow would bring a barrage of phone calls. Every

board member with an ax to grind would be checking in.

The Mountain Men were on the move and Lozen was with them. Listening to the incoming reports on their radios, they took a run at every fire within a ten-mile radius of the Reiman farm, canvassing every nook and cranny. The men saw nothing, but Lozen and Hunter were on high alert. "They are here," she repeated over and over each time the location changed. "They are not of this world."

Dick, the unofficial leader of the Crew, said, "We need to get together with Cable, and soon." Shortly after that, it was agreed to meet up at ten the next morning at the lake, Area 17.

"Tell everyone to say absolutely nothing," instructed Cable, "until we talk this over tomorrow. Be sure to bring Lozen and Hunter. And stay out of The Kitchen," he added as an afterthought.

"That might be asking a little too much, Sheriff," said Dick. "These are all grown men who seriously dislike formal instruction. Some will be a little hung over and may not be able to travel."

"That would be just like any other day," Cable retorted. "Ten a.m. Do you want to help or not?"

Cable waited through the most prolonged belch he'd heard in quite a while.

"I know, I know," said Dick. "Not bad manners, just good beer."

"I'll take that as a yes. See you at ten." Cable disconnected.

8

◆◆◆◆

HOPING FOR A GOOD TURNOUT, CABLE GOT TO THE LAKE WELL BEFORE TEN AND HAD HIS LARGE COUNTY MAP SPREAD OUT ON A PICNIC TABLE AS THE CREW STARTED ROLLING IN.

GETTING DOWN TO BUSINESS, THEY CHECKED THE highlighted locations of each fire from the previous night and positioned an overlay with all the previous fires on top of the map.

"Okay, men. Check out the maps. See any clues, any patterns?"

Everyone studied the maps, moving around to get different views. They yawned and scratched; after all, most of them were up much earlier than accustomed.

Dick broke the silence, "Well, Coach, I don't see a pattern about the where, but there sure seems to be one about the what."

Cable raised an eyebrow. "We don't need any code talking, Dick. What are you trying to say?"

"No one's been hurt, that's what."

He spread his hand across Cable's highlights.

"Nobody's lost a house, a barn—shoot, not even a shed. That right?"

Cable nodded and said, "Yes, it's always been a brush pile or a tree. Never any real damage. I guess we can be thankful for that. What we need, though, is to get there first—one time would be a start."

"I can help you do that," said Lozen, silent until now.

The Crew nodded in agreement.

"At some point, the violence will escalate," she said. "Luck will run out, and people will die. The fire-starters are not of our dimension; they are spirit beings with no form. Shadows that are unseen in the darkness."

The twelve men looked at Cable with furrowed brows.

One of the Mikes finally spoke, "You want us to be seers, divine the future?"

Cable smiled. "No, just make sure Lozen and Hunter are with us."

"We can do that, Boss," said Dick. "We absolutely can."

From a list he'd made earlier that morning, Cable assigned six two-person teams to open field locations throughout the county with Lozen and Hunter in the middle. While he didn't have enough personnel to cover every square mile, the spacing ensured a rapid response of thirty minutes or less for eighty percent of the open farmland in the county. The dice had been rolled, but the odds still favored the unknown.

9

◆◆◆◆◆

THE TEAMS DEPLOYED AS AGREED, BUT FOR TWO DAYS AND NIGHTS, THERE WAS NO ACTION OF ANY CONSEQUENCE.

A DOMESTIC DISPUTE AT THE KELLER FARM DID HELP relieve the monotony. Such is life in rural America.

Late in the afternoon on the third day, while sitting and staring at his scarred oak desktop, battling discouragement, it crossed Cable's mind that perhaps a change in procedure would relieve the boredom that was surely setting in.

He picked up his phone and dialed the familiar number. "Dick, Cable here. Call everyone now before they head out to their assigned areas. Have them meet at the lake right away. The usual place. We've got to make some changes." He hung up without waiting for a reply.

Darkness was descending as the last man pulled into Area 17, covered now by security lights and shadows.

As the Mountain Men gathered, their usual chatter trailed off. Although most had been lifelong friends and even soldiered together in Iraq, none of them had fought ghosts. They had entered uncharted territory.

"I can only imagine your anxiety," Cable said, trying to maintain a monotone. "I've been in my office the last two nights waiting on that first report, and everyone knows as well as I do, nothing's happened. But what has been happening is the chatter on your radios. Since nothing's been going on, I believe they, whoever they are, are monitoring our frequencies and are aware we're on the lookout. If they are sharp enough to get in and out of these locations without leaving any evidence, they've probably got plenty of technology helping them. I know you get bored with nothing going on, but cut the chatter. Turn your radios to monitor only. Dispatch will announce any incidents being called in. Any questions?"

When no one spoke up, the Crew headed to their vehicles.

10

CABLE RETURNED TO HIS OFFICE,
HIS MIND STILL OCCUPIED BY THE MISTY-
FACED STRANGER FROM THE KITCHEN.

SITTING AT HIS DESK, HE KILLED TIME BY REVIEWING the material for the pending County Board meeting. It was merely a self-contrived distraction. He needed a break in the storm.

He was rechecking his equipment one more time to confirm the tuning when the police scanner crackled, "County to Unit 3, fire reported near the intersection of 127 South and Cedar Lake Road."

Cable spun his chair to look at the county map on the wall behind him. Lozen and Hunter were on the other side of the county. *Crap.* He rushed into dispatch. "Any details on the fire?"

Judy looked up to him from her chair. "Sheriff, from what I gathered, it's more of the same. We are standing by. No requests for backup so far."

"Thanks, Judy."

Going back to his office Cable continued monitoring the radios. Time slowed to a crawl. He couldn't shake the thought that the fires were just camouflage. Something bigger was in the works, but he didn't have a clue as to what it might be. They were dealing with the unseen and unheard, the invisible.

Finally, the tracker frequency crackled. "Dale here. Got one. Nothing special. Same old brush pile stuff." Then silence, nothing else reported. Ten minutes later, County Unit 3 called in with the same report.

As the morning dawned, Cable called off the troops and headed home for a hot shower and a few hours of light dozing. A couple hours later, he rolled out of the rack, showered, and headed back for more punishment. None was forthcoming. Until the fire mystery was resolved, no one would rest easy. It was bizarre, to say the least. Not so much as one living suspect. The events of the past few days felt weird. Twilight Zone weird. Disappointment battled frustration, and they both fought anxiety.

11

-◆◆◆◆-

SONTA WAS DEALING WITH A DESIGN FLAW OF HIS OWN DOING, WHICH WAS UNSETTLING AT BEST.

THERE WAS NEVER GOING TO BE ANY PROMOTION or reprieve from Koal should results go south. The blueprint was dragging its feet. Sure, headway was being made daily. Businesses were being taken over through manipulation and mind control. Neighbors vanished as they were caught up by the Corruptors. The fires were unsettling, but something more would up the ante. There were more churches than Christians he reasoned in his demonic mind. Burning a church would be a step forward.

Sonta summoned Zorah to bring the maps of the region. There was a pleasant little Apostolic Openness Church in a town called Pomona. Out of the way it was. What made the site an outstanding candidate for destruction was the rumored open conflict between the literalist faction of the church and those less convinced of the strict interpretation of the Bible. The congregation was so caught up in the argument, they had, for the most part, abandoned prayer, which Sonta knew to be a wicked opening.

"You will need to inform Master Koal of your plan," ventured Zorah.

Sonta was vexed at this reminder but acknowledged the

reality and sent the message by telepathy.

Koal's eyes burnt blood red as he deciphered the true meaning of the request. He had to agree that the logic was sound, based strictly on the warring tribes within the small congregation and their abandonment of the most significant deterrent to demonic activity bar none—the power of prayer. Without exception, the Angelic Warriors could not act.

"Burn it," came the reply. "Do it on Sunday."

12

HAVING THE CREW STOP THEIR RADIO CHATTER APPEARED TO HAVE PAID OFF.

A WHOPPING SIX FIRES ON THE FOURTH NIGHT could have put someone near the goal line. That didn't happen, which meant they were still too far apart. A small strategy tweak was in order.

Cable remembered hearing a story one of the Crew told about an "arc light" operation during the Vietnam war. High altitude B-52 concentration bombing allowed ground forces to close on enemy positions without detection. The Crew needed to decrease the gaps between themselves, his inner voice told him, get closer to the fire.

Little did he know, eighteen minutes, the long lead time, was seventeen minutes and fifty-nine seconds too long. They were going to have to be deadly close to the crime scene to have a positive result. It was bound to happen.

13

------◆◆◆◆◆------

WITH HIS CLUTTERED OFFICE ALL AROUND HIM, JONES O'BRIAN WAS DEEP IN THOUGHT WHEN HIS CELL PHONE RANG.

"HEY THERE, SHERIFF," HE SAID, PUSHING BACK THE stack of reports on his desk. "What's up?"

"Well, to be honest, Jones, I'm about to lose it over these fires. I can't seem to slow them down. How would you like to become a volunteer deputy again?"

Cable laughed as he said, "I can't pay you."

Lt. Jones O'Brian was a veteran who had fought with the 75th Ranger Regiment in the Khmer Kush region of Afghanistan. He had done his share of long-range recon, otherwise known as Lerps, and lived to tell about it. Basic, AIT, OCS, Ranger School at Ft. Benning, Georgia. Then the Taliban. Jones had been down the road a time or two.

Over the ensuing years, he had assisted in several search and rescue operations in the county. He saw what most didn't. When Cable called Jones, it was past time.

Jones rearranged his pile, which uncovered his appointment calendar.

"I should be able to juggle some things around," he said,

"but first let me see if I understand. You want me to work without pay, take time off from my job to do it, and look for invisible fire-starters. Is that about right?"

"You got it, Jones."

"Well, the truth is I've been checking this out for a while. A change will do me good.

"I'll need to check with my boss and then stop by later so you can bring me up to speed."

Jones disconnected.

14

CABLE ARRIVED AT THE LAKE
FOR THE TWO O'CLOCK MEETING
TO FIND THE MOUNTAIN MEN,
AND LOZEN, ALREADY GATHERED, TALKING
AMONG THEMSELVES ABOUT
THE PREVIOUS NIGHT'S ACTIVITIES.

"TRY NOT TO BE DISCOURAGED," CABLE SAID. "WE STILL don't know what we're up against.

"Anybody got suggestions for me?"

Silence met its match. The perplexity of the situation was challenging to comprehend. Each face validated that conclusion.

Dan finally spoke, "My time in Iraq was sure different from this. When we looked hard enough, we could always find some clues. The rag-heads weren't perfect. Here, there are no clues. It's like a ghost started these fires and watched us try to find them while they burned. At least no one is shooting at us, yet."

"Yeah," Terry added, "in Iraq, there were always indications of movements. We didn't know their plans, but we knew something was up. The fire watch is totally different."

"Well, I'm not giving up!" said John, "we've got to reposition ourselves in our territories and move faster. Something will break our way."

The others shook their heads and grunted in agreement.

"Boys, ma'am," Cable added, "we've got to move so close together an ant couldn't escape. I've been doing some tactical research. Think spokes on a wheel. Lozen and Hunter are our hub in the middle of the wheel, no more than five minutes to our farthest location. We are going to have to use extreme camo, silent running, boys."

"Good idea, Sheriff," John agreed.

Cable appreciated the vote of confidence. There were times he wasn't sure if they were the hunters or the hunted.

Cable pulled out his map. "Let's focus on the northeast quadrant; it's more populated than the rest of the county. There have been more fires there, so whatever or whoever we're after knows that too.

"Everyone, pick a spot on your spoke as near to the middle as possible. That will put you two and one-half minutes out from our farthest point.

"Stay away from any point on your spoke where there's already been an incident. We haven't had any repeats up to this point. Anyone have any other ideas on how we can do things differently?"

One of the Mikes asked, "How about getting pizza and beer delivered to our posts?"

It was good to hear the laughter; it relieved the tension.

"Not in the budget," Cable responded. "Remember, what you're doing is off the grid."

As they stood to leave the picnic tables, Dick said quietly, "I couldn't find any evidence last night, but I know someone was there when I arrived. No way could I've been detected. I was on foot for only seven minutes. Did you ever see a shadow, but not what cast it?"

The remark caught everyone off guard, but some of the others had seen shadows that moved. Those five looked at one another as if agreeing with Dick. To a man, they believed something was at each of their locations last night.

"Spooky," Cable said. After thinking for a moment, he asked, "Are we dealing with goblins?"

"No," said Lozen, speaking for the first time, "we are closing ranks with the other world. The shadow traveled from another dimension." She walked toward her truck, Hunter in tow, and everyone followed.

God have mercy on us if she's right, thought Cable, starting to come to grips with this reality.

15

-◆◆◆◆-

KAZ IS GONE, JONES KEPT TELLING HIMSELF. PINCH YOURSELF FOOL; SHE ISN'T COMING BACK.

SOMETIMES HE JUST CRIED, ALL BY HIMSELF. THERE were days he believed God had forsaken him. His faith was eroding as it endured the absence of belief.

Approaching his front door, Jones stared at two years of emptiness, holding sway inside an empty house. He was lost in place, as they say in the military, having much more than reluctant moments. It had been two years since Kaz's passing, and he was unable to extract himself from the same old rut. Longing would not bring her back. God's will had been done, and Jones was forced to accept it. Isn't that what good Christians did? Don't question, take it on faith. What kind of will was that? He didn't know. He just knew there had to be a path to his new reality. It was up to him to find it, since it appeared God wasn't around to help.

As he entered the house, the odor of the trash can in the kitchen brought him back to Earth. Digging through kitchen drawers until he found a zip tie, Jones closed off the stench and took it outside to the trash bin.

A quick shower and a change of clothes brightened his outlook so much that he grabbed a leftover turkey sandwich and hit the door running. The sheriff was about to educate him about the fires.

Smiling to himself, he burst through the courthouse doors and headed directly to the sheriff's office.

"Is the sheriff in, out on patrol, or at the golf course?" he asked.

Clarence Merritt, the Chief Deputy, gave Jones the same kind of antagonistic look he'd given him for years.

"Jones, quit bothering Merritt," said someone from behind a door marked Deputy and Records Administrator.

He grinned. That would be Abby.

With a nod to the still-silent Merritt, he stuffed his hands in his pockets and obeyed the command. As he entered the office, Abby Solomon, who had been Kaz's best friend, rolled a chair in his direction. Protecting himself, he instinctively snatched it and sent it wheeling back at her.

Abby laughed as she stopped it with her foot. Tall and slender, Abby looked like she had just stepped off the volleyball court. Her short hair projected a person who hated hat hair. She had been a deputy for over ten years with several of those spent as a shift commander. Recently, state compliance had become a hot button, and Abby was the only person on staff who could install the new digital platform, which upgraded the record-keeping functions of the office, while maintaining their sanity.

Jones and Abby were a mutual support group. Friends since high school, they'd always enjoyed playful banter. Funny though, in spite of knowing each other for years, it wasn't until recently that Jones noticed Abby's eyes were green, and when she looked at him, and he looked back, they seemed to have a story to tell.

Merritt got up from his chair and started toward the file room. Pretending not to notice, Jones closed the door.

Merritt had a problem with Jones going back to their high school years. Cable had told his staff that Jones, who assisted on cases sporadically, was to be considered an honorary, unpaid, volunteer Captain. Chief Deputy Merritt disapproved and would demonstrate his displeasure by withholding information whenever convenient.

"Quick," Jones whispered, "where's Cable?"

"Out driving the county," Abby whispered back, "looking for clues and meeting with the Mountain Men."

"Thanks," Jones said, opening the door, looking at her sideways. She had a look about her, no doubt about that, a beautiful look. He nodded in her direction, knowing he needed to keep his feelings under control. Couldn't go there, not now, anyway.

Jones nearly ran over Merritt as he opened the door and stepped outside the room. *Heard every word*, he thought, grimacing.

As Jones walked by him, Merritt did a 180.

"What should I put on the visit report, Captain?"

"No need to put anything," Jones replied.

"I have to make a record of everyone who comes in, and why they were here," said Merritt.

"Do what you gotta do," replied Jones, moving steadily toward the door.

16

ABBY ALWAYS EXPECTED THE UNEXPECTED WHERE MERRITT WAS CONCERNED.

A S SHE HEADED TO THE DISPATCH ROOM, MERRITT, who was running, caught up with her. He grabbed her arm and was beginning to talk when a dull thud interrupted the proceedings.

Elbert, one of the two deputies in Dispatch, seeing an incident was about to happen, had dropped a telephone directory.

Stooping down to pick it up, he said, "Sorry, my bad."

Trying to hide her shock at the sudden intervention, she turned to look at Merritt, who had unhanded her and stepped back. A black mist was beginning to cover his face. Abby barely blinked, and just like that, the fog vanished, revealing his all too familiar features. She knew he hated her friend, that was plain to see, but what was happening?

17

-◆◆◆◆-

"YOU CAN
SEE THEIR
CONFUSION."

SONTA SAID TO ZORAH AS THE TWO FALLEN ANGELS
walked through the Wondren, their partially built headquarters located in a remote wooded valley with easy access to
the major highways of southern Illinois, which led to everywhere.

"Humans are like mad ants in a firestorm," Sonta continued,
"not knowing where to go or what to do."

Zorah uttered what passed for a laugh but, in reality, was no
more than a hiss.

"When we hit that little dump of a church tomorrow evening
during services, their God will be smitten. There will be no
warning, which means no messages will rise to the Heavens
summoning the Angelic Warriors. We will prevail." The plan
to hit the Apostolic Openness Church made Sonta salivate,
the drool emitting a particularly foul stench that incapacitated
regular flossing.

Zorah, who would lead the attack, was hopeful he would be
able to kill a Christian or two, see the terror in their eyes before
he gutted them with his talon-like nails, watching their body
parts sag as life fled. He would drink their warm blood, which
he preferred much more than Earth water.

Watching the preparations for an escalation in the battle for the souls of Earth citizens from his vantage point in Chicago was most pleasing to Master Koal. Like any Field Marshall, he valued the element of surprise, especially when it compromised the Angelic Warriors. They had to be asked, and there would be no time for that. There was also the notion, to which he held firmly, that Sonta's plan, which had been adopted by the high council, was indecisive and riddled with uncertainty. Time would tell all. Meanwhile, a change in tactics would invigorate the troops.

The USA had been divided into four quadrants, making it only natural that competition would arise among the Field Commanders, who were all members of the high council and on a par with Koal. It would be career-enhancing to make a bold move pay off in advancing the darkness, the uncertainty, and suffering that the Lord High Satan was bringing to the human race.

The quadrants had been determined by size, not population, which meant the eastern half of America was the most fertile territory. Rude humanity lived there. But that was not his assignment. Instead, he was given the Midwest Bible Belt farmers and workers of all types. It was a tough crowd. Poor and rich mingled, or rather existed, in close proximity. Church, drugs, promiscuity, and guns were all caught up within the Christian community. After all, they were humans, a crowd that worshiped Jesus and belonged to the NRA. Indeed, Koal reasoned, Jesus would have condoned all the violence and belonged to the NRA himself. He would more than likely have owned an M-16. He laughed, there had to be some amusement, even for demons. WWJD. A real slogan if there ever was one.

The choices to make lay hard in front of him. There would be no easy decisions here. The Fallen would have to carve their way forward, throwing away the fat while consuming the remainder.

Koal had been in the top tier of the angelic hierarchy when Lucifer, which means morning star or bearer of light, suffered a name change. Satan was cast out when it became known that he intended to replace God as the Most High. He said, "I will ascend into Heaven and exalt my throne above the stars of God." He was a chief in Heaven alongside Michael and Gabriel before tumbling from that high place to his new home that the demons call Second Heaven. Pride was his downfall. One-third of all the angels in Heaven fell with him, Koal being one of those in close proximity. Satan and the Fallen Angels took satisfaction in being the source of all evil on Earth.

Make no mistake; they were hard at work.

18

⬥⬥⬥

SHERIFF BOB CABLE WAS SITTING ON A PICNIC TABLE TRYING TO ENJOY THE VIEW, BUT THERE WERE TOO MANY UNCERTAINTIES SWIRLING IN HIS HEAD TO RELAX.

A DISTANT RATTLE OF AN OLD TRUCK GRATED ON HIS ears. That would be Dick. The old junker screeched to a halt. Dick exited and bee-lined straight for Cable.

"The cool don't say how they got that way," he said as he approached.

Cable had never quite learned what made the man tick, and that thought encompassed his mountain friends as well. He had also learned never to underestimate them. To a man, they were veterans who had survived only God knows what and lived to tell about it. The hand of Death himself had occupied their lives.

Although Dick could put together some strange sentences, he could be a voice of reason. He hadn't become the de facto leader of the Mountain Men because his fear factor ran wild.

Before Cable could respond, Jones' truck came into view. When Jones opened his door, Cable yelled, "I'm not here. I'm driving the county looking for evidence!"

"If that's a fact, you're driving slow, Sheriff," Jones said as he closed the truck's door and started moving in his direction.

"Do you still have the overlay maps with you?" Jones asked.

"They're on the front seat."

Jones made an about-face and retrieved the maps from the squad car.

"What gives, Dick?" Jones said as he approached the table. "What have you found out that we don't know?"

Jones smoothed the maps out on the picnic table. One overlay had the date and location of each reported fire; the other included those from last night.

"What's going on?" Cable asked, looking from Jones to Dick.

"I don't know," said Jones. "I think Dick is going to enlighten us. Okay, Dick," Jones challenged, "we're here, the maps are here. Let's hear it."

The three stood looking at the display on the picnic table. Dick walked around the table a couple of times, his eyes never leaving the map. He opened his mouth as if to speak while continuing to circle the table.

Cable broke the silence, "Earth to Dick!"

Dick stopped walking and stared out across the lake. Then he turned and pointed at the map.

"Look at this." He took a toothpick out of his pocket and stuck it on the map.

Cable and Jones looked at the map, then at each other. They had spent so much time trying to analyze where each fire had occurred that the overall picture was never appropriately considered.

Where Dick placed the toothpick was a blank area.

Knowing Dick had seen this map only a short time before, Cable asked, "How'd you know about this area?"

Dick, with his shaggy hair and unkempt beard, looked at both of them. Tears started to form in his eyes.

"Two nights ago, I thought I'd gone over the edge. I was sitting on my porch waiting for a call about another incident when I heard voices. No, it was only one voice.

"'Look at the map,' the voice said.

"I heard it three times. I'm sorry I didn't tell you a while ago, Sheriff. I had to be sure I wasn't crazy. I was still trying to put it all together when I saw Jones downtown a while ago."

Without speaking, Cable walked to his car and got another overlay, this one with a grid outline. He took the toothpick out, laid the grid on the incident map, and put the toothpick back in.

Cable abruptly turned and walked several steps toward the lake's edge, stopped, threw his hands up in the air, and let out a yell.

He returned to the table with a big smile on his face and said, "Looks like we're finally making progress."

Jones, living in the moment, said, "Hey, I see it now!"

Dick was overcome with emotion, wiping tears from his eyes.

Jones said, "When you were a kid, Coach, did you ever get out to the old brick plant? That toothpick is where the old Paving Brick Company stood. Remember the story? It opened in 1909 and operated for a couple of decades. The plant sent bricks to Panama when the canal was under construction but went bust in the Depression and has sat empty ever since. Not a soul ever tried to buy it or repurpose it. Now it's just a landmark. We all used to play there as kids."

Dick chuckled, "Rumor has it some of us were conceived there."

"Of course, the brick plant," Cable said, going back in time. "You say that toothpick is where the brick plant stands?"

"True enough," said Jones. "That would make it the epicenter of the fires. Every incident is a radial, in a direct line to the plant. If our logic is correct, then there must be planning behind the events. Something or somebody is creating all this. The brick plant appears to be ground zero."

Jones' mind was working feverishly, but he could not quite connect the dots. The input was coming from somewhere he could not pinpoint.

Cable picked up on his turmoil and said, "Spill your guts, man."

"Sheriff, I'm considering a couple of things, but I need to think this through. Why don't you head back to the courthouse? I'll get with you real soon. Whatever you do, don't let Merritt know what we are talking about or that we have seen each other. I've got some serious issues with that man."

"That goes for you too, Dick. Don't say anything to anyone about what we've discovered here. Not that anyone would believe you, anyway." Jones laughed a little and briefly clasped the man's shoulder.

"We'll talk later about that voice you heard."

"Jones, what are you going to do now that we think we might know a way to focus our surveillance?" Cable asked impatiently.

"This is the best lead we've had."

"Our plans need to be solid," said Jones, "and solid takes a little time and thought."

Cable had known Jones for more than thirty years. He had watched him go off to war in Afghanistan with the 75th Ranger Regiment and come home alive. Cable could only imagine what it took to survive in those conditions. Hungry, dirty, stinking, hurt, wouldn't begin to describe what some had endured. Cable realized that 1st Lieutenant Jones O'Brian

2/506th Infantry, 101st Airborne Division, had been tried under fire. A Silver Star with oak leaf cluster hung in his bedroom. The army doesn't give those out as souvenirs.

No wonder he was a quick thinker. It was required. Jones had been known to say there were two kinds of soldiers: the quick and the dead. Over the years of their friendship, Cable had come to value Jones' ability, and despite a tendency to second-guess himself, Jones was much more often right than wrong.

"Take the reins, son," Cable said.

19

CABLE PUT THE PEDAL TO THE METAL AND HEADED BACK TO HIS OFFICE.

HIS ROUTE WAS IN THE DIRECTION OF THE OLD BRICK plant, so close, in fact, that he was tempted to do a drive-by, just a little close area surveillance. All it took was a left turn at the bottom of Cemetery Hill, but he had given his word that he would go along with the program. Jones had said sit chilly. Cable turned the car south.

Employees came in all shapes and varieties. Knowing individual capabilities allowed the wheel to turn with less friction. It was important for the sheriff to understand the skills of his employees or lack thereof. Some were always going to be better than others—that was just performance data talking. Cable trusted his perception, which was not exactly foolproof. Results were mixed. He needed to remember that people required supervision, whether he was providing it or not. Merritt had been more than lax the past few months, letting some things slip by that should be routine. Jones could be right about Merritt. Where there is smoke, something is burning.

20

ABBY PICKED UP HER RINGING PHONE. "AB, WHAT IS MERRITT UP TO NOW?"

C ABLE ASKED THE SECOND SHE PICKED UP. "He's at the front desk typing some reports."

"Has he taken his break?"

"Yes."

Grumbling to himself, he asked, "Can he hear you?"

"I doubt it. I'm in the file room. Did Jones find you? He was here about two hours ago."

"We met. I'll fill you in on it later. I'll be there in about five. Don't tell Merritt I called." Hanging up, he arrived, parked his car and considered his next move.

His space was private, hidden from view. He liked that. He carefully separated the overlays from the county map and grid and locked them in the bin under the passenger seat. Taking the map and the grid with him, he headed for his office.

Merritt looked up from his work as he passed by but said nothing.

"Anything going on, Deputy?" Cable asked, heading to his office.

"Nothing out of the ordinary, Sheriff. A couple of mailboxes knocked over last night. A fender bender up by Dowell, nobody hurt. How was your drive?"

Not hearing it mentioned that Jones had stopped by to see him, he replied, "Nah, nothing, just a trip into the countryside. It's amazing, though, how fast people slow down when they see me coming."

Merritt nodded, seeming to agree.

With the maps under his arm, Cable went into his office and, as always, pulled his door partly closed. No need to raise any red flags at this point. He pinned the map up and, using his pocketknife, gently pushed the little edges around the pinhole back into the paper fabric. It would take a very close inspection to see the tiny hole. Going into his bathroom, he flushed the toilet as a distraction, stepping out just as Merritt walked into his office.

Before Merritt could speak, Cable enlisted his assistance, "Help me put the grid map up."

Once the grid was in place, Merritt unleashed a barrage of questions.

"Do you think there will be any incidents tonight?"

"Do you plan on calling the 'hillbillies' to help?"

"That's what they are here for," Cable said.

It was evident that Merritt was doing verbal surveillance.

Hoping to deflect further interrogation, Cable busied himself by opening a logbook and perusing some entries.

Merritt persisted, "Are you and Midge going out tonight? Where can you be reached if you're needed?"

Realizing no answers were forthcoming, Merritt paused and in a demanding tone asked, "Are you going to answer me? Hello?"

Abby, listening intently through the open door, took Merritt's tone of voice as her cue. As the barrage mounted, she gathered together the papers that needed signatures and walked into the sheriff's office.

Merritt mumbled to himself as Cable picked up a pen and began reviewing the documents Abby laid one-by-one in front of him. As he did, the phone in the outer office rang and Merritt—with a huff—went to answer.

Cable thanked Abby as he handed the papers back to her. "Perfect timing, Deputy," he said.

"Yes, sir," she answered with a faint smile playing on her lips as she left the room.

Cable picked up his cell and called Dick. While the call was going through, his thoughts turned to Merritt. There was no doubt that several years earlier, shortly after he had hired Merritt, the man had been an asset to the office. Hard work earned him the promotion to Chief Deputy.

In the midst of it all, though, it was hard not to notice his solitary life, the absence of friends. Merritt was a loner who lived with his mother; his only family as far as anyone knew. His mom was aging, and her boy was very attentive. When she passed less than a year ago, things changed, Merritt changed. While not exactly a GQ man, he dressed more in tune with the current fashion, bought a restored 1957 Chevy hardtop, and drove the wheels off of it. On his days off he was frequently out of town, reportedly in the company of new friends he'd made among the many newcomers to the community.

"Hello," came the voice through the phone, "are you there?"

Cable realized he must have drifted off thinking about Merritt, "Hey, Mountain Man."

"Whatcha need, Sheriff?"

"Just want to thank you for figuring out the map situation this afternoon."

"It just fell together for me," said Dick. "There are too many things I still can't explain. I'm still not sure about the voice I heard."

"Let's cover our bases and send the trackers out for the next three nights," Cable interjected.

"Nah, these spooks will come to us," said Dick. "No need to go thrashing around with everyone out in the field. Let's send a tracker, one if you must, or not."

No mistaking that intention. Dick meant Lozen and her dog, Hunter.

"Do you mean what I think you mean?" asked Cable.

"You're reading my mind," said Dick.

"She's got something we don't. She's not much of a volunteer, though. She has to be asked, and she is hard to find to ask if you get my drift. She and that dog are always inseparable and always out at night. Maybe she can see in the dark," he said laughing.

Cable wasn't sure that was an impossibility.

"I suppose you're right. Let's work our plan, though. I didn't mean to scatter everybody around. If we have everyone in place on the spokes, we'll be positioned to provide our tracker backup if needed.

"Can you get her out there for a little recon before everyone's in position?" Cable asked.

"No need," said Dick. "I suspect she's already there."

"How would she know?" asked Cable. "How could she know?"

"She just does, that's all. She just does. Lozen knows things before they happen. It's weird, hard to explain," said Dick.

"Well, be advised to keep all of these plans to yourself. We don't want anyone else, including Merritt, in the loop. Something is going on with that man that's not right."

"Roger that," said Dick.

"I think Jones is right. My office is bugged or under close

observation. Merritt just tried to pull information from me that I believe he was planning to pass on. He was asking questions that he's never asked before."

"We need to set up a Red Herring," said Dick.

"Great idea," said Cable, "I'll run it by Jones."

At that very moment, Cable's cell phone chimed.

"Got to go now, another call's coming in on my cell. Be sure to contact everyone about the next three nights. Be ready to roll that wheel."

He hung up and connected his cell. It was his wife, Midge.

"Honey, it's me," she said in a strained voice. "You know I'm not one to panic, but there has been a van parked down the road a ways for hours. There were two people in it; now they are gone."

"Maybe someone broke down," Cable said.

"Well, they're not there now," she said, her voice shaky, "and no one so much as opened a door."

Cable had confidence in Midge being able to handle most any emergency that would come up. She was familiar with every weapon the county had in its arsenal, especially the AR-15, the civilian baby brother to the M-16. And—like pretty much everyone else in the boondocks—there was more nearby.

Cable answered calmly, speaking a code they'd developed after he won his first election.

"Plan Alpha?"

"Yes," Midge acknowledged.

He bolted upright from his chair. An affirmative answer meant—"Help, come now."

He knew the necessary steps had been taken to secure the house. Doors and windows were locked. Fully loaded weapons were in plain sight.

"Okay, tell me what you see." Cable stood poised to rush to her.

"There are at least fifteen men headed toward the house, and..."

"Hold on," he interrupted Midge as he rushed out the office door.

Abby looked up at his haste. Cable made brief eye contact with her, hoping to convey the depth of his concern, but kept moving toward the exit.

"Something up, Sheriff? Another fire?" Merritt called after him.

"Keep hanging, Hon," he said into the phone, then raised his voice and glanced back to Abby and Merritt.

"Have any units close to my house converge and wait for me at the crossroads!"

He headed to his car.

21

✦✦✦✦✦

AS SOON AS CABLE HAD CLEARED THE PREMISES, MERRITT DUCKED INTO A NEARBY ROOM PUNCHING NUMBERS ON HIS CELL.

ABBY WATCHED IT ALL UNFOLD AND KNEW, RIGHT THEN and there, that Merritt was the mole others suspected him to be.

He's probably trying to alert someone, she thought, sprinting down the hallway toward dispatch. Merritt caught a glimpse of her running and took up the chase. As he dashed after her, trying to catch up, he yelled out, "All units close to Eagle Nest converge at the crossroads!"

As Abby entered dispatch, she confirmed the order to the dispatchers on duty, who rushed to comply. Starting back to her station, she ran headlong into Merritt, who slid to a halt barely inches away. Their eyes locked. Merritt backed up slowly. He had seen Abby in action before and wanted no part of it. He met her glare for only a second, then whirled around and walked back down the hallway.

Abby silently followed Merritt. With his back still to her, he sat down at his desk and picked up his cell.

Abby spun his chair so fast the phone flew from his hand, hit the wall, and shattered. "What's more important than getting units rolling to the sheriff's house?"

When Abby looked at Merritt, she couldn't see his face; only a black mist confronted her. It was a hazy darkness, like earlier in dispatch, just as the sheriff had described the stranger in The Kitchen a few weeks ago.

Merritt stood to face Abby and began to draw his gun. A nanosecond later, an unexplained light flashed.

Merritt's hand froze as his trigger finger stopped. He had fired one round, but couldn't squeeze off another.

His facial features reappeared; a terrified look now covering his face. He ran out the door, jumped into his car, and sped out of the parking lot.

Abby looked at the front of her shirt. No blood. No feeling of impact. Walking to the window, she watched Merritt driving off. *He's not okay*, she thought, *not even close*.

Abby went back to dispatch. "Elbert, Merritt just fired on me, missed, thank God, ran out the door, and I don't know when or if he'll be back. Call someone else in to cover for you, and go to the front desk. I'm headed to the Eagle's Nest to see if I can help the sheriff and Midge."

Elbert, a tall, thin, Afro-American who had been around the block, said, "I heard the shot. And that light flash, what was that?"

"Merritt pulled the trigger," she said, "not sure about the flash."

With that said, Abby was gone.

As he entered the front office, Elbert smelled the gunpowder. With instincts honed by education and experience in crime scene investigation, he stopped and surveyed the area. Debris from the shattered cell phone lay on the floor. There wasn't anything else lying around, so Elbert turned to get some yellow tape to cordon off the area. It was then that he heard a shuffling sound in the front hallway. When he looked, there appeared to be a little more light than usual, but nothing stood out. Maybe there had been someone there. Whatever it was had gone.

A shiny object on the floor caught the light; he bent down to examine it. A spent 9mm shell casing lay in the sunlight. Looking up, Elbert saw a hole in the wall, about head high.

22

-◆◆◆◆◆-

THE TINY SOUTHERN ILLINOIS TOWN OF POMONA, AN UNINCORPORATED VILLAGE, LAY JUST OFF STATE ROUTE 127 SOUTH OF MURPHYSBORO, ILLINOIS.

THE TOWN'S POPULATION NUMBERED A LITTLE OVER 300 brave souls. The Apostolic Openness Church had been organized by settlers coming into the region after the Civil War and had somehow survived until present times. The congregation's head-count stood at forty-two strong and, until recently, were unified in their literal interpretation of the Bible. A slight disagreement among some of the newer members had changed their dynamic. They had been known to handle snakes and for some time had outlawed singing, but all that was in the past. Their young minister, Rufus Cornwell, was a full-time employee of Southern Illinois University in Carbondale some twenty miles northeast. Many of his flock were from families who had settled the area. Rufus was a devout Christian who strove to follow God in all his daily activities. He received a small pittance for Sunday sermons and funerals.

The church held regular services each Sunday morning, and evening Bible study began at 7 p.m.

Sonta, fully aware of the calendar of events as it pertained to church activities, instructed Zorah to assemble a forty-man assault team, which consisted of demons and Fallen Angels. Using the unseen parallel dimension, the team transported to a small wooded area that lay just beyond the gravel parking lot flanking the small church's south entrance. Advancing on foot and wing, the group surrounded the church in short order and at 7:23 p.m. came through every opening, sealed or not. Windows shattered, doors splintered, as evil poured inside. All light was extinguished as the living servants of God paid with their blood. As the pulpit ignited, the flames spread rapidly throughout the old wooden structure.

Zorah reached the young minister first and, grabbing him by the neck, lifted him five feet off the floor, cutting him from throat to groin with one savage slash of his thumbnail. Only a groan of agony escaped the preacher's lips as life fled. Others suffered similar fates before they could so much as speak.

But one small child did speak. Amidst the din of savagery, a little girl, overlooked by the attackers, called out, *"Help us, Lord; we are sorely set upon."*

In an instant, everything changed. The fury of the attack had been so explosive that none of the congregates had offered up a prayer for protection. But, the little girl's cry for help, her intercession, set Heaven in motion.

Every demon and Fallen Angel was instantly staring directly into the face of one of God's Angelic Warriors, who unleashed tremendous bolts of light into them. Demons died. Fallen Angels, Sonta and Zorah included, were hit and driven into retreat. Only a few survived. It was over in seconds. The fire that started with the pulpit consumed the church and all its ascending souls until only ashes remained.

The little girl, who had asked for help, remained among the living. The leader of the Angelic Warriors held her tightly. Putting his hand on her head, Arrow asked God in Heaven to heal her memories, erasing the demonic intervention forever. "Out of the mouth of babes," said the leader's lieutenant.

"Yes," was the only reply. Not everyone would ask for divine protection, which could be fatal. The angels would, however, strive mightily to save those who did.

A neighbor seeing the glow from the fire called 911 and rushed down the road. Only the brick chimney remained standing as the fire smoldered.

Seeing the little girl standing at the far edge of the parking lot, the wife rushed to her. Wiping away tears, she carried her back to the car.

23

LOZEN ROLLED OVER,
STRETCHED HER ANGULAR FRAME,
AND STOOD UP. HER DOG DIDN'T MOVE
A MUSCLE, SO SHE ROLLED HIM
OUT AS WELL.

EVERYTHING ABOUT HER COTTAGE, SITTING DEEP within the Pomona hills in a tiny enclave of ninety-eight souls called Etherton Switch, was authentic. The Native American log cabin built by early settlers to the region in the late 1800s was in dire need of repair when Lozen and the Mountain Men came along. They shored up the timbers, added new crossbeams, bolstered the foundation, and sealed the numerous openings in the walls. The small structure was rendered bone dry and once more was capable of holding heat. The wood-burning stove Dick brought from his farm near the Little Grand Canyon accomplished the mission.

Tall by Apache standards, lean and remarkably fit, Lozen moved about in a continual conversation with an unseen director. She walked closer to the Lord than most. People called her prescient, but it was a strong spiritual relationship with the Great Spirit, the Apache's recognition of the Creator, that gave her this ability. Lozen's heritage had brought her to this place, and she walked much like great, great, great, great aunt Lozen, a hero and legend to the Apache, the first of Lozen's bloodline.

The Warm Spring Apaches referred to her namesake as a woman of spirit. She would inherit that title as well. In the 1870s the Apache had been forced onto reservations. Some escaped. One of those was Victorio, leader of the Warm Springs tribe. In 1877 they were on the run, eluding U.S. and Mexican authorities. Among the warriors at Victorio's side was his younger sister, Lozen, who had a very unusual gift. She had a knowing, seeing things that had not yet happened, items and objects that were invisible to the naked eye. Her hands would tingle when she faced the direction of the enemy. The strength of the sensation indicated proximity. Her tribe migrated to this remote part of Illinois years ago.

Lozen of the Mountain Men, whose age was unknown, was her direct descendant and keeper of the gift. She appeared to be in midlife, but looks could be deceiving. When she reached out to Jones, it signaled trouble that was unseen but expected. No one knew much about her, and she preferred it that way.

The atmospheric shift in her surroundings had not gone unnoticed. Mist-faced demons, and the dark vans that carried them, were visible on her radar. Hunter was tuned in as well. He was in continual growl mode.

"Yes, Hunter," she said, "darkness occupies those vans. Stay alert."

There had been little contact between her and the Mountain Men recently, so she piled into her truck and headed for The Kitchen. Someone would be there drinking coffee. As she closed on her destination, the old truck, without her assistance, started turning right, indicating an assignment was imminent. Parking across the street from Shooter's Alley, Lozen exited her vehicle with Hunter hard on her heels. She took a long look at the business front. No visible merchandise was the first take. Not like the old days when shop windows stayed full.

Opening the door to Shooter's Alley set off her internal alarm. The lights were low, but not from an electrical malfunction. It was the darkness, descending like a dense rain cloud. At the same instant, Hunter dropped to the floor in attack mode.

Swiveling her body to the left, she could see two teenage girls near the back of the store, backed into a corner by two scruffy-looking men with no features.

"In the name of Jesus!" hurled from Lozen's lips as she made her move. Quicker than the eye could register, she closed on the demons. With her right hand she pulled a beautiful bone handled knife from her belt. In a U-shaped cutting motion taught for thousands of years by Samurai swordsman, she cut them both up and down, their wounded bodies collapsing to the floor before dissipating in a pool of blood. Their blood.

Calling Hunter to heel, she rubbed his head.

"We've seen that before, haven't we, old boy," she told the dog. Dimension shifters were a clear and present sign of the evil around them.

Lozen gathered up the girls, who were speechless at the force of their rescuer, and sent them off to the police department around the corner. Her name was unmentioned, just a girl and a dog would be the only report.

As she returned to her truck, a thought locked itself in her heart. The Darkness was here for a reason, and her game needed to step up. That would not happen if she were too fatigued to act, and the day's activities had been draining. With that thought in mind, Lozen headed for the Switch to get things ready for the evening and take a little nap.

The small siesta didn't seem to accomplish much as the evening advanced. Too soon, it was time to move out towards her cabin at Little Grand Canyon. Something was afoot in the Shawnee National Forest, but she felt no fear of death. "The Lord is my shepherd; I shall not want," she repeated to herself, meaning every word. There would be no mercy if she were captured, for either she or Hunter would be as good as dead if such a calamity occurred. That did not change the fact that she was here for a reason.

The trip each evening from Etherton Switch to the Canyon was her part in the play, an assignment of duty duly followed. Her place at the Switch was mainly a cover. It gave her an address, a place to get mail from her family, a landline phone, and somewhere to park her truck. Etherton Switch was so out of the way it kept questions about her identity to a minimum.

The Switch was out there, as the locals liked to say. In years gone by, it had been a shipping point for the peaches and apples raised in the area. The orchards were long gone, but it had been a good location for her, being close enough to the Canyon and surrounding towns. As she set out on the rugged six-mile hike through the forest, a strange feeling she had experienced many times before rolled over her body. This disturbance was intense. Something terrible was happening.

"Father, lead me!" she called out and, turning back, jumped into her old Chevy truck and headed towards Pomona.

Hunter jumped into the bed of the old '53 Chevy, and together they roared down the road. Topping Tom Cat Hill on State Route 127, she could see a glow in the distance. Two hills later, the light became an inferno. Turning right towards the little settlement, she saw the disaster. A standing chimney was all that remained of the Apostolic Openness Church. She had met the pastor, Rufus Cornwell, and admired his commitment. There would not be another meeting in this place.

As she pulled into the parking lot, a lady left one of the

arriving vehicles and ran to the far end of the lot, picked up a little girl, and carried her to safety.

Lozen silently commanded Hunter, who took off around the smoldering debris. Nose to the ground, the dog howled while twice circling the burnt-out structure. Suddenly the dog stopped and dashed northward. At the edge of the woods, he dropped to the ground, not making a sound. Lozen got out of the truck and made her way to the spot. Standing over Hunter, she knew, intuitively, this was the portal, the entry point for the Fallen. She had seen too many of these over the years.

Hearing a siren wailing somewhere in the distance, she knew her time to leave was at hand. The only witnesses to this tragedy had flown. Not being one of those, she would be of no help to the investigation that was sure to commence.

Pausing, observing, as the still-standing chimney smoked its last, tears poured down her face. Believers had been ruthlessly murdered this evening, and she keenly felt the loss.

Calling Hunter, she returned home, parked the truck, and set out overland for the Canyon. Arriving just as darkness set in, she opened the windows of the cabin. Breathing the fresh air deeply into her lungs, she walked to the edge of her garden, noticing a few of the vegetables were ready for picking.

Standing quietly, Lozen felt the air chill. Zorah, a Fallen Angel, flew silently over the Canyon wall rising above Chalk Bluff searching for a prize human to present to Master Sonta for his pleasure. Putting her hand on Hunter's head to indicate silence, Lozen watched as the beast cast his wide net. Seeing no quarry, Zorah departed. There would be no prey gathered for his master this evening, but time was not the friend of the Fallen.

24

-◆◆◆◆-

CABLE FORCED HIS PHONE INTO ITS BLUE TOOTH HOLDER AND ACTIVATED THE LINK. "WHAT DO YOU SEE, MIDGE?"

HER VOICE WAS STILL CALM. "THEY'RE GETTING CLOSER. The vans are gone. Yep, there are fifteen of them."

Anxiety crept into her tone. "When I got the binoculars on them, I thought they had black ski masks on, but it wasn't that. They, um, I don't know how else to say this, they didn't have any faces!"

"Didn't have faces, or was it a black mist in front of their faces?" asked Cable, wheeling the squad car furiously around Cox's Corner. The sun had started sinking toward sunset, and deepening shadows created by the house would make it hard for Midge to see any movement.

Then he heard it, the unmistakable bark of Midge's AR-15. He could hear glass shattering and the distinct sound of a door disintegrating. The house he cherished was under attack, he thought, losing count of the shots now being fired.

"I've hit at least three of them, Bob," she yelled, "but they aren't slowing down."

Midge dropped the phone as she screamed, "Dropping back to Dog Trot!"

Hearing the commotion sounded like a transformer humming on overload. Cable started to say something when the connection went dead.

He grabbed his radio mic and yelled, "Code Red at Eagle Nest! Code Red at Eagle Nest!"

There was precious little traffic as Cable raced to his house. What seemed like forever was merely a few minutes. He was the first arrival and came in hot. Throttling back on his adrenaline, he called up years of training, tapped the brakes, and eased up to the driveway. The scene was nothing like Midge had described. There were no visible combatants. No one was moving in the fields, no vans.

Nothing.

As Cable stepped out of his car, two squad cars arrived. There was no sign of his wife anywhere. On his command, the two officers set up a roadblock one hundred yards out. He didn't need gawkers disturbing any evidence.

"Keep everyone back. I'm going in alone," Cable said, getting back into his car and driving slowly toward the house. Drawing his Sig 26 as he got close, he exited and moved cautiously through what remained of the front door.

If Midge had been able to make it safely to Dog Trot, she was probably alive. Dog Trot was the Cable family code name for a fireproof, hidden chamber between the two floors of the house. The room ventilated via a long underground shaft that surfaced as an innocuous-looking structure in the garden out back, far enough from the house for safety. There was ample food and supplies for two people to last several days. It was their secret place and would remain so. He went in alone.

The diminishing light of day no longer shone through the downstairs windows. Every pane was broken. Both entry doors off the front porch stood in shreds. Inching his way through the house, watching for any movement, Cable could see everything in the living room had been demolished. Tables, chairs, sofa turned over. Lampshades crumpled, broken glass everywhere. Years of experience and instinct told him the culprits were long gone. Nevertheless, he stayed alert on his way to the safe room.

Utilizing their unique code, Cable knocked on the safe room wall.

A panel slid open, and Midge cautiously poked out the barrel of her AR-15.

He smiled at the sight of the weapon.

"It's me, Honey," Cable said.

"Thank, God," Midge said as she drew the gun barrel back and came out with tears streaming down her cheeks.

He held her tight for a while. When her shaking subsided, they walked to the kitchen, sat down on two of the unsmashed chairs, and were silent. The breakfast room was in tatters with glass everywhere.

"Who were these people, Bob?" she asked.

"Did you find the three I dropped on the front porch?"

"Sweetie, there are no bodies on the front porch. No bloodstains. Maybe in the morning, we'll be able to find something, but for now, let's keep the body count to ourselves."

"Agreed," said Midge, "but where did they go?"

Cable's two-way radio crackled, "Seven to Eagle."

"Go ahead, Spec."

"The ambulance has arrived."

"Send them back. Midge is fine."

"Roger that. Solomon is here."

"Send her in. I'll be out there in five."

Cable turned toward his wife and said, "Midge, you are the sole witness to date of all this mayhem and uncertainty. That is a breakthrough."

He then brought her up to date on the fires.

"Looks to me like they picked us out of the pack. Someone had to furnish the intel. We'll find out who, you have my word on it. I got here as fast as I could, but when I pulled up out front, there was nothing, I mean nothing. I didn't see anything like what you described. That's the MO for these players." They sat at the table and held hands.

Wiping her face dry, Midge said, "It all happened so fast, Bob, but you can see I'm okay. It was scary, but this was no hill for a stepper. We've been through a lot over the years and survived."

"Yeah, but never anything like this. You've shot a lot of rounds through that AR of yours, but never to defend yourself."

Hearing a car in the driveway, he got up and went toward what used to be a door and met Abby on the front porch.

"Can you spend the night?"

"Of course. How's Midge?"

"She's okay, but her adrenaline is still pumping."

"Yours would be too," said Abby.

"Right. You bet," said Cable.

"Midge, Abby's going to spend the night with you. We are trying to catch these guys in action, and tonight is our first close encounter. I'll have a perimeter set up just in case of a return visit."

As Cable exited onto the main roadway, three more deputies arrived. "Gentlemen, nothing moves inside these two hundred yards, understood? Abby will spend the night inside. Ellen, call Elbert. We need to have you guys relieved at four a.m. I want to protect this area until daybreak unless something else happens. You guys cover the front. Stay alert. Having never seen the enemy, we are still in the dark. I'll be out back of the house to keep watch if you need me."

He turned to walk away when one of the deputies down the road caught his attention.

"Sheriff, is that Merritt?"

25

------◆◆◆◆◆------

ABBY LOOKED AT THE SHATTERED WINDOWS, BROKEN FURNITURE, AND OVERTURNED LAMPS IN DISBELIEF.

HOW COULD MIDGE HAVE GOTTEN THROUGH THIS alone? Midge seemed to read her thoughts.

"At least it's not supposed to be cold tonight," Midge said. "It would be hard to keep the house warm with the new ventilation we have."

Abby smiled. At least she still had a sense of humor. "What kind of tea do you want? I'll put the water on."

"Forget the tea, Abby. We need expresso!"

Observing Midge's condition caused Abby to remember her first shoot-out. One of the Wilson twins, a stone-cold junkie if there ever was one, got out on parole after a five-year stint for armed robbery and possession with intent to distribute. He promptly walked into the local Walgreens with a handgun and shot the clerk. About two minutes later, Abby's Walther PPK380 pumped five rounds into Mr. Wilson, effectively ending his criminal career and his life. That experience alone told her that Midge's adrenaline was still pumping.

The dream house that Bob and Midge had always wanted was gone. Someone or something had taken it from them.

"Midge, I'm so sorry for what you've been through," said Abby.

"I've never seen anything like it," said Midge. "These things that attacked didn't even have faces!"

"That sounds weird. Like the guy the sheriff saw at The Kitchen a while back," Abby related.

"That's right. Bob told me about that. And when he looked for him outside, he had disappeared. You know, I could see them moving around, obviously having conversations, driving vans, but no faces," Midge said.

No faces. Kind of like Merritt earlier, Abby pondered.

Midge tried to get up from her chair and grimaced. "That hurts, really bad!"

Rushing over, Abby saw blood oozing through Midge's sweater. "Let's get this off, and your blouse," she said, removing it carefully. "I see blood."

"Blood? No way! I felt something hit me in the back when I escaped out of the living room, but I know I wasn't shot."

Midge tried again to get up from the chair, but couldn't move her left shoulder. She looked to see if her fingers wiggled, and they did. Her elbow worked but not her shoulder.

No way around it, Abby would have to cut the garments off. She grabbed some scissors from a drawer in the kitchen and started cutting.

She gasped as she peeled the clothes from Midge's back.

"What in the world is there, Abby?" Midge demanded.

Abby has seen a lot of wounds over the years, but she wasn't prepared for this. She grabbed her two-way radio to call Cable. "Sheriff, Midge is, uh. . .hurt." As Abby looked out the back window, she saw the sheriff standing next to an old oak tree, about thirty yards away. He quickly covered the distance to the house and came through the opening where a door had been, just behind Midge.

"What is it, Bob? Abby won't tell me." Midge was getting

testy. The effects of adrenaline were wearing off, and the pain was settling in.

He took a deep breath. "It looks like a laser beam went across your back, starting at your left shoulder and angling toward your right kidney. The bleeding has slowed, but it looks like a burn, a severe sunburn with blisters and lacerations."

"We need to bandage Midge as best we can, Sheriff," said Abby.

"Do you have a first aid kit?" she asked.

Midge pointed toward the bathroom with her working arm.

"She can't move her left shoulder, Sheriff," Abby called as she went to get the supplies.

Bob saw the pain in his wife's face as she tried to move her shoulder again. "Does it hurt, Sweetheart?"

"The shoulder just won't work."

She paused for a few seconds as if trying to remember.

"Bob, it was quite a sight seeing fifteen men dressed like commandos rushing the house. Now that I think about it, they didn't have guns. They just threw up their hands in front of them and some, some. . ." She stopped in midsentence.

Looking at Bob, then at the AR-15 on the table, she tried to gather her thoughts. "I know this sounds weird. No guns, just streams of black light seemed to come out of their hands."

Abby came back with tape, gauze, and disinfectant. Infection was her biggest worry. She carefully dressed the wound, noting that the bleeding had ceased.

"We'll get you to a hospital at first light," said Cable, helping his wife to a bed that had somehow escaped destruction.

" I need some peace, Bob. Go do what you have to do," said Midge.

Kissing her forehead, Cable acknowledged the request and resumed sentinel duty in the back yard. As he moved around the property, his phone rang, but he didn't recognize the number. Picking up he heard a woman say, "Sheriff, this is Lozen. I am west of Elkville at a fire site. The darkness has injured Dale and Dan. They'll be okay, though."

"What happened?" asked Cable.

"The men were in position on their spokes and saw a fire starting midway between them. They arrived at the same time and walked straight into an ambush. Hunter went off, growling and howling at the fire-starters, demons I suppose. He held them at bay while I got the boys out. Both of them are burned and beat up. When I confronted the evil and used the name of Jesus, they returned to the shadows and slipped into their alternate dimension. This is not my first experience with these creatures, Sheriff, and it will not be the last."

Lozen disconnected, failing purposefully from informing Cable about the church fire. He would find out soon enough.

26

JONES' TYPICAL WORKDAY WAS ENDING WHEN THE REPORTS STARTED FILTERING IN ABOUT THE FIRE AT THE CHURCH IN POMONA AND THE ATTACK ON CABLE'S HOMESTEAD.

HAVING STOPPED AT THE QUICK SHOP, HE LISTENED to his radio as news teams reporting at the scenes called in their reports.

Things have picked up, he thought nearly out loud. Just then, four eighteen-wheelers with no visible registration information came into view. As the big trucks approached the intersection, their right turn signals went on as they turned south. Every law enforcement officer in the area was in motion or being called up. Those trucks were probably going to get stopped. Two local events were now active cases, one an attempted homicide by persons unknown and the other a tragedy of unspoken proportion. There would be no going back from tonight.

Being tired and more than a little concerned about the recent turn of events, Jones pulled out of the parking lot and headed east, listening to his radio as he drove. *Those boys are picking the wrong time to drive unregistered,* he thought, looking directly at the four eighteen-wheelers making their move southbound.

Jones was a man who trusted his gut, which had proven to be a reliable course of action.

As Jones approached highway 127, he felt something nudge his consciousness. Without knowing exactly why, he turned right at the intersection, the same direction the trucks had taken.

27

CHIEF DEPUTY MERRITT SAT
SECLUDED, HIDDEN FROM ALL BUT
THE SHARPEST EYES, IN A WOODED
AREA JUST INSIDE THE PERIMETER
THE DEPUTIES HAD ESTABLISHED
IN FRONT OF CABLE'S HOUSE.

HIS VEHICLE, PROVIDED BY ZORAH, WAS LOADED WITH all types of electronic devices used to monitor any wireless communication, including cell phone traffic. There was also equipment that could intercept telephone conversation when parked in proximity to the lines carrying the signals. Merritt sat quietly, listening to a conversation between Jones and Cable. Jones was on to something. He wasn't saying much about exactly what, just that he was following a lead and would be "out of pocket" for a while. Cable responded that "help would be in the woods tonight," whatever that meant. Zorah, who was sitting next to Merritt, expecting an explanation, got none. The deputy scratched his head and shrugged his shoulders as Zorah looked on in contemptuous disbelief.

Zorah, humanized as William Zorah, had no respect for this weakling human. He was merely following Sonta's blueprint, which was designed to take control of large areas of terrain from their human inhabitants. The plan relied on using the powers of darkness to control citizen's minds. In this case,

Zorah, or William, had befriended Merritt and piled the man with attention before bringing him into the fold.

Merritt had met Zorah in a bar on Gartside Street. The conversation initiated by the stranger had brought Merritt out of his shell. In Merritt's life, any attention was preferable to the opposite. Zorah took his time ensnaring Merritt; it was never wise to rush. After all, patience was still a virtue, and time was immeasurable to the demonic hordes, or always had been. The deputy became a staple at parties where beautiful women offered their favors. Compliments were the order of the day. On more than one occasion Merritt was flown to St. Louis and Chicago to meet influential people, eat at expensive restaurants, and visit with prominent state and national political figures. The program was a sophisticated image building model with a proven track record.

Zorah eventually convinced Merritt to join his team. His job would be to monitor and report daily activities in the sheriff's office. Since everything comes with a price, there was the small matter of upfront whip-out, twenty thousand dollars to be exact. Merritt took the money and became a spy on the payroll of a foreign power, watching his people for money, paid by powerful strangers with an agenda to which he was not privy. Regardless of how it might end, though, and there was that reality, he did not want out.

As he became one of the bought, Merritt, no master of rocket science, eventually deduced that, no matter how he shook it, Zorah was more than likely not on his side.

The man had powers that set him apart from Merritt's frame of reference. You might call them otherworldly. As he met more of Zorah's entourage, his doubts transitioned to belief.

The day finally came when Deputy Merritt sucked up his

courage and confronted the demon with his suspicions. Having some experience at this crossroads moment, gleaned over eons of time, Zorah ignited an abandoned garage just by pointing at it, which confirmed, if there were any mitigating factors, the seriousness of Merritt's situation.

"I want out, Zorah," Merritt had said, his voice shaky and full of fear.

"I'm afraid it's not that easy," Zorah said, his eyes glowing red in their humanized sockets, his face losing its outline under a black mist.

"You see, Deputy, you know about us now. You are probably under no illusion as to our intentions here, on Earth. The information you give us is vital to our planning. Knowledge is king, you know. Well, maybe not king. That would be someone else.

"Let me assure you that a withdrawal is not your best option. In any event, you are due for a raise."

At which point Zorah doubled Merritt's salary and repurchased him.

"Now, Deputy," said Zorah, "I need to know where all the troops are, all the time. You can do that in your sleep.

"This new man, Jones, needs our attention. The other deputies see him as 'special' since the sheriff brought him on. He has elevated status among them. Sow discord there, Deputy, make them resent him, turn on him, who knows what else. Keep an eye on the trackers, the Mountain Men I believe you call them, and especially the woman and her dog." Zorah laughed as he contemplated offing this pathetic human at the first opportunity.

Merritt got the message and the clear understanding that this relationship had finite limits, some of which were foreseeable. Failure would be termination. He was sure of that.

28

-◆◆◆◆◆-

EIGHTEEN-WHEELERS MOVING THROUGH SMALL TOWNS WERE COMMONPLACE IN SOUTHERN ILLINOIS, ESPECIALLY SOUTHERN ILLINOIS, WHERE SEVERAL HIGHWAYS CONVERGED.

EVEN SO, THE ONLY CONVOYS JONES HAD EVER witnessed were Fed-Ex trucks at Christmas on their way to Nashville, Tennessee. There wasn't much night traffic either, so four unmarked trucks, obviously traveling together, defied the norm. He caught up with the trucks as they left the city limits. As the big rigs picked up speed, Jones dropped back. He wasn't committed to long-range recon but interested enough to spend an hour or two. You never know what's in the Cracker Jack box.

At that moment, feeling he wasn't alone, Jones scanned his cab and saw a faint glow. Sure enough, it was Ephram, his guardian, sitting beside him. Arrow had assigned his second in command to Jones. His status had changed from "angel assigned" to "angel on assignment."

"Turn off your headlights, Jones," said Ephram.

Reaching over, Jones complied. Before he could object to running dark on an extremely curvy road, the whole countryside lit up like noon on a cloudless day. Jones could see the trucks running up ahead.

Ephram reached for the radio scanner and activated the unit, punching in numbers for a frequency unknown to Jones. The language he heard was gibberish. Jones understood nothing, not a word, but something beyond his understanding was happening.

He glanced at Ephram. By the look on his face, Jones could tell that Ephram wasn't in the dark.

Looking at Jones, he waved his hand forward twice. Jones took that gesture to mean to keep going, and that's just what he did.

The road they were on would eventually take them into Union County. Thirty minutes later, having never slowed down, Jones glanced at his gas gauge. He hadn't filled up for several days, but his half-empty tank was now full.

Jones' mind worked to accept this reality and not lose focus. He looked at Ephram and started to speak, but stopped. They were surveilling. What else was there to say? He doubted that Ephram could be put on the spot, even if Jones wanted to do that. The trucks began to slow as they approached the Jonesboro exit. Turning left would keep them on the main highway, but the big rigs went right. Jones knew that this road would become a rugged country lane within less than a half-mile. These boys were too heavy for gravel. Still, they continued.

Ephram shifted in his seat.

Without warning, he put his left hand up in the air and clenched his fist. Jones knew the hand signal for "Stop" and looked for a place to pull over.

Up ahead, Jones could see that the old country road ran directly into a concrete highway that he had never seen before. There hadn't been a contract let for any roadbuilding west of Jonesboro in twenty years. All the roads were old two-lane oil and chips, in various stages of disrepair, which intersected with connectors to state roads that had sprung up from time to time.

"Pull in up there," said Ephram, motioning to a small gravel side road up ahead.

The name on the mailbox caught Jones' eye: Flowers and Gifts by Ellie.

Ellie Moore had been an old classmate and close friend of Kaz. She had come to the funeral. Jones hadn't seen her since. It was twelve-thirty at night when they pulled over. Up in front, three cars sat in the driveway, and lights shone from the windows of the nearby house.

Jones got out of his truck and went up to the door before he realized his lights were on and would eventually time out. Ephram was gone. It was very dark, and his eyes had not adjusted.

A piano inside the house was playing praise and worship music. Jones knocked on the door while simultaneously running a hand through his hair and tucking in his shirt. The porch light came on.

As the door cracked open, Jones saw one eye, then two, and then Ellie's broad smile appeared.

"We were expecting someone else to arrive, but you are a surprise, Jones."

Ellie had been a jock, and Jones could see that the years since graduation had been kind to her. She was still athletic, her red hair longer than he remembered, which was pulled back into a ponytail. She took his jacket and laid it on the bench by the door.

"Come on in and meet everyone, Jones. I think you know them all."

Jones recognized the three couples as he entered the room. They were local and had been known to help out in the girls' home when Kaz was still alive. "I'm a little surprised to find people up at this time of night," Jones said.

Ellie smiled. "It's not normal," she said, laughing. "For more than two years, we have felt the need to meet and pray over all these strange goings-on. Quite a few people know about our group. You are not the first person who has dropped in unannounced."

"Who might some of the others be?" asked Jones, more than a little curious.

"That Apache girl, Lozen, and her big dog have been here several times," said Ellie. "She is a Christian whom God has blessed with prescience ability. She is an excellent person to have on your side. We count her as a friend."

She brought Jones a cup of coffee, her face an untraveled roadmap of bottled thoughts.

"Tell me about the highway, Ellie," Jones said. "The last time I was up this way hunting, it was a gravel road full of potholes and ruts."

"A lot of outsiders have located here in the past couple of years, Jones. I've never looked into who it was, but someone purchased all the land from my place west to the county line. They bought several parcels in Jackson County, too. Supposedly, it was all done in the name of some land trust in Delaware. None of the sellers were aware of what was taking place, and most didn't care, since they were paid a premium for the land, some fifteen thousand acres, all told."

"Fifteen thousand acres!" Jones was stunned. "Why that must be the equivalent of, of. . ."

"About twenty-three square miles," Ellie said. Jones stared at her, hardly comprehending.

"And get this, Jones," Ellie continued, "nothing about the land transfers were ever reported in the county paper."

"Same for Jackson County, Ellie."

Jones managed to find his voice. "I don't recall any notices about land transfers along the border between our counties. *The Southern Illinoisan* is good at reporting that kind of news."

"It gets better," Ellie continued as she slipped her shoes off and pulled her feet under her in the chair. "Once the land trust owned all the land on both sides of the road, they proposed road improvements to the county board to be paid for by the landowner. The board approved their proposal with the only stipulation being the added construction of sufficient drainage ditches. It was a done deal. Now we have this concrete road. And, since they own all the land beyond my place, there is no public access allowed, strictly 'private.' The county government doesn't care, since the county didn't build it, doesn't maintain it, and there are no other landowners involved."

Everyone else in the room nodded in agreement.

"So now you have a practically new road that the locals can't use. What else is going on?" Jones asked.

"Well, about twelve new families have moved into town. Nobody paid much attention at first. It's exciting to have new people come and be a part of a small community. Being the only florist around gives me a good vantage point to watch what's taking place. But when none of the kids went to school, people started to pay a little more attention. It appears they all home-school their children. None have jobs in town; the men travel a lot. They pay cash for everything, buy all their clothes, groceries, and cars locally, and eat out a lot, but always with each other."

Ellie paused to take a deep breath. "This is the strangest peaceful invasion we have ever witnessed here, Jones. These people, whoever they are, have not attempted to make close friends in town. They are good neighbors, but not friends. And, none of them attend any of our churches."

Ellie watched Jones take a drink of his coffee before she continued. "When the land was being gobbled up, I often wondered why I didn't get an offer. Well, after the roadwork was finished, a couple of guys came to see me. You know, Jones, when people arrive during the day, they always come to the shop door. But, about three weeks ago there was a knock on my private entrance.

"My impression was that the men were part of the newcomers in town. They asked if I'd be interested in selling my property." She took another deep breath. "There are two outstanding things I remember from that meeting: when I asked why they wanted my property, I never received a direct answer—they just talked around the question. And, I can't remember either of their features."

Point two jolted Jones. He interrupted Ellie. "You can't remember what they looked like?"

"It's embarrassing, Jones. They stood right in front of me, no more than four feet away, and to this day, I can't describe them."

"You're not the only person with that problem, Ellie. You can't recall what they looked like because there was a mist in front of their faces."

"That's it!" Ellie yelled. She sighed with relief. "I've even lost sleep over that. They were here, talking to me and each other. They were courteous when I said I wasn't interested in selling. And, strangely enough, they didn't give me a number to call if I changed my mind."

When the other families voiced some of the same concerns, Jones related Sheriff Cable's incident at The Kitchen several days earlier. He felt some relief discovering that this "mist" thing had happened in Jonesboro, too. But he was gripped by the thought that the problems they were having in Jackson County were here in Union County as well.

"It's a good thing you pulled in here, Jones," Ellie said with some concern in her voice. "They have installed a guard post a little farther up the road. If you had traveled another few hundred yards, you would have been stopped."

"I've heard they don't treat uninvited guests very well," Jewell Abercrombie interjected.

Jones realized Ephram was looking out for him but said nothing.

"I was in downtown Murphysboro earlier and saw four semis rolling through town and thought I should follow them. They all went right down that road, so here I am. But, Ellie, you said when I came in, you were expecting someone."

"Jones, we feel like watchmen on the wall. From my property line on, something dark and sinister is happening. When we started our prayer time this evening, the Lord spoke and said light would arrive. At first, we thought it meant we were to pray until daylight. But, when we saw your headlights appear in the driveway, we understood."

"Well, I guess I brought the light," Jones said, shrugging his shoulders. "Maybe I was guided here."

"Is that why you showed up here tonight, just following some trucks?" Jewell asked.

"Maybe; it's complicated. You probably won't read about it in the paper tomorrow, but there was an attack this evening at Sheriff Cable's house. His wife is lucky to be alive. Midge Cable described them as faceless. Ring a bell?

"Appears it was a group of people who had no faces. Every law enforcement agency in the county is on standby. Then these four trucks came running through town." Jones chuckled, "I think I now understand the phrase, 'Like a bat out of Hell.' I don't know what their cargo is, but they weren't slowing down for anything."

Suddenly Jones slammed his fist into his palm. "That's it!"

"What is it?" Ellie asked.

"Whatever happened at the sheriff's house was a diversion! The trucks were able to make their run without any fear of being stopped and searched, since they didn't have any ownership markings. They are hauling something that is top secret."

"I don't know what they had on board tonight," Jewell interjected, "but there've been many truckloads of building materials going through town headed down this road. Hardly ever in the daytime, though, mostly at night. Their going past here a while ago isn't unusual."

As daylight approached, Ellie's guests sensed it was time to bring their session to a close. Gathered together, the small group sent forth their final fervent prayers. Jones joined in, trying to believe that good could, and would, triumph over evil, but not sure of anything. He might have to lose his faith to get it back. *These people do know how to pray*, he thought silently, seeing Ephram kneeling in the kitchen, his arms lifted toward Heaven. Jones certainly hoped that God would protect these warriors for Christ, who sought to protect them. Sometimes he felt as though God allowed people to pray because it did them good, not because the prayers ever were going to be answered.

"So long to you all," Jones said as the three couples were leaving.

He grabbed his coat as he headed for the door.

"Just asking," Jones said, turning to Ellie, "has anyone been successful in getting past the guard shack on that road since it was marked private?"

Ellie looked Jones in the eye. "Except for the newcomer families, no one that I know of has been allowed down that road. Even the people working the land are outsiders.

"I guess," said Ellie, putting her hands on her hips and sounding defiant, "there is a way to check it out."

"Without getting past the guards at the entrance? Sounds a little iffy to me," said Jones.

"These people who bought the property, whoever they are, might have a lot of money, but they aren't very savvy when it comes to the great outdoors," said Ellie.

"I haven't figured out entirely what they are up to, and they do have a lot of security, but it's mostly in the wrong places. This part of the country is pretty rugged. I think they are afraid of getting too far off the beaten path." The smirk on Ellie's face was giving her away.

"I give, Ellie. What have you been up to?"

"You ready to saddle up and take a trail ride, Jones?" Ellie had a Cheshire cat smile on her face.

"Okay, but I have to get some chow before riding off into danger," Jones replied.

"Give me a few moments to change. We can grab a bite and then saddle up at the stable on this side of town."

Ellie disappeared into her bedroom and changed into outdoor gear, put her phone on autopilot, and hung the "Closed" sign. Their exploration would take a few hours.

As they headed into town, Ellie related, "I go riding regularly. Whoever these people are, they have a lot of money. They've built miles of concrete highway that dead-ends a few miles from here. They have some service type buildings about a half-mile down the road. As far as I can tell, guards and maintenance people live in them. About eight miles out, another road heads into the woods. You would've thought if they wanted privacy, they would've gone due north into the heart of the backwoods country. But no, they followed Buck Creek and came back toward civilization."

Ellie started laughing. "Their main complex is only five miles from town. The going is tough, but we can get there. There probably isn't a soul out there except a few snakes and wild animals. Believe me, when I say rough, I mean rough."

The sun was making an entrance when they got to town. They weren't first. Several cars and pickups were already in the parking lot at the café.

"Reminds me of The Kitchen," Jones said as they went in a side entrance. As the door closed behind them, Jones caught a flash of light out of the corner of his left eye. Ephram? Jones grabbed the back of Ellie's sweater and pulled her to a stop. As she turned, he put his finger to his lips. She froze in place.

The light flash had come from across the room. Nobody else seemed to notice, at least none of the locals. There was a low wall dividing the café into two seating areas. Jones pulled Ellie down into a chair at an empty table close to the door, which partially hid them from most of the people in the front area.

"Jones, I think the two men who came to my shop are seated up by the front entrance," Ellie said hesitantly.

"Take a good look," said Jones.

Ellie stood halfway up and took off her sweater. It was an ingenious way of looking around the room while partially concealing her face.

"Yeah, that looks like it could be them. Their faces are still fuzzy, but, maybe."

The server came to take their order. Ellie was still adjusting herself after removing her sweater, so Jones ordered for them both. Scrambled eggs, bacon, biscuits and gravy, coffee.

Glancing toward the corner, Jones saw Ephram standing upright, a satisfied look on his face. He gave Jones a thumbs-up signal just as the two men up front rose to leave. Their eyes were glowing red through a black mist, and both were shaking their heads as they went out the door.

Jones was amazed no one noticed.

Their food came and they quickly consumed it. Small talk

and banter filled in the gaps as they caught up on news of mutual friends. Much too soon, it was time to go.

Jones handed Ellie some money and asked her to pay the bill. "I'll be in the truck waiting for you," he said, ducking out the door.

After paying and leaving a tip, Ellie headed straight for the truck and climbed in. "What just happened, Jones?" she asked. "And don't try to change the subject."

"Do you want the long answer or the short answer?"

"Short will do for now."

"You saw the light flash, didn't you?"

"It took my breath away! What happened?"

"Short answer, it was needed to confuse the two guys up front who had come to see you at your shop. The light emanated from my bodyguard, who happens to be an Angelic Warrior."

"But. . .," Ellie started before Jones cut her short.

"El, we need to get on the horses and head toward wherever we're going before too many people begin stirring this morning."

Ellie looked at Jones quietly for a moment and then nodded. "Head back toward Murphysboro," she said, "and pull in at the white barn with the scriptures on the outside walls. Justin should be moving around by now."

As they drove, Jones said, "Do you remember the story in the Old Testament about Elisha asking God to open his servant's eyes after the enemy's army had surrounded them overnight?"

"Yes, I remember," Ellie replied.

"You'll have to trust me on this, but in your prayer time today, ask the Lord to do for you what he did for Elisha's servant. Meanwhile, rest assured we have help traveling with us today."

Over in the passenger's seat, Ellie was quiet.

After a short drive, Jones saw the stable and pulled into the drive. At Ellie's direction, he drove around to the backside of the barn. They both got out just as a man walked out of the machine shed. He had a bucket of white paint, a roller, and an extension pole in his hands.

"Hey, Ellie!" he called.

"Justin, I'd like you to meet Jones O'Brian, an old classmate of mine from Murphysboro."

"Jones, heard a lot about you. Good to meet you face to face," Justin said as they shook hands.

Justin handed a rag to Jones. "Sorry about the paint. Just about every morning now I have to touch up my barn. It's like someone comes and scorches everything. The vandals try to burn off the scriptures, but the Word of God cannot be touched. They sure do make a mess on the rest of the barn, though."

Wiping the paint from his hand, Jones said, "Nothing like the truth to shake up the neighborhood."

Justin Bryant was short and stocky with reddish hair. He wore bib overalls and a plaid shirt. Used to hard work, he stood erect and had a vise-grip handshake. His blue eyes told a story of a man living in peace, no matter the circumstances.

"Justin, we need two of your best trail horses," Ellie said as she moved toward the stable.

"They're already saddled. Sandwiches in the saddlebags. Tea in the canteens. Your favorite Henry rifle for you, a .30-06 for your friend. And I do not want to know where you are going."

Ellie looked surprised.

Justin continued, "Don't ask, Ellie. I got the message this morning during prayer time to have everything ready."

Jones slapped Justin on the shoulder. He reached behind his truck seat, pulled out two pistols, and gave one to Ellie. "I assume you have had some experience with these?"

"Smith & Wesson? Yes, I can handle it."

Nothing else was said. Justin went back to painting over the scorch marks on his barn. Ellie and Jones checked the cinches on the saddles, mounted, and rode toward trouble.

Jones followed Ellie but stayed some twenty-five yards back. It was an old Ranger tactic, stay far enough back to be unnoticed yet close enough to intercede. If one of them were spotted, the other wouldn't be. It was a hard ride as they traversed an old dry creek bed that provided more cover than the meadow above them.

After about an hour, Ellie dismounted and led her horse under a small bluff. She turned in Jones' direction, a worried look on her face. Noticing her concern, Jones closed the distance between them and drew alongside.

"I felt deserted there for a moment," Ellie blurted.

"I'm sorry, El. Until we know what we are trying to find, we shouldn't take any chances. I have a bad feeling about this. I only hope I'm wrong."

She appeared satisfied with the apology.

Grabbing a stick, Ellie cleared some leaves so she could draw in the dirt. "Okay, we're here," she said, drawing several lines and placing a big X on their destination. "It puts us two miles out."

"We better leave the horses here," said Jones. He had done way too much recon in the Kush that demanded stealth. If it were two miles to target central over rough terrain, they would have to proceed on foot.

"I figure that's why they don't like to patrol this area," said Ellie. "Lots of rattlers, not a friendly area for city slickers."

The pair hobbled the horses, grabbed their rifles and binoculars, and headed toward the first ridge with Ellie in the lead.

The sky was a radiant blue, and the sun was shining, but the thick woods and underbrush were still dark and foreboding. Maintaining separation was difficult but necessary. It could easily be their only advantage.

As they came closer to the top of the second ridge, Jones closed the distance. They hadn't backtracked once.

"How many times have you made this trip, El?"

She smiled and winked at him, "Five or six. After stumbling on this place the first time, I couldn't stay away. Hunker down when we reach the top of this ridge and be careful."

The other side of the ridge was a cliff face with a vertical drop that Jones estimated to be at least thirty feet. It was surrounded by a small canyon that ran away into a distant wood line. He breathed in deep.

"Steep, huh?" Ellie whispered.

"Straight down, more or less," Jones replied.

They shared the binoculars, scanning the ravine, talking out of the sides of their mouths.

At some point in Earth's history, most likely the Paleozoic, the whole canyon had been carved out of solid rock. The road running in and out ran well away from the inhospitable cliff face. Who would attempt to traverse such an obstacle? It would be hard to imagine, especially for urbanites.

As they continued their surveillance, Jones made a mental diagram of the building locations. Four trucks stood side by side near one of the outbuildings. Several men were unloading what appeared to be cardboard boxes of food supplies when one of the men accidentally dropped a smaller, more extended, all-wooden crate. Out tumbled an M-16.

Taking note and exercising extreme caution, they continued to watch the activity below. Then a light flashed, like at the café.

"Ephram!" Jones thought he had only said it in his head.

"Who?" Ellie quizzed.

"My guardian," said Jones.

"I'll explain later, but it must mean some of them, those beings, they might be demons, are close. See that tree on the left," he motioned to her, "slide down a little to your left where that tree has fallen. I'm moving to the right to that draw. Stay quiet. Let's see what happens. Follow my lead."

Sensing Ellie's discomfort, Jones said, "Ellie, remember whose side those demons are on."

As they watched, two people approached from the wood line in the distance. As they noisily shuffled along, Jones made out the figure of the first one. The man was dressed like some English dandy on safari in Africa, but with a dark mist where his face should be. Both men were walking directly toward them.

Suddenly, there was the unmistakable chica-chica-chica sound of a timber rattler in full locked and loaded position somewhere in the path of the advancing duo. The noise stopped the men in their tracks. They scanned the surroundings, saw nothing, conversed for a moment, and took off in the opposite direction.

Yes, I would say the crawlers represent hostile territory for those boys, thought Jones. They certainly aren't in tune with Mother Nature. Jones waited until the men were out of sight before moving. When he stood up, Ellie also did. He motioned her to start back down the hill. It was midafternoon when they got back to the horses.

Jones asked, "Are you hungry, Ellie?"

"Yes, but let's eat on the ride. I need to get back to the shop and check for any orders. If I don't respond to the phone calls, it might raise some questions that I wouldn't want to answer."

"You're right, Ellie," Jones said as they were getting sandwiches out of their saddlebags. After they were mounted, he continued, "That's a mysterious place. At least six large storage buildings, barracks, men everywhere. Those were the trucks I followed."

Finally, they reached the creek bed and made their way back to Justin's. As they arrived on the backside of his property, he was there, still painting. When they dismounted, Justin took the reins of the horses and moved off to feed and stable them.

As the duo drove back to Ellie's place, she said, "Jones, that's the first time I stumbled onto anyone in my visits up there. I'd never seen a soul. Those guys were the same fellows, more or less, who we saw at the café earlier."

"Had to be," said Jones.

When they arrived at Ellie's florist shop, Jones went in to check for unwanted guests. As he was leaving, Jones said, "Keep the handgun. You might need it. Better safe than sorry."

Jones and the enemy had both been busy.

Driving back to Murphysboro, he pondered the events that had just transpired. As the afternoon drew to a close, he turned on his scanner and tuned in to civilization.

"Eagle, this is One."

"One, go."

"Let's mix. Our regular place."

"Roger," Cable replied.

Jones had suspicions that the beings, whatever they were, monitored all communication going to the sheriff, and maybe to him, too.

They would have to figure out for themselves what regular meant.

29

------◆◆◆◆------

JONES AND CABLE DROVE
UP TO AREA 17 WITHIN MINUTES
OF EACH OTHER.

"I'D HOPED TO HEAR FROM YOU LAST NIGHT, JONES. Bring me up to date. Did you get to the brick plant?"

Jones cut him off, "First things first. How is Midge, Sheriff?"

"By the time I got to the house, it was all over."

Cable repeated Midge's story about the faceless men.

"They trashed the house?" Jones said in disbelief.

"Pretty much," said Cable. "Here's the stunner, though. Midge shot three of them, so she said, and I believe her. There should've been blood all over the porch, especially around the bodies, but there wasn't any, and the bodies were gone. You know how good a shot she is."

"I do," said Jones.

"Midge is sure she hit several of 'em. Something left a burn mark on her back. She can't move her left shoulder because of it."

"I think you all need to relocate to my place," said Jones.

"Abby is still there with her," Cable interjected.

"She goes, too. My place is the safest."

"Before you leave, Sheriff, I need to fill you in on a few things." He proceeded to do exactly that, starting with the four trucks and ending with the rattler.

"You should've been along for the ride, he said, skipping

the incident at the café but electing to thoroughly cover the diagram. "Are you sure you were in Jackson County? I don't recall any big construction taking place in that area," said Cable.

"Yes, we were in our county, no doubt, but close to the county line."

Cable chuckled. "Whatever those things are, those snakes got them right, didn't they?"

"Yep," Jones said, then asked, "Will Dick and the others be out tonight?"

"Yea, they are scheduled again tonight and tomorrow."

Jones thought for a few moments.

"Call Dick on the radio and tell him to contact the others to stay home tonight. I'm sure these people, or whatever, are listening in on all our communications. We need to set them up by letting them think we aren't watching tonight. I'm going to check out the brick plant after nightfall."

"Where do you want me to meet you? You'll need backup."

Jones could see the concern on Cable's face.

"I've got backup with me and at my house," he said. "Not to worry. I told you about the guy with me last night, right? He and his friends are my backups. Besides, you need to be with Midge. She needs you close, and Abby needs some rest. I'll be okay."

30

-◆◆◆◆◆-

JONES WAS BEGINNING
TO PUT THE PUZZLE TOGETHER.

THE KNOWING THAT HE FELT WHILE READING HIS Bible was making sense, mainly where it dealt with battling the powers of darkness, although he still couldn't square it with Kaz's death. That had to be God's will. Why else would she have been taken from him. Why would his God do that? What kind of a God does that to his faithful servant? Jones didn't feel the need to be tested in that way, but he knew his faith was potentially an issue. Why was the phrase *"For such a time as this"* playing over and over in his mind? He didn't recall ever reading those words, but they must be there, somewhere.

After a short prayer together, Jones and Cable went their separate ways. Jones' concern for his old friend lessened when he saw the small glow on Cable's bumper as he drove off toward town. The sheriff now had a real backup.

The sun was beginning to set when Jones got back into his truck. Realizing he hadn't slept last night, he laid his head against the door, drew his 9mm, placed it in his lap, closed his eyes, and dozed off.

One hour later, Jones awakened, feeling as if he'd slept for six hours. Must be something supernatural, he reasoned. Feeling stronger, rejuvenated, as consciousness returned, his watch affirmed that one hour had passed. The sun was beginning to disappear below the horizon.

Stepping out of the truck, stretching, Jones felt renewed. Darkness was coming on the land, but the entire picnic Area 17 was filled with light. Then he realized why the light was so bright. It was more than the sun disappearing on the western horizon, yeah, for sure. It was angels, lots of them, crowding Area 17 and glowing brightly. Around the perimeter, he saw what appeared to be guards. But in the dock area, Warriors relaxed, talking and joking, pushing and shoving, just like a bunch of regular guys out having fun. The scene reminded Jones of football days gone by when the practice was over. It made him think back to his first meeting with Arrow and the army that traveled with him. Then, of course, there was always Kaz.

Scanning the crowd, Jones saw Arrow, who was accompanied by Ephram and three other angels. He walked over to say hello. The angels greeted him warmly. They were, however, serious men, with stern countenances. Warriors all, with deep creases overlaying faces covered with scars of many battles fought over vast periods of Earth time.

Jones was mesmerized, no mistaking those scars for tattoos. Arrow had been wounded so many times it was impossible to imagine the number or level of those conflicts.

"You are getting too close to the Fallen," Arrow stated. "They know you were in Jonesboro, but don't know why. It has caused quite a stir in their camp."

"Well, is that good or bad?" Jones asked.

"It just puts things into motion and accelerates the inevitable," said Arrow. "You are about to have an interesting evening. Standing down the Crew for the night was a smart call. The enemy focused on you has momentarily let down their guard. Your instincts were correct. Merritt is passing on all your communications. He has been drawn to the darkness and has recently lost favor with the Corruptors, making him expendable. Redemption is available to him. Time will tell."

"Corruptors? You used that word again."

"Yes, our name for the Fallen Angels who work in darkness. Fallen Angels are everywhere. Their evil caused the great flood in Noah's time. Our Lord refers to them using that name in the book of Jeremiah. They have been active throughout the centuries, standing on the sidelines, watching the victims from Auschwitz, Dachau, and Treblinka go to their deaths, watching men die in wars they helped foment. Most of all, their deceit and trickery have disguised the gospel of our Lord and confused many who would follow. The Fallen have supported and promoted false prophets who weakened the path to righteousness instead of leading the way."

"I guess my only real question that matters is will you intervene if the going gets too rough? Ellie and her prayer meeting friends, Justin with scriptures on his barn, they're standing at the gate," Jones said.

Arrow looked intently at Jones. "We can't give mortals ideas. We can act only when a believer has set his heart to serve our Lord."

"You can, but don't always, intervene," declared Jones, tears swelling in his eyes. "You took my wife, or let them take her to punish me."

"No," said Arrow, "that is not so."

"Then you are saying God does not intervene in the lives of Earth citizens but lets us find our way, deal with all this misery, suffer because we have created the framework for the suffering. We are too alone in this battle," Jones lamented.

Arrow and the others were watching Jones intently and

could see the pain etched like delicate filigree on the man's face.

"All I can tell you at this time, Jones, is you are not even close to alone," said Arrow softly, but with authority. "The ways of the Lord are known only to him. Each person's destiny must be worked out according to God's plan.

"Your friend Justin wants others to have access to the word of life, so he chose the spot and put it on his building. For that unquestioned devotion, he is held safe. His outreach is praiseworthy, or a hindrance, depending on your point of view.

"We are here with you. Now, go to your work," Arrow said, his look deepening.

"When you enter the enemy camp tonight, be watchful and learn. Ephram's Warriors will be with you. They have battled many hordes of Satan."

Suddenly Arrow snapped his head to the right, listening to an unseen voice. "Now," he said.

Jones looked around in awe as the entire body of angels moved instantaneously back to their dimension. It felt like a gale-force wind one moment and then, quiet. They were gone.

Jones shook his head. *Amazing Grace, how sweet the sound.*

31

---◆◆◆◆---

WARM RAIN FELL FROM UNTOLD HEIGHTS AS DARKNESS GRADUALLY PULLED ALL THE LIGHT FROM THE SKY.

JONES CALLED OUT, "EPHRAM, ARE YOU HERE?" He saw a clump of light move near the shoreline and then saw it move again. Ephram was not only present; he was not alone. "Get a move on, Jones," said Ephram, "we'll be close. Focus, stay in control. You have a lot to deal with right now, control your thoughts, stay strong on the inside. All things will be revealed."

Jones fired up his truck and headed east on Illinois Avenue. Turning north on 23rd Street, he drove directly toward the brick plant. Jones turned off the road onto a small rutted lane leading down to a slag dump near an old mine site, went about twenty yards, and parked in a clump of trees. He got out and did a final equipment check. It was another two miles to the plant. He decided to hump the minimum. Burdened soldiers were always compromised. Holstering the 9mm, he pocketed three extra magazines and picked up the Winchester Model 12 pump his daddy had given him years ago. Chambering a round, Jones secured his Zeiss binoculars, with their night-finder lens, grabbed his flashlight and compass, and set off down the railroad tracks. He would follow them until they turned east, at which time he would go due north until he reached the old brick plant. He reached for his flashlight but thought better of it. Night missions were no place for an amateur. He would never forget the recons he and his fellow Rangers had sortied back in Afghanistan. The rugged mountain ranges made his current terrain look docile. There was no room for complacency in the dark. All facets of self-preservation magnified when visibility decreased. Sounds were louder. The night creatures were out and about. Jones needed to call on his old training, and he knew it.

As he secured his Magna light, a small flash off his starboard bow let him know that reinforcements were present and available.

That's how it was going to be.

After a careful fifteen minutes on the tracks, Jones slid down the embankment and made his way through the brush. He crossed a ravine he and his buddies had played in as children years ago and continued north.

The Murphysboro Paving Brick Company ruins emerged in the distance. The old brick company had been abandoned during the Depression of 1933. Several old buildings and kilns remained standing, but nature had taken over and covered most structures with vines and native plant growth. A plant that had employed over two hundred people in its heyday and churned thousands of bricks daily sat silently in the night.

Some of the surroundings looked familiar to Jones, but time had dulled his memory, and it was dark, too dark to see clearly. The building walls were beginning to crumble. Debris piles formed all around. The kilns stood proudly in two neat rows, reminding all who could remember of a time long passed.

Inside the old complex, Jones moved slowly and cautiously, staying close to a ravine that ran along the south side of the second row of kilns. It was just then that he saw what appeared to be people, with red coals where their eyes should be, walking around the perimeter. *Guards,* he thought, sinking into the ravine. From his horizontal position, Jones saw several men moving toward him. A light flashed in the distance, causing the men to head back. Ephram must be in action. Time for him to do the same.

With one motion he dropped into a section of old-growth scrub and brought the 12 gauge into a right ready position. Be patient; all things come to him who waits.

A large crowd of men and women with torch poles had come into view, moving toward the front of what once was the main office building.

There appeared to be a stage between him and the crowd, where several men and women were dancing wildly. *It must be some form of ritual,* he thought.

Not all of the participants had misty-faces, but Jones didn't recognize any of them, which meant they were not local.

A hush came over the crowd as a man took center stage and started speaking the same distorted language Jones had listened to from the truckers the night before. When applause broke out, Jones realized the crowd was getting the message.

Somewhere over his right shoulder, Jones heard Ephram say, "He is congratulating the people for their success in distracting the locals while the Wondren was under construction."

"What is that?" asked Jones.

"Their headquarters. You saw it when you were there with Ellie," said Ephram. "Now that it is complete, the battle to take control of this area can begin. Their goal is to turn or kill believers. The nonbelievers are fodder, which they randomly collect. Complete physical and mental occupation is a result of their darkness."

As Jones turned to respond, three men rounded the kiln and moved in his direction. He slid farther into the brush as one of the beings sent a wave of darkness from the palm of his hand in Jones' direction. The wave missed him, hitting a tree, blowing a massive hole in its outer surface. Splinters spewed out from the trunk. Suddenly, two of the beings crumpled, their bodies hit by bolts of light. The third went down as Jones squeezed the trigger of the Model 12. Hit in the chest by double ought buckshot, the being went down, momentarily, before staggering to his feet.

Time to go, thought Jones, noticing the speaker pointing in his direction.

Moving toward Ephram's voice, Jones navigated his way through the brush, preferring briars to confrontation. Suddenly, the night sky lit up, revealing waves of blackness pouring toward Ephram's Angelic Warriors. Jones was spellbound. Forty of the quad surrounded Ephram as he headed toward the Corrupters. Some Warrior Angels were big, some smaller, but all were encompassed by a glowing light that functioned as a protective cocoon.

Ephram had said the number in a quad was equal to the situation. That appeared to be true. The demons fired blackness that flowed forward like streams of water coming from a hose, all sent forth by a mere raising of their hands, only to see it splatter on the Warriors outer glow. Proving the theory that matter in motion tends to stay in motion, the blackness was redirected like a power surge, a ball of fire, back to its source with the strength of lightning blowing all but the fastest Corruptors into bloody pieces. Few escaped. Demons hit with raised hands in the act of sending more darkness paid the ultimate price.

Just like that, it was over. Jones felt a tug on his sleeve and followed the glow toward the train tracks. Not soon enough, the truck came into focus and Jones climbed in, started the engine, and lived to fight another day. As he drove back, all he could think about was these beings were here to take over.

32

AS JONES MOVED TOWARD HOME, THE COURTHOUSE CAME INTO VIEW.

IT WAS HARD TO MISS ABBY'S CAR AND MERRITT'S truck in the parking lot. It was apparent that his instructions to stay with Midge had not been heeded. There had to be a reason for that, and this was no night for coincidence. Jones blocked the parking lot exit with his truck and went in, taking the Model 12 with him.

Not knowing what to expect, Jones moved cautiously. As he entered, he saw Abby in the radio room with two deputies, but Merritt was not visible from his position.

"Hey, Abby," Jones called out, entering the room where she was working. Abby turned and smiled at Jones, her right eye closed. Without moving his body, he followed Abby's lead and shifted his gaze to the left, where the door leading to the records room was open.

At that moment, something moved in his direction. Merritt, a black mist covering his face, came toward him with his service weapon drawn. A voice sounded from behind blood-red eyes, "It's always been you, Jones," he hissed, "blocking my path, causing trouble. Ever since high school, it's always been you. You crippled me, you bastard. You thought you were better than everybody else. I never had a shot when you were around, and you were always around. I still have trouble accepting the notion that you are a believer. Have you had a sighting, maybe seen a miracle? Has God revealed himself? This Christian faith is a giant hoax hoisted upon the backs of humanity.

"I've finally gotten a chance to be a part of something," Merritt continued, moving slightly forward, the handgun leveled at Jones' chest, "and here you are, just like the plague, spoiling everything for me again! You gotta go away, but you're not going to do that voluntarily, are you, old buddy?"

"Probably not," said Jones, trying to remain calm when that was virtually impossible. "If all this was like you say, the bad guys wouldn't be trying to kill all the Christians, now would they?"

"I think I'll just eliminate my biggest problem in life," said Merritt, who was posturing like he was through talking.

Jones remembered at that moment what his instructors at Ft. Benning had told him: he who hesitates is lost.

As Merritt moved his arm to aim, Jones raised the Winchester to hip level and fired, pumped in a new round and fired again.

The shotgun blasts echoed in the confined space, drowning out Merritt's gunfire. A flash of light accompanied its discharge.

Merritt's body was blown backward against the wall, knocking over a bookrack and a trash can that sat nearby.

Merritt's round had splattered the wall behind Jones, right where his head had been, yet he was still standing.

Abby had hit the floor when Jones fired. The two deputies with her drew their weapons and rushed toward Jones. Jones looked intently at their eyes but saw no red. Ephram didn't seem alarmed. Jones put the Model 12 on the floor and raised his arms.

"Call 911, Abby," he said, not thinking clearly.

"We are 911," she replied.

"Well, then call an ambulance!" Jones ordered.

"Don't think we'll be needing one of those right away," said Tom, the first officer to reach Merritt.

Tom, a former police chief in Murphysboro, rolled Merritt over. His eyes widening as he looked at a man who has just taken two loads of double ought buckshot to his chest, which was mostly gone, its pieces splattered everywhere.

Abby walked to the phone and called the Coroner.

"Mr. Ragsdale," she said when the line picked up, "this is Deputy Solomon at the sheriff's office. Weapons have been fired here; two officers involved, one is deceased."

"What in the world happened, Abby?"

"One officer had to fire in self-defense; he is okay."

"Self-defense?"

"Yes." Abby looked over to Tom and the other officer, who both nodded in resolute agreement. "We have multiple witnesses."

"I'll be there as fast as I can with an ambulance. Be sure to cordon the area off; don't let anyone touch anything."

"Will do."

Abby ended the call and sat down on the closest chair.

The rest of the evening was a blur. The Coroner came and went. Jones gave his statement to the senior officer on duty.

"Abby and I are going to my home," he said, motioning to her as he headed for the door.

"Safety is my principal concern; she'll be at my place. Cable and Midge are there. I'll fill the sheriff in on what happened. Come on, Abby."

Abby grabbed her jacket and followed Jones.

"What just happened, Jones?" she said as they came out the door, her eyes welling with tears.

"I just killed a man," replied Jones, "who would have killed us all. He had gone over to the dark side. You do get that, don't you?"

Seeing that Abby was stunned and in shock, Jones knew he needed to be direct. The time for evasion had passed.

"We have a war going on, Abby, for the hearts and souls of our people, our folks here. I don't know if it's just our small part in a bigger play, but the stakes are deadly serious. There is no easy way to tell you. Hell is erupting on Earth. The battle is in our backyard. I have no idea for how long or for how much longer. There are scores of Angelic Warriors battling the Fallen Angels. Merritt was lost. He had crossed over."

Abby just shook and kept shaking as Jones put his arms around her and held her closer than he could ever remember. Gradually, she calmed and pressed herself even tighter to him, seeking shelter from this terrible brewing storm.

"Yesterday Merritt pulled a gun on me," she said. "The light flashed then, just like now. I think it saved my life." She started to say something else, but her knees gave way, her head coming to rest on his shoulder.

Jones felt a sense of déjà vu, knowing he had to be there for her right now. Sometimes we all need to be held. He had abdicated his responsibility with Kaz and vowed to do better with Abby.

"Let's get you to my house, Ab. Sheriff and Midge are there. My bodyguard Ephram is close. You will be safe there."

Jones' faith in Ephram's ability to protect them all was beyond doubt. He had seen the angel in action.

"It's been a crazy time Abby," he said as they made their way to his truck. "If I hadn't stopped by the department instead of just going home, Merritt might have hurt you."

"It was gonna happen, Jones," Abby said haltingly.

"He was in a mood. Before going into his office and closing the door. . ." her voice trailed off.

Abby was in shock. She had been trying to bury her feelings

for Jones with work and distraction. What would her life be like if Jones weren't there? Worse, there was a war going on around her that she had not so much as noticed, not really. Events were moving at the speed of light, or so it seemed, and yet, what everyone wanted was right in front of her, how to get from here to there was the question. Life with Jones would be so natural.

Abby had one leg in the truck when she noticed a light in the bed.

"What is that glow in the truck bed," she asked.

"That is safety looking you in the eye," replied Jones. "When we need extra help, the Lord sends an angel."

A wave of peace, inner strength, came over her. She pulled her other leg in and closed the door. Jones reached over and took her hand. It felt good.

The short drive to Jones' house was uneventful. Abby's eyes closed. As she took a few deep breaths, a sense of comfort washed over her. It was good to have a man close by, especially the right one.

As they came around the corner, Abby gasped. Bright lights surrounded Jones' house.

33

-◆◆◆◆-

SATAN SCREAMED,
AND THE VERY FABRIC
OF TIME SHOOK.

SECOND HEAVEN, WHERE THE FALLEN ANGELS RESIDED, trembled as the wrath of his Most Extreme Highness manifested itself. Known for his many disguises, Satan currently bore the shape of a dragon whose slithering coils undulated continuously as he spoke.

"We killed a church," he said to Balzar, one of his high council members. "Killing believers is on our list, but our first and highest mission is turning them into workers for our cause, destroying their faith in this God they worship."

"Yes, Your Supremeness," agreed Balzar, knowing better than to offer any dissension.

"Fortunately for us," said Satan, "the Warriors wrapped the girl, turning her memory of the destruction into a fire. That decision was probably the work of Arrow, the angelic commander in charge on the ground. No doubt both sides are protected by such action, as it enables our battle to continue unnoticed by the populace. Still yet, the attack was an escalation of the blueprint, which was approved by the high council."

"Perhaps Sonta and Zorah grow weary of the pace of our proceedings," said Balzar.

"Perhaps," replied Satan, "or tired of the tactics being prescribed by Koal, especially the daylight attack on the house, which resulted in mass casualties."

"That was not Koal, your Highness," said Balzar, "that was Sonta."

"So," said Satan, "what we have are two outcomes, the first fueled by a strategy that brings us new scrutiny, while the second demonstrates a dangerous impatience."

"Yes, Your Grace," replied Balzar.

"The council will be divided over the decision to fire the church," said Balzar, "which raises the stakes prematurely."

"Nonetheless," Satan said, "killing Christians is never all bad."

He smiled.

Oblivion's Reach | 138

34

❖❖❖❖

THE CHURCH ASHES WERE STILL SMOLDERING WHEN COUNTY COMMISSIONER BILL REDMOND AND HIS TEAM ARRIVED ON THE SCENE.

THE VOLUNTEER FIRE DEPARTMENT HAD BEATEN HIM by twenty minutes, but the fire had raged unchecked for more than two hours, and there was little left except charred bodies. As Fire Chief Russell Riepe examined the burnt-out hulk, there was no apparent cause or accelerant as a starting point for the fire. When Charlie Schmidt, from the Coroner's Office, arrived, he was hard pressed to identify the piles of ashes that were scattered among the corpses and around the grounds. He took samples for analysis, hoping to arrive at some idea that would help the investigation. About an hour after the locals had been actively dissecting the scene, the IBI landed a chopper in the parking lot and joined the party. There was no way to know if anyone got out or if there were any survivors. Primitive ruled out here in the Shawnee Forest. People could have scattered and simply gone home. There must be a few who lived. It was hard to believe a fire could engulf such a small structure quickly enough to prevent some of the faithful from escaping.

An hour later, the situation was clarified. A young girl, who turned up at the local hospital suffering from smoke inhalation, had somehow escaped. Pictures were taken and ambulances called as the gruesome task of removing the bodies began. Someone must have seen something.

35

〰〰

CABLE SAW JONES COMING
AS HE SAT IN THE LIVING ROOM
WATCHING THE LIGHT SHOW.

MIDGE WAS SOUND ASLEEP IN THE GUESTROOM. The strange burn wound on her back was inexplicably healing. She could already move her shoulder without pain. There was no rational explanation. The doctor couldn't say. He had indicated that it would take weeks for the wound to heal, and even then there might be skin grafts to consider.

Turning on the porch light, Cable walked outside. Abby opened her door, put both feet on the ground, and collapsed.

Cable rushed to help her to her feet.

"Jones, what happened to Abby?"

"Let's get her inside. I'll explain in a minute," said Jones.

As Jones picked Abby up, their faces touched. He could not help notice her crooked little nose. It was cute, though. She smelled nice, too. Getting her inside, he took her into his room just as Midge entered.

"Put her to bed, Midge. She's had plenty of excitement for one day," Jones said, leaving the room not a moment too soon.

Cable handed Jones a cup of coffee as he walked into the living room.

"Tell me all about it, Bud," Cable said, getting comfortable on the couch. Jones started talking and in a few minutes had related the whole evening's business before the sheriff had a chance to get a question in crossways.

Cable could see the claim of self-defense in Merritt's demise was strong. Jones' story would more than likely check out. The report of the happenings at the brick plant triggered more questions with no clear answers.

"We have a distraction on our hands, Sheriff," said Jones.

"More like a cover-up of significant proportion," said Cable.

"Unless I miss my guess you could call this a war," said Jones.

With the two bedrooms in his house occupied, Jones said goodnight and headed back to his truck to get some rest. As he went out the door, all the activity of the past two days settled in on him. The neighborhood was quiet. Dim lights glowed at the four corners of his property and each window of the house.

"Everyone is safe," the words echoed in his head, as though he had spoken them aloud. The clock on his dash read two thirty. Releasing the lock on his seat and pressing tilt, Jones was asleep before it stopped moving.

Ephram looked in on the passenger. He was well aware of Jones' confusion and loss of belief in Kaz's passing, but amazed and pleased with the resolve the man had demonstrated the past two days. Rescue from the abyss was possible. The result of years of Bible study would stand him in good stead.

Ephram placed several guards from his quad around the truck, since the vehicle was outside the secure perimeter. Chances were fool's gold. The enemy surely knew where Jones lived. He also stationed several scouts throughout the neighborhood, sure that the Fallen had figured out Jones' involvement by now.

36

—◆◆◆◆◆—

FLOATING IN A HALF-ASLEEP, MEDITATIVE STATE, JONES OPENED HIS LEFT EYE TO SEE IF WHAT HE WAS SMELLING WAS REAL OR A FIGMENT OF HIS IMAGINATION.

IT WAS ABBY, STANDING INCHES FROM THE WINDOW with a cup of steaming coffee in her hand.

Raising the seat back, he opened the door. A light mist was falling as Abby, sounding exasperated, said, "Jones, what are you doing out here? This is your house. I was praying for you all night, hoping you were okay."

Tears streamed down her face as she blurted out, "Jones, I can't stand the thought of losing you!"

Abby covered her mouth as she jammed the coffee into Jones' hand and bolted for the house. She had said her piece and Jones heard it all. There was fire in the rain.

He lifted the cup, drank, and savored the aroma. Dark Roast was his favorite blend, strong Colombian with a shot of caramel syrup and cream. How did Abby know this? He hadn't told her, that's for sure.

Before he could ponder the question further, the front door slammed, and Sheriff Cable made tracks in his direction. "The morning's getting away from us, Jones. It's ten o'clock already. Give me the recap again of your brick plant visit. What you told me last night is still buzzing in my head. Just what is going on out there?"

"More than we realize," Jones said. "The enemy is building a fortress or a series of them. After the shoot-out last night with Merritt, I know you'll want to get to your office, so let's postpone a full debriefing on the plant visit until I get a shower, change of clothes, and a little chow. I'll be there shortly after that.

"Abby's car is at the office, so why don't you take her with you. That way she can come back here later and take Midge home."

"Sounds good," Cable said. "I'll see you in a little while. Midge is in the kitchen."

The sheriff gathered up Abby, who refused to look Jones in the eye as she walked by, and departed.

Women are strange beings, thought Jones, but it was a blessing to have them.

He took another sip of coffee and headed for the house. As he approached the front door, he could smell the bacon frying. Just then, Midge yelled from the kitchen, "Hey, Jones, you want those eggs scrambled soft?"

"Yep, that's how I like 'em," Jones said. Then he remembered, "Wait, I thought you were hurt. Let me take over the cooking. The way they described your injuries, your entire back must be out of business."

"I can't explain it, Jones, and the doctor can't either," said Midge. "Ever since you had Bob bring me here, that wound across my back just faded away, not even a scar. My shoulder has healed, as well. Come on, eggs and biscuits need to be eaten hot."

Jones hugged Midge and sat down. She poured him another cup of coffee, slid a full plate of food in front of him, and cleared her throat.

"While you eat, tell me what's going on. Who are those people?" Midge asked.

Jones stalled, searching for the right answer, so long that Midge cleared her throat again, spun around, and started putting dishes in the dishwasher.

"You know, you're treating me like Abby now, Jones. She says you never answer her questions directly, either. Trying to get information from you is like talking to fog."

"I'm still trying to put the pieces together, Midge, but this I do know. We are under attack by Satan's Fallen Angels. I don't know their game plan, but it has elevated considerably in a short period. God's Angelic Warriors are guarding us. I don't have all the answers you need, but I intend to get them. The sheriff and I need to go over a lot of details from the past two days. Maybe by tonight, we'll have something figured out."

Midge's mouth was slightly ajar.

"No wonder I couldn't kill them," she said. "They are not of this world."

"No, they are not," said Jones.

"While I am working on this puzzle, you need to pick yourself up from here and go home," he said.

"Why should I go home to that mess? You haven't been there, have you? All the windows and doors downstairs are wrecked. My kitchen is destroyed. I don't even want to think about it." She sniffed back a tear.

"Midge, arrangements were made. By noon today, all the repairs will be completed. You and Abby do some grocery shopping for your place. By the time you get home, the mess will be cleaned up."

"Impossible!" Midge said.

"Your back healed. Was that impossible? Go see for yourself," Jones said.

37

SHERIFF CABLE PULLED INTO HIS
SPOT AT THE COURTHOUSE, LOOKED
AROUND THE PARKING LOT AS WAS
HIS CUSTOM, AND IMMEDIATELY
NOTICED TWO BLACK VANS
AT THE END OF THE LOT.

THEIR DARK WINDOWS AND WHITE PLATES SUGGESTED the federal government. Maybe the FBI was making a social call. Slim chance of that happening, although it was a possibility.

After giving Abby her marching orders, the sheriff headed for his office, only to notice that one of the vans, attempting to follow Abby, suffered an engine failure before it could intercede. The driver was not a happy camper, as he could be seen cursing and frantically banging the van with his fist as Abby departed to look after Midge.

Many unknown characters were popping up on the local scene that Cable did not know or had never met. It wasn't difficult to make the connection between these new arrivals and the trouble that was now an everyday occurrence.

The shoot-out was bound to bring hordes of reporters. It was the last thing he wanted to deal with, but homicides were the downside of his job, and the devil seldom rested. Cable determined to refer all questions about Merritt to the Coroner. That would buy some precious time.

Entering the office, Cable blinked. The blood and broken door were gone. Cleaned up. Elbert, sitting in Merritt's usual spot, said, "Sheriff, two men here to see you."

Cable turned toward the waiting area. What he saw was *Men in Black* revisited down to the suits, ties, white shirts, and sunglasses. *Nice look*, he thought.

"I'll be with you in a moment, men," Cable said, moving toward his office, but the men were already on their feet, walking in his direction.

"We need to see you now, Sheriff Cable," they said in unison as both started to reach inside their suit coats.

Elbert was up immediately. "Whoa, boys, easy does it," he said, his hand moving to his side-arm.

The two strangers each held up a badge and ID card. Unreadable from where Cable stood. Elbert stood down, and they reluctantly gave their IDs to him.

"What's on your mind, gentlemen?" Cable asked.

The taller of the two said, "It's our understanding that one of your deputies is deceased. We want to know the circumstances. Has the shooter been identified?"

"I don't know you from Adam, boys," Cable said, moving closer and taking the badges from Elbert. "Illinois State Police investigators, from where? Where is your home office? Who is your commanding officer?

"While you are taking your time answering, I'll let my deputy here scan your badges." Elbert headed to the copy room.

Cable was on high alert. The parking lot, now this. The enemy was active.

"For the record, once your organization begins its investigation with verifiable detectives, I will be forthcoming. Until then, I have no official comment. This investigation is in the Coroner's hands. I want to put you both in cuffs, but that is probably not a viable option. Sorry, that's all I have."

Elbert stepped back into the room.

The men took their ID badges back. "We didn't mean to get you stirred up, Sheriff. If that's all you have right now," the taller one said, "we'll be on our way. If you don't mind, we'll check back in a couple of days."

"Leave me your number, and I'll be glad to give you a call."

"That's okay; we'll check back later. Thanks for your time."

Cable watched as the two phony detectives made their way across the parking lot and got into the second black van. The van that had stalled started, and they both sped away. Elbert smiled his crooked smile. "Those guys are dumber than a box of rocks, Sheriff. Has the law changed, and you haven't told us? The Coroner can't be a part of our investigation."

"Right," said Cable, never too amazed at Elbert's grasp of a situation.

As he headed back to his office, Elbert called out, "Come here quick, Sheriff!"

Cable did an about-face and saw Elbert holding up a blank sheet of paper for him to see.

"What?" said Cable. "Where's the copy you made?"

"This is it! The moment I started to look at it, everything just faded away." Elbert looked confused.

"Creepy," Cable said, his suspicions confirmed.

"We'll deal with that when they come back, if they come back. Any calls for me this morning, Elbert?"

"No calls for you, no calls or any reports in the county. You need me to do something for you, Sheriff?"

"What are the other deputies saying about last night?"

"As far as I know, Tom and Kent gave their statements to the Coroner last night. There's a copy on your desk. The way Merritt was acting the last few months, I think they're almost relieved he isn't around anymore. They all understand that he tried to ambush Jones. He got what he deserved."

Cable thanked Elbert and said, "Release all the deputies who are keeping watch at my house. Everything's under control, someone's control."

At that moment, Cable's cell went off. It was Jones.

"See you in thirty, usual place."

38

JONES DROVE TO THE KITCHEN LOOKING FOR DICK THE MOUNTAIN MAN.

HE NEEDED TO BRIEF HIM, AND THE MEETING WITH Cable was the right starting place.

Approaching the restaurant from the north, Jones drove to the back entrance, where he spotted Ephram in what appeared to be a locked and ready position. It was late morning, and the lot was nearly empty. Hard to put the pieces together with what he was seeing and feeling.

Backing into a parking space as was his country custom, Jones looked around for Ephram, but the angel had relocated. Nothing left to do but go in.

Jones walked to the rear entrance with apprehension and carefully opened the door. Waiting for his eyes to adjust to the darkness before opening the second door took an eternity, but he had learned that lesson once before. The restaurant was quiet, snoring. Slowly opening the dining room door to keep the cowbell from announcing his arrival, he scanned the room.

Everyone looked frozen in place, listless, almost drooling. Upfront, there was his A-Team. The usual regulars occupied various tables around the room, but none of them were moving or talking.

At that moment, his vision came to rest on the reason for the shutdown. Four large men, with heavy beards, were sitting across from the Mountain Men. Jones didn't recognize any of them. *No doubt now*, thought Jones as he noticed the glaring red eyes and mist-covered faces.

Jones felt heaviness settling on him, as if something was pushing down on his shoulders. His mind started to wander, and he couldn't concentrate on what was taking place in the room.

"Help me," he muttered.

Help arrived in a flash.

From nowhere, Ephram and two of his Warriors appeared directly behind the Corrupters. Surprising them completely, bringing them to their feet without a command, they herded the strangers out the back door. Then came a bright flash.

Ephram touched Jones on the shoulder and said, "It's a type of mind control, an illusion. It's how they develop followers and bring them to their side."

Jones nodded his understanding, feeling the heaviness lifting. Ephram continued, "You can change the atmosphere by speaking calmly, but it's probably best to omit the details. When they hear your voice, a familiar voice, they'll be free of the control."

Jones felt stupid but did as Ephram directed.

He walked over to Dick and said, "It's clouded up outside. Think the fish are biting?"

Dick slowly turned his head toward Jones and said, "The sun was shining when we came in. That sure happened fast."

Just like that, the usual chatter and ambiance of The Kitchen resumed, just as Ephram had promised. Jones got the message to Dick to meet at the lake.

As Jones went out back and left for the meeting, he stepped over a fresh pile of ash in the middle of the sidewalk. It was as if someone had burned a bunch of newspapers. He assumed it was what remained of the four demons forced outside. He stomped his feet, making sure no residue stuck to his shoes. Ephram was a shooter.

The lake was smoother than a baby's butt when Jones and Dick arrived. Cable had gotten there first and laid the maps on the picnic table. He and Dick were soon listening to Jones' story about the restaurant elimination.

Dick was in a state of disbelief. His eyes bulged as he slumped over the picnic table. "You're telling me this happened just now? Someone was taking control of my mind?"

Jones put a hand on his shoulder to assure him everything was okay and said, "Dick, this is real. It's happening in our town. You need to understand. Know also that we are not alone in this fight."

After a few more details, Jones laid out the skirmish at the old brick plant.

Cable threw up his hands. "How can we fight against this, this, whatever it is?"

"We use what we've got to slow them down and let the Angelic Warriors do the heavy lifting. They have bigger guns," said Jones. "Make sure you are out of their way."

"Well, it's good to know there's some defense," Cable said.

"At least we can halt their progress for a moment. It also proves these beings can't be human. So the bottom line is we can't get too excited about shooting them," Jones said. "Midge had the same result. All I know is the 12 gauge stopped one of them long enough for me to escape. The demons were celebrating their success in taking over our county, I guess, celebrating a little too soon."

Cable straightened up. "This starts filling in the blanks on all the fire reports."

"There is more, guys," Jones said, spelling out what had happened at the church. "The powers of evil we are facing have upped the ante. The conflict is growing. We need to hold a town meeting and inform the populace."

"It will scare people half to death, Jones," said Cable.

"Better scared than ignorant or dead," Jones replied. "Besides, that has to be a part of their plan. A silent takeover. Too far gone before everyone wakes up and the town is captured or gone missing.

"I forgot to ask," said Jones, almost as an afterthought, "but did you have a chance to get a plane in the air?"

"I was going to call the operator at the airport," Cable replied, "but I wasn't sure what we needed to have done."

"First," Jones asked, "do we have someone we can trust out there?"

"Terry has a plane at the airport," Dick said. "He flew choppers in Iraq. Getting him in the air for us would probably be an upgrade."

"Okay, Dick, here's what we need him to do." Jones put his finger on the map, "With Jonesboro as the starting point, fly a grid ten miles north and twenty miles west. About right here," his finger drew a circle, "is where Ellie and I saw a building complex. We need to know if those busy demons are building any other structures. Tell Terry to stay above twenty-five hundred feet and use Visual Rules only, not instrument rules. That will eliminate a flight plan. If, by chance, anyone asks him about his route, tell him to say he is just getting certification time."

"You got it, Jones," Dick said. Within seconds he was in his truck speeding toward Terry's place a couple of miles away.

39

~◆◆◆◆~

ABBY AND MIDGE DEPOSITED THEIR GROCERIES ON THE KITCHEN TABLE AND PLOPPED ON THE COUCH JUST AS ABBY'S PACK RADIO ANNOUNCED THE CALL FROM THE SHERIFF.

"GO, EAGLE."

"Where are you and Midge?"

"At your house unloading supplies and groceries."

Midge stuck out her hand, took the radio, and said, "What happened here, sweetheart? Everything looks like it never moved. Oh, never mind, we'll talk about it later."

"That's a plan, dear," said Cable. "Remember not to leave the property under any circumstances. You will be protected as long as you are there."

40

THE MEETING ENDED, AND CABLE HEADED BACK TO HIS OFFICE.

JONES STOOD SILENTLY IN PLACE AS HE DROVE AWAY. Walking back to the picnic table, he heard a voice from somewhere behind him say, "And now it begins."

Arrow and his Warriors appeared in an instant. Like sentinels on watch, his commanders stood right beside him. Jones stared at them, strength and calm filling his body, realizing that there were no words to capture this moment.

"I know there are many questions, Jones," Arrow said softly. "It is important for you to continue in the direction you are going. Your faith will be rewarded and restored."

"That will take some doing," said Jones.

"Your leadership is needed now more than ever," said Arrow. "This is the beginning of many battles."

Silence.

Then he and his men were gone.

41

-◆◆◆◆-

TERRY HEARD DICK'S OLD BEATER COME TO A SKIDDING STOP IN HIS DRIVEWAY.

THE BACK DOOR OPENED IN A DUST STORM. Fanning dust from his face, Terry asked, "What's up, Dick?"

"We're about to be," said Dick. "Fire up the bird, I'll tell you on the way."

"Sorry, old buddy, flying isn't on my agenda this afternoon. Janet's laid another 'to do' list on me," Terry said as he grabbed the coffeepot.

Dick took a deep breath and shot back, "You've got to take me up. Jones needs some information, and we can only get it from the air."

"Jones needs this? Is it about the fires?"

"More than that," said Dick.

Terry moved with vigor and purpose. He grabbed the phone and called the airport, instructing them to roll his plane out on the tarmac, fueled and ready to go.

"Where are we going?" he asked.

Dick fumbled and said, "For a joyride, getting in your certification time. Jones needs us to fly a grid and get some intel."

Terry just nodded, went to his computer, and called up the

current weather. As soon as the printout came, they headed for their trucks.

Arriving at the airport, Terry saw the black van parked at the far end of the parking lot. *The whole county is under surveillance,* he thought. As they entered the flight office, he noticed two strangers sitting quietly in the corner and mentally tied them to the van.

"Humm," Dick muttered, "those boys resemble the out-of-towners we saw at The Kitchen earlier."

Terry called over to the men and asked, "Where's the manager?"

One of them stood up and came to the counter.

"Name is Ed. I just came up from Paducah to relieve the manager for a couple of weeks."

"That's my Cessna out on the apron," Terry said as he grabbed the fuel ticket on the counter and signed it before walking toward the door.

"Going to file a flight plan?" the man called out.

"No. Visual Rules today," Terry responded. "I'm just getting in my required time. Gotta keep my license current," he said.

"Where will you be going?" the stranger asked.

Terry pretended not to hear and walked briskly to his plane, Dick in tow.

The plane was a beauty, a Cessna 172 Skyhawk high-wing aircraft that gave its occupants an unhindered view of the ground.

"Clear skies and no wind, a great day to fly," said Terry. "A quick preflight check and we're on our way."

Having flown with him before, Dick watched over Terry's shoulder as he took care of business. In about fifteen minutes they would be ready to go.

As Terry went through his procedural walk-around, he examined various moving parts. He checked the fuel to be sure there was no water present. Reaching through an opening in the front cowling, he tugged and pulled on all the belts and tensioners. There was a moment when his inspection halted. The alternator belt was loose. It had too much play when it should be taut. Without the proper tension, a malfunction could easily happen. As he checked the bracket holding the belt in position, he discovered two loose anchor bolt nuts. Attaching the bracket to the frame, they were barely tight. It was an accident waiting to happen. Full throttle would achieve that condition.

Dick noticed the concern on Terry's face.

"What..." he started to ask, but Terry cut him off, speaking in a whisper.

"The engine starts on battery power, and then the alternator provides electricity during flight. The same way a car runs. If the alternator fails, the battery takes over. If that happened while we were airborne, we'd have to immediately return to the airport, hopefully before the battery failed. Emergency landings are never fun. This alternator was fine the last time I flew. These nuts couldn't have loosened that much on their own, and the plane has been in the hanger since then. Someone has tampered with my plane. Bring me the adjustable wrench from my flight bag. Rules say I need to have the airport mechanic do this, but we need to get going. Move slow and casual, try not to draw any attention."

42

-◆◆◆◆-

"AND NOW IT BEGINS."

ARROW'S PRONOUNCEMENT ROILED JONES' thoughts. Connecting the dots amidst all the uncertainty was no easy task. There were lots of new faces in the local communities. Were they all from the darkness? The struggle was in full play but as yet undefined. The people were at risk, being uninformed. That was about to change.

Jones gave up on the possibilities and drove back to town. His company had built their offices and warehouse years ago in a small area adjacent to the shopping district in the middle of the tiny burg. It was a quiet spot and next to a park-like location where senior citizens, out for a little shopping, could take a breather.

Not wanting anyone to know his whereabouts, Jones parked down the street in an alley. Remembering what had happened at The Kitchen earlier, he substituted a five-shot .357 revolver for his 9mm and tucked it into his belt. It was easier to conceal and had more stopping power. He might need it the next time he confronted the demons. Grabbing a backpack that contained his laptop, he walked the half block to the corner. He got his computer connected and checked his emails. One of them was a note from Judith, his assistant, informing him that two men had been to see him but had not left any identification. She made it quite clear they intended to return.

Judith had been raised on a farm in the deep country and was a keen observer of the human condition. She had a paralegal background and ample time to practice her craft since his absences had been increasing lately. Judith was a pretty girl, tall and angular with long black hair and big blue eyes. She was the focus of many, especially the opposite sex. Judith was a keeper.

Jones responded to most of his messages and assigned Judith the task of obtaining a count of new businesses, ones that had changed hands, and new people that had moved in the past two years. Judith proceeded to check the courthouse database for individuals and newspaper filings of businesses that were either new, acquired, or had a recent name change.

The business landscape had evolved.

Although there had been no announcement, the local paper and its fellow competitors throughout southern Illinois identified new corporate managers and owners. No details of land transactions in several counties were being published, at least not all as required by law. Reporting for the published record had taken a vacation. All news distribution in the southern part of the state was now controlled by one source.

Other legal records were sketchy at best, so Judith dug in. Information requiring a filing with the County Clerk's office was being rerouted. This process aborted public disclosure. As she updated Jones, he could only imagine who was responsible.

Especially troubling was her notice about the ownership changes for the gun shop and sporting goods store. The dark brothers appeared to have gone for the ammo. There were many other changes, including the airport, groceries, and the biggest bank. None of which portended good from Jones' perspective.

The strategy was disturbing but merited real potential for evil. The end game of gradually ratcheting up discontent had a proven track record that could slowly yield a coordinated stranglehold on the people and commerce of a community. Raising prices on merchandise, increasing fuel costs, changing loan conditions, and making home ownership more difficult eventually agitate people, who then take out their discontent on one another and their elected officials. This type of maneuvering takes time to pull off but is generally more successful than a raid across the border.

Jones realized he needed to leave before his guests came calling. Time was moving quickly. He closed his programs, emailed Judith, and shut down his computer.

Pausing briefly, Jones looked around the entire, nicely landscaped corner, built by his company on his recommendation. It was a shady little spot in the summer that the locals called Jones' Corner. It was hard to make yourself believe it might not always be there.

At that moment, Jones heard a voice say, "Jones, Jones O'Brian, so good to see you. I have been thinking about you. How are you doing?"

Mrs. Elfred, an old friend of his grandmother, was sitting on one of the benches, looking in his direction. Seeing her flooded Jones' memory with thoughts of the happy times he had spent growing up in the church, years ago.

"Mrs. Elfred," said Jones, "you look spiffy as usual."

"I know you are busy, Jones," she responded, "but the Lord has asked me to tell you that only he knows the plan for each person's life. Do not lose yourself questioning Kaz's death. Keep your faith in God."

Jones thanked her. The realization that God knew about his questions brought him some consolation. He moved toward his truck and started the engine. Ephram appeared in the passenger seat.

"Be alert," he said. It was more than a subtle warning. He turned around to respond, but Ephram had disappeared.

"Thanks," Jones said to no one present and put the pedal down.

As Jones started to drive, the thought occurred to him that Terry lived nearby and maybe, just maybe, he could get that aerial report. As he passed Shooter's Alley, the gun shop now under new management, the ever-present black vans were parked in the rear. The store was open, but the window displays were noticeably bare. The place looked deserted.

Casting aside his well-thought-out reasoning to go low profile, Jones parked his truck and walked in the front door. His pretense of buying a box of shells should provide adequate cover and avoid suspicion, or so he reasoned in this moment of sheer bravado.

As Jones entered, three figures came in from a side room. When the door shut behind him, Jones immediately felt the weight of his decision. There was no exit route. Having been a combat soldier, Jones quickly realized the danger presented. In his former Ranger résumé, this whole event would have been a nonconsideration. Suddenly, without warning, the same heaviness he'd felt at The Kitchen began to settle on him.

A man, maybe not a man, more like a being, came toward him. One of the mist-faced demons, a Corruptor, Arrow called them, stopped inches away from Jones' face. There was a red glow where his eyes should be. He said nothing.

Realizing he needed to leave before the heaviness overcame him, Jones spun around and headed toward the door. "Sorry, I don't see what I wanted," he said, exiting. Stupidity had taken precedence over common sense. No purpose had been served except to announce his presence.

As he got into his truck, disappointed in himself, Ephram

said, "Well, you have confirmation." While it was a relief to hear Ephram's voice behind the seat, the tone was unmistakable.

"You violated your intention to remain under the scope of visibility, and you are fortunate to have walked out. Follow your feelings, your gut I believe you call it, but understand, the darkness has been alerted."

Unannounced, Jones walked in Terry's back door. Dick and Terry were sitting at the kitchen table, staring at their cups. Hard to say what condition their condition was in at the moment.

Terry looked at Jones and shook his head. Dick was more forthcoming. He said, "Thanks a lot, Jones, for sending us to an airport full of suspicious characters who tried to sabotage Terry's Skyhawk. We landed in a crosswind with the sock showing calm. We barely got out of the plane alive, and the new security people practically chased us away from the airport. Why don't you send us to the Bermuda Triangle next?"

Jones smiled, aggravating Dick even more. "Spare me the theatrics, Dick. What did you see?"

"Nothing! It was a clear day, not a cloud in the sky, and we couldn't see anything when we flew over the area you designated. It's like they had their own private fog bank. We could see the ground everywhere else. We could see Cairo and the Ohio River flowing into the muddy Mississippi. We saw Metropolis and the casino boat. We could see Bald Knob Cross and Alto Pass. But nothing to report where you wanted us to look."

Terry threw his hands in the air. "I surrender," he said.

"We've been together a long time, guys," Jones reminded them. "We're in a massive fight that goes way beyond us. Always remember, our backup can take out their backup. I am sure our support brigade knows who they are, even if we don't, so hang in there."

Jones felt reassured listening to himself, which can be very dangerous, as he had already proven. He had unexplainably lost his wife. Now, these monsters were here, in his backyard. It must be God's will, and maybe this was his burning bush. But was that necessary? For a man who had spent years studying the Bible, Jones despised his confusion. He knew in his heart that those who remain faithful to the Lord were always victorious. Mrs. Elfred had reinforced that belief.

43

MIDGE PULLED A CHAIR FROM THE TABLE
TO THE MIDDLE OF THE KITCHEN AND
SAT QUIETLY, TRYING NOT TO CRY,
OVERWHELMED BY HER SURROUNDINGS.

WHAT WAS DESTROYED DAYS AGO HAD BEEN restored. The smell of fresh wood permeated the kitchen, emanating from the newly installed cabinets.

She had never seen anything in her rural life like the past two days. Her upbringing was a training platform for hardship more so than understanding. The farming world in her neck of the woods demanded constant effort. There were strict rules of behavior. What was acceptable elsewhere did not pass muster in the isolation of southern Illinois. People were largely uneducated. Those who had an education seldom stuck around. The grass was greener elsewhere. Bob had courted and married her before she could so much as think about college. She had spent her life married to a football coach, a high school principal, and now a sheriff. Time had taught her to keep, as the British would say, a stiff upper lip. With an absentee husband, she had managed to raise two children. Midge was no shrinking violet, having had the opportunity to wilt on many previous occasions.

Now she stared blankly into space as Abby brought in the last of the groceries, opened a cabinet to stuff them in, and gasped. "Midge, come here!" she said.

There was no room for the groceries, the cabinet was fully stocked, as though nothing had ever happened.

Abby opened the refrigerator. It was full, too.

The two women spoke little as they found a place for the overflow.

It didn't take long to finish their tasks, as the heavy lifting had somehow been organized and executed without their assistance. Abby went outside and moved her squad car into the garage. Best to appear gone. She also snatched up the snub-nose .38. Being armed was a positive, even if she was in the presence of the supernatural.

As Abby entered the mudroom off the kitchen, she called out to Midge but got no response. *No matter, she's somewhere in the house.* Swinging into action, Abby started making tea and toast. "Midge, soup's on," she called out, but Midge didn't answer. After filling both their cups, Abby walked over to the front window and saw Midge almost at the end of the driveway walking toward the mailbox. Jones had issued a clear directive to stay on the property. For some reason, Midge had chosen to ignore that warning. Abby ran outside and yelled at the top of her lungs, but to no avail, Midge was too far away.

A black van, parked off to the side of the road, started to move as Midge neared the mailbox. The minute Midge stepped across her property line, the black van pulled onto the road and headed in her direction, rapidly closing the distance between them.

Abby yelled again, and when Midge still didn't respond, she drew her .38 and fired two rounds into the air. That got her attention, but as she turned, Midge slipped in the loose gravel and fell. As she rose to her feet she passed back on to the Cable property. The van skidded to a stop, and two men jumped out and attempted to snatch her up. A blinding flash of light stopped them in their tracks.

Where the men stood was now a small pile of burnt ash. The van sped away before suffering the same fate.

Abby corralled Midge, and together they headed back toward the house with a clearer understanding of why Jones had insisted they stay on the Cable property. As Abby turned to look back at the intersection, there was no missing the glowing light that hovered over the driveway.

"Shots fired," Abby said, relaying the incident to the sheriff.

"Do you need an ambulance?" Cable was instantly on his feet.

Realizing she had unnecessarily raised a red flag, Abby said, "No, our guardians here took care of business. Midge is fine, just a little confused.

"Tell Jones I get it now. He'll know what I mean."

44

—◆◆◆◆—

IN THE RADIO ROOM AT THE WONDREN, THE UNDERLING MONITORING ABBY'S PHONE CALL TO THE SHERIFF SHRUGGED HIS SHOULDERS.

"THIS IS ANOTHER CRYPTIC MESSAGE, MASTER. THEY speak in code."

Dismissing him with a growl, Zorah paced. It was times like this that made him realize how useful that cretin, Merritt, had been. At least he knew the local language. Now they had no interpreter.

Zorah had received a lashing from Sonta over the failure to eliminate everyone at the church, which had resulted in the little girl calling for help. *Sonta was there too,* thought Zorah to himself. He could have killed her, which would have eliminated this dilemma. They just missed the child in all the excitement. Everyone was caught up in the killing. The Corruptors needed revenge for the losses incurred at the farmhouse. Instead, the church soiree turned the demonic hordes into casualties of war.

A dominant quad was sitting on them, in the parallel dimension, crossing over when asked. Zorah had faced many Angelic Warriors in the countless battles between the two warring factions. The Angelic Warriors were not to be trifled with unless living had ceased to be an option.

The Fallen Angels knew how to affect an advantage. Why they weren't using that knowledge baffled him.

Zorah realized Koal was also under scrutiny. Word traveled fast on the demonic hotline, and rumor had it that the Grand Master himself was displeased. That was not good for anyone in Koal's position. Waste runs downhill, and there is always a bottom. Zorah resided there, much to his chagrin.

His role was clearly defined, even if he didn't like it. Quadrant one was the test case for Sonta's blueprint to take over the planet Earth. They had all been here for quite some time but never organized entirely like they were at the moment.

The three other quadrants were mobilized and watching. Stand-by mode was probably chafing the field commanders and their lieutenants. Success was paramount for Koal, Sonta, and himself. Failure was not an option, and there certainly was no going back. God had been quite specific about that.

The grand design would not move forward unless their boots on the ground in quadrant one ripped the faith right out of those Christian believers and converted them to the Satanic hordes. There was fruit on the vine, and Zorah was in charge of the picking crew. He had been amazed for centuries that the Earth citizens had remained so unaware of the battles that had been going on around them. The decay in morality should have signaled danger but instead led to other equally dangerous declines. Murder was rampant in this world. The proliferation of weaponry was enormous. Greed prevailed. The sanctity of life was a divided issue.

The Fallen Angels were sowing discord at every opportunity, breaking down the citizenry, and yet, the resistance was fierce, if only from a diminishing number of humans. Zorah and his comrades were wired for winning. It was the path to salvation.

45

CABLE BREATHED A SIGH OF RELIEF, SAT DOWN, AND LEANED BACK.

DARKNESS HAD VISITED THE GIRLS. SHOTS HAD BEEN fired. He knew Abby would give him a full report as soon as she could do it personally. The demons had listening devices throughout the area. Wires were tapped. There was no room for a retreat on either side.

When he heard Abby say details were forthcoming, it took him a while to understand she meant Jones, tell Jones. That presented a problem, but maybe there was another way.

Knowing Dick was dispatched to Terry's, Cable reached for the phone book to look up Terry's number.

Terry answered his phone on the second ring, "Yell-o."

"Sheriff here, Terry. If you happen to see Jones sometime today, let him know that Abby needs him."

"Jones is right h—."

Cable cut him off. "Give him the message. Bye."

Terry slammed the receiver down and looked at Jones. "I tried to tell him you are here, but the sheriff just hung up on me. He said to tell you that Abby needs you."

Jones got it. So did the Corrupters.

"See you," Jones said, heading for his truck. Stopping

momentarily, he said, "Terry, you and Dick set up on the airport. There are some woods on the northeast. Good cover. We know what's going on now, but anything you find out will be helpful. Stay safe and report your findings in person to either Sheriff Cable or me. Maybe we can fit some more pieces into this puzzle."

"Sure thing, Jones," Dick yelled as Jones went out the door, climbed into his truck, and headed off down the dirt road that connected Terry's house to civilization, spewing a dust trail so intense it made Terry grimace.

Eventually, Jones worked his roundabout way through the country roads until Cable's homestead came into view. He slowed to a crawl, pulling in behind a brushy outcropping about three-quarters of a mile from the house.

Jones grabbed the 12 gauge and his Zeiss binoculars and walked about twenty yards to a wooded trail that exited the old roadbed. As he climbed its slope, Cable's house lay before him in full view. At first glance, everything seemed peaceful enough, but on closer inspection, the usual black van revealed itself parked in a clump of trees just beyond Cable's property line.

Staying covered, Jones slowly descended toward a pole barn standing at the back of the house. The building shielded his approach as he quietly slipped into the mudroom adjacent to the kitchen. It was then that he heard voices that he recognized as Midge and Abby. They were discussing the flashing light that signaled divine intervention.

Being careful not to startle the women, Jones puttered around the kitchen, making noise. "It's just me," he called out, stepping into the dining room.

"How is life on the old homestead?" he asked.

Abby took the initiative, explaining in detail what just happened out at the mailbox. Midge started to apologize, but Jones cut her off.

"This is uncharted water, Midge. There are no ground rules. We have the heavenly host here helping us. The battle lines have extended to your home whether we like it or not. The Darkness has surveillance all around us. All you can do is your part in the play. I'm going upstairs to check the enemy and get a better view of the surroundings. Finish your tea and relax."

All it took was one thorough scan of the property lines to see the swarm of vans, box trucks, and SUVs pulling up, full of bodies.

"Ab, someone up here wants to meet you," Jones called out.

As she entered the upstairs sitting room at the front of the house, Abby's face reflected her amazement when she saw Ephram for the first time.

"Who, who are you?" she stammered.

"Ephram," he responded without further explanation.

"Everything's fine," Jones said, seeing the confusion in Abby's eyes.

"This is one of the Lord's Warriors, Abby."

"Okay," Abby replied. What else was there to say about that.

Ephram just stood there, observing the movement.

"Have you ever seen an angel, Abby?" Jones asked. "You can see him, can't you?" It was a dumb question, since her mouth was ajar, speechless.

"Remember I told you we have help. Ephram's in charge here, and believe me, he's not alone."

Abby said nothing. There was nothing to say. She was looking at an angel.

Ephram reported, "I've contacted Arrow, since it appears the Corruptors have moved up their timetable. We didn't expect this kind of action, especially in the daylight. Have Midge and Abby arm themselves. They will both be able to see us, so be sure Midge is informed."

Jones reached for Abby's arm but she seemed stuck in place,

still trying to understand the situation. Jones led her downstairs and asked, "Midge, where's the armory? Unless I miss my guess, we are about to have some unwanted visitors."

Midge sucked in a big gulp of air, opened the door to the closet, and tapped a small button hidden innocuously beside the light switch. A part of the wall slid back, revealing an arsenal any Navy Seal would have been proud to own.

Midge Cable wasn't dancing Dixie. Reaching for two AR-15s and four magazines, she handed the first load to Jones. A full-sized .45 became Abby's weapon of choice, along with three extended magazines holding twenty-two rounds each. All that was lacking was a grenade launcher, which was Jones' weapon of choice in a previous lifetime. Enough time had passed to make him realize he would probably injure himself with it. Still, it would have been a suitable addition.

46

——◆◆◆◆——

THE DEMONIC FORCES UNDER THE COMMAND OF SONTA AND ZORAH WERE UNSETTLED AT THE RESTORATION OF A PROPERTY THAT THEY HAD RECENTLY DESTROYED.

IT WAS AN UNUSUAL OCCURRENCE EVEN FOR THE Angelic Warriors. There had been carnage beyond description in their respective pasts. What made this piddling homestead special? It didn't matter. They would destroy it again.

At the northeast corner of the property, carefully placed outside the property line, Zorah set up a command post whose sole purpose was to organize the assault. The location was remote enough to fall into the no sight, no rules category. With the territorial escalation well underway, this would be a good training exercise for his fighters, some of whom were recent recruits and had yet to see combat.

The restoration could not stand. Zorah wondered aloud how he could have missed such an angelic feat. It was all supernatural and reeked of righteousness. His minions had seen or heard nothing, not so much as a hammer or saw. The repairs just happened.

The main problem, as Zorah saw it, was the potential presence of real power. There was no telling who his adversary might be or the strength of the opposing force. It might be Arrow, which was not a healthy thought. The two field officers who escaped from the first encounter had been severely punished. He had difficulty dealing with weakness in his warriors. Throughout the ages, whenever dark forces fought the angels of light, death was the outcome for defeat or retreat.

Zorah hadn't picked this time and place. It was Sonta's creation. The task had been handed to him to execute. Every demonic fighter within a fifty-mile radius had been called up, but some had not arrived. The possibilities were serious. What if he was about to take on a quad? What if a top field commander like Arrow had come across the parallel dimension. It smelled like a battle to Zorah, not a routine training exercise.

There was one more factor that tilted the balance of power away from his control. For some unknown reason, Sonta had decided to attack in daylight. This tactic alone terrified Zorah and many of his field officers. They had to be wondering about the urgency of taking this risk for such a pitiful reward.

"I don't think Zorah has his act together on this fight, but he's the boss," said a nameless demon. "Have you heard the higher-ups saying all the fights over the past few months show us winning?"

"I've heard that," came the reply, "but I think it's all rumors. All I've seen are the wounded, lots of them."

Silence surrounded them as they waited for Zorah's command.

47

FOR HIS PART, JONES WAS LOOKING
AT AN INCREASING NUMBER OF MEN
AND MATERIAL GATHERING IN
FORMATION OUTSIDE THE
CABLE PROPERTY LINE.

EVERYONE INSIDE THAT BOUNDARY HAD TO BE READY. There was the possibility of facing an overwhelming force. Going upstairs, he encountered Ephram, watching the buildup intently.

"What do I see out there?" Jones asked.

"Corruptors," said Ephram, "and demons they have turned. They will be bringing streams of darkness, but I cannot believe they will attack in daylight, which it seems they are considering. The Corruptors fight in the darkness. Sunlight is not their friend."

Jones could sense his companion's concern but also understood that there was always the quad to consider. Arrow had told him, "We always have enough." That in itself was a reassuring statement that could not be easily forgotten. Was it possible to be overpowered by numbers? Not if you believed Arrow.

Ephram had not moved a muscle. The man had not even acknowledged Jones' presence in the room.

Then he spoke, "Yes, you are thinking correctly. Don't lose faith; there's always enough. Besides, we intend to fight this skirmish on two fronts."

Thinking back to some old World War II movies he'd seen, Jones replied, "Well, yes, a frontal assault with a flanking movement creates a two-front fight."

Ephram said nothing, nor did he move.

Jones noticed his stillness and pondered where he was with all this. *Maybe I need to occupy the same space*, he thought.

"What do you mean by two fronts?" asked Jones.

"Not what you said, that's not what I meant," said Ephram. "I mean from the front and the back, simultaneously." At that point, Ephram smiled.

"Not only have I positioned my quad surrounding the house, but Arrow has also arrived. His Warriors are behind the entire force of Corruptors."

"I see," Jones acknowledged. "A true two-front battle."

Zorah's two battlefield commanders, Ashima and Zoboth, notified him of their readiness. The plan was to destroy Cable's home and anyone who happened to be there. Sonta would not be happy with anything less.

Destruction outcomes are horrific, creating fear on the ground among the people. It was a tactic for the ages, one that eventually led to total submission.

Orders were delivered. The demonic horde readied for combat. In fifteen minutes, there would be chaos as the house was leveled. With Sonta's plan in place, Zorah slipped noiselessly down a nearby ravine and away from his possible close encounter of the angelic kind.

Zorah, deep inside, knew he should have stood up to Sonta and told him he was aware, like the other pawns in the game, that the darkness had never won a daylight battle with the Angelic Warriors, at least not in his memory. He didn't do that. Instead, Zorah went along with the plan, always doubting.

Ashima surveyed his troops one last time, concerned about

his front line and possible reinforcements. Those present would fight this battle, which might not be enough. He needed options that he could not envision.

The moment felt wrong to Ashima, who remembered a similar feeling several months earlier. He survived, just barely, and still carried wounds and scars that had not completely healed.

"This is no good," Zoboth declared. "With the battle in the daylight, we lose our cover of darkness. No wonder Zorah left."

The clock timed out. Calling a halt to the engagement was above their pay grade. Retreat was not an option. The battle was on.

From his vantage point on the second floor of Cable's house, Ephram watched Corruptors emerge from every hidden venue on the perimeter.

Even with his quad in place, Ephram winced at the number of demonic hosts advancing toward the house. His most experienced commanders were manning their battle stations, instructed not to move until the enemy crossed the property line. These were seasoned Warriors whose skill and fighting experience were not in question. They had proven themselves countless times throughout the centuries and were about to do so again. Ephram's confidence in them was high, knowing full well what the Corruptors were about to face. His men would move and mobilize at precisely the right time.

While Ephram stood looking at the formation that fronted his position, he noticed a large oak tree on the house's south side. The leaves had gone still, and what few clouds were drifting across the sky had suddenly solidified. Sunlight disappeared; the entire area darkened. It was a moment reminiscent of battles past when evil darkened the world. Here, now, the quiet became overwhelming. The Corruptors came to a dead stop.

Ephram looked to the left. About six hundred yards away, on

the northeast corner, a single Corruptor crossed the boundary fence, triggering the bugle-like sound of a Shofar, an ancient Israeli battle horn.

"Now," Ephram said under his breath.

Jones watched as many of the Corruptors froze in place, unable to unleash their blackness. Their stopping was no accident. The legendary sound of the Shofar was a deadly warning, and they all knew it. One demonic presence had crossed the line. The battle was on. Ephram's quad moved with fierce resolve.

As Corruptors charged, Angelic Warriors appeared in their path. The ground shook. Heaven and Hell met head-on.

A Corruptor crossed over the roadside hedges guarding the eastern flank. As the Fallen Angel moved into position, a withering blast caught him just below the sternum. His field jacket was consumed by fire, effectively ending his day. Another suffered a similar fate as he was confronted by two Warriors simultaneously as his unit approached the front steps.

Abby watched the battle unfold, her AR-15 in readiness. The enemy fought with streams of pure darkness—in broad daylight. Hideous screams filled the air. No one could ever get ready for this. Somehow amid this carnage, she felt inexplicably safe. Midge, who had seen the demonic beings a few days before when they attacked her, was frightened but not running. There was some kind of a line around the house that the demons could not penetrate. Both women were speechless as they watched.

The demons varied their battle group formations as they advanced. Ephram's quad parried. When a Warrior was about to be overrun, a flow of his comrades, like waves crashing on the land as they build toward high tide, moved to assist against the attack and terminated it. The quad flowed from area to area until there was nothing left to cover.

Zoboth, having fought angels for eons, watched his troops falter. He had fought this fight before. "These aren't humans," he reminded his troops. "You can't kill them with darkness by yourself. Take on a Warrior one-on-one, and you'll die every time! It will take two or three of you to stop an angel."

While this strategy might have worked on a smaller quad, the warring angels had all the numbers. The Corruptors' wounds and causalities mounted as streams of darkness encountered flashes of light that became fireballs. Puffs of smoke heralded the demise of the Fallen.

Zoboth studied the battle in horror and contemplated the unthinkable.

Retreat?

As the battle raged before him, Arrow nodded toward the keeper of the Shofar, and once again the sound blew through the winds of war.

The Corruptors, engrossed in the battle and their losses, didn't react. What happened next was brutal.

In overwhelming numbers, on the second front—from behind—Arrow's Warriors entered the battle. Ashima, and then Zoboth, fell under the onslaught. No prisoners were taken.

48

-◆◆◆◆-

CABLE SAT AT HIS DESK, ENGULFED WITH A FEELING OF HELPLESSNESS.

ABBY'S REPORT OF GUNSHOTS AND JONES' MESSAGE, which had been delivered by Terry, were disconcerting. He felt glued to his chair, unable to move.

Finally, words begin to form, "Lord, being sheriff is enough of a challenge. Midge and Abby need you now. I'm sorry I'm not with them. Get Jones to my house safely. Be a protector for them. Amen."

He'd never prayed quite like this before. Relief washed over him like a tidal wave.

The intercom buzzed. Elbert blurted, "City police are reporting a lot of strange activity happening all over town, Sheriff. People are fighting and shouting epithets."

"Do we need to call for backup?" asked Cable.

"No, I reckon not yet," said Elbert. "City dispatch sure sounds exasperated, though.

"Oops, look out the window, boss. Two more of those vans just pulled up."

Cable watched the vans park. Four men exited the vehicles

and started toward the courthouse steps when they crashed into an invisible barrier. The men acted confused and disoriented. They even tried moving forward again but were stopped, unable to mount the steps.

Finally, they gave up and returned to their vans, shouting and cursing, and drove off. As Cable watched the demons leave the parking lot, he saw the glow on the sidewalk next to the building and knew with certainty that the Lord's hand was indeed upon them.

Cable had never seen that phenomenon, and although city dispatch didn't ask for help, he decided to take a drive around town to see what else was going on.

Just then, his radio crackled, "Eagle, Elbert here."

"Go, Elbert."

"City dispatch just called. Someone hit the off switch. All's calm on the western front."

"Copy that, out," Cable said, smiling like a Cheshire cat. He parked his car in front of The Kitchen, chuckling as he looked at the OPE sign, wondering if the N would ever be lit again. The light had been out for so long townspeople were referring to The Kitchen as Mayberry in honor of Opie, one of the characters in the TV series, who was probably born and raised nearby. Cable stepped through the door only to confront total quiet. The place was empty. He called to out to Cindy, the owner, who was helping her employees clean up dishes scattered across the floor.

"It was like a storm rolled into the restaurant," she said. "Everyone got jumpy and nervous and ran out of the doors. No one stopped to pay their bill, but you can bet I'll collect when and if they ever come back."

49

CABLE REMOUNTED AND WENT FOR
HOME. AS HE APPROACHED HIS
DRIVE WAY, HE SLOWED TO A CRAWL.

DEBRIS LAY EVERYWHERE. SOMETHING BIG HAD happened while he was away. The grounds were torn apart except a fifty-foot perimeter that started with his front driveway and circled the house, which lay untouched. Some invisible wall had stopped all encroachment.

He turned down the driveway and stopped about halfway to the house.

Cable honked his horn and Midge came running out the front door, down the steps and toward the driveway.

Cable tried to get out, but Midge jumped him, almost pushing him back into the car. She kissed him so hard you'd think he had just returned from a deployment.

"You won't believe what's happened, Bob. I almost got snatched up right there at the end of the driveway," she said, pointing to the spot. "Abby scared them off with that little .38 of hers. There was also a big flash of light."

"It was the light, baby, that's all it was," Cable said, trying to calm her down.

Holding her tighter, he said, "I was praying for you. Whatever you say happened, it did happen. Just the way you saw it. Our world is at war with something very, very evil, but we have help, the most powerful kind I have ever seen. This whole thing is way beyond me. I truly believe there are more for us than there are for them."

Seeing Bob and Midge embracing in the driveway propelled Jones up from his chair and down the stairs. As he walked into the dining room, he came face-to-face with Abby. It was an awkward moment, neither knowing what to say.

They found themselves in each other's arms before thinking any further. Abby pressed herself to Jones so tightly he could feel her heartbeat. Trembling, she started to cry. Holding her face in his hands, Jones kissed her on the lips and meant every bit of it. "We have a lot to talk about when we have time, Abby," Jones said when he could no longer hold his breath.

"I am sure you pretty well have this all figured out anyway."

Hand in hand, they walked into the kitchen. Bob and Midge came in and joined them. There was lots of catching up accomplished in the next thirty minutes.

"What's your next step?" asked Cable.

"I need to check on Ellie in Jonesboro," Jones said abruptly, pulling Ellie's business card out of his pocket. In short order, she was on the line.

"Hi, Ellie, it's Jones."

"Hey, Jones. I was thinking of calling you."

"Why? What's going on?"

"I don't know. I don't know," Ellie stammered.

"Tell me what's on your mind," said Jones.

"There are so many vehicles coming and going by here; I don't know what to make of it."

"Okay, let's meet at the barn. Maybe we need to revisit our friends."

"The barn. Like the last time?"

"Yeah, like the last time. See ya."

Abby walked Jones to the back door.

"Just so you know," she said, drawing him close and kissing him with everything she had, "that wasn't a one-time shot."

Jones smiled and moved off silently into the woods.

50

-◆◆◆◆-

EPHRAM AND ARROW DISCUSSED AND REVIEWED THEIR STRATEGY SURROUNDING THE BATTLE AT THE HOMESTEAD.

THEY HAD SLAUGHTERED THE CORRUPTORS. MORE than 90% of the enemy breathed their last that day. The angels had only suffered two seriously injured and several wounded. All would recover and be back soon.

Ephram's duty to protect Jones had been accomplished. This battle was different from any of their past conflicts, though, which numbered more than it was possible to count. Never in their long history of intervention had the two Warriors faced an attack in broad daylight.

"There will be hell to pay for that decision," said Arrow.

"It was a battle they could not win, so why engage?" said Ephram.

"Rage against Heaven can fan an inextinguishable fire," said Arrow. Both men could feel, without acknowledgment, the darkness around them growing more intense and unpredictable. With knowing looks, they departed to their assigned positions.

51

·◆◆◆◆·

ZORAH HAD EXPERIENCED
MANY DEFEATS, BUT NONE LIKE THE
ONE HE CURRENTLY SURVEYED.

HE FAULTED HIS COWARDICE, BUT THERE WAS NO
precedent for such a confrontation. Not only had The
Darkness been unprepared and shorthanded, but they had
chosen to fight in the daylight. All demons knew the risks of
such a strategy, and yet Sonta had forced it to happen. While
that might protect him from Koal and the high council, it would
certainly not bode well if Sonta learned of his recusal. It was an
inescapable fact that Satan himself would hear of this catastrophe.

Trouble was coming, and he knew it. Entering the area after
the battle, Zorah was staggered by the loss of demonic lives.
There were very few injured warriors left to load and take away.
Most were gone, reduced by the power of the fireballs into little
piles of ash scattered over several acres, already forgotten like
last week's trash left at the curb.

As Zorah surveyed the area, a deep, horrific, growling
moan came from his throat. His nostrils flared at the sight of
ash piles so numerous as to defy description. The red from his
eyes flooded his entire facial area. How could Sonta make this
his reality?

Instead of slipping into a different dimension and transporting himself back to the Wondren, Zorah climbed into one of the vans and rode. He needed every excuse that would give him more time to think. A wound would help prove his involvement and improve his chances of living. With extreme prejudice, he ripped open his thigh, inflicting a jagged cut on himself. It was a terrible injury that just might be enough to save his life. Both field commanders that saw him leave were dead. There were no witnesses to report him slipping away before the battle started. Zorah groaned as the self-inflicted pain shot across his system. He immediately induced a coma upon himself.

52

-◆◆◆◆-

JEREMIAH KOAL'S INVITATION TO ADDRESS MAJOR SUPPORTERS AT A FUNDRAISING LUNCH ON EAST WACKER DRIVE WAS ANOTHER NOTCH IN HIS BELT.

A S ONE OF THE LEADERS OF THE DARKNESS ON Earth, he needed to raise money for the restoration of several acquired properties on the near southside. These locations provided refuge for demonic emissaries. Their presence would morph into positions of influence over time, a commodity, he realized all too well, that was in increasingly short supply. It was also confirmation of the clout his organization was gaining. The mayor and his staff, the Governor and several state officials, had all clamored for inclusion in this photo opportunity. A meet and greet of this stature did not come along every day. Over fifteen hundred tickets had been sold, raising well over a million dollars.

Events this large, with so many political alliances on display, became a protocol nightmare. Being the third public appearance that month was stressful to Koal. Not so much for Gozan, his majordomo, who had worked for many bosses.

189 | OBLIVION'S REACH

The security team was more than up to the task, he reassured, freeing Gozan up to meet many of the available ladies who would be there for the face time. The parties that took place at Jeremiah Koal's penthouse were always in need of fresh flesh. Gozan made sure to carry a pocket full of invitations at all times. These were needed to gain access to the private elevator. Seldom were there refusals to what became the gold standard as the hottest party in town.

Koal's speeches were full of hyperbole and platitudes. It was important always to mention the mayor's name several times while simultaneously giving him undeserved credit for doing such an excellent job. No matter that the city was floundering in debt, corrupt beyond belief, and drowning in a tidal wave of crime. The praise bought him space to operate from a struggling police department overwhelmed by every manner of criminal activity. There was no shortage of targets. Going looking for more was unnecessary.

At the end of Koal's speech, he had said nothing. Everyone applauded. There were so many demons in the audience controlling the atmosphere that nothingness was the theme for the day. Even the newspaper reporters, masters of the short form, had trouble writing anything convincing. No reports of substance would be originating in Koalville.

As the reception room finally began to clear, Koal continued to work the crowd. It was just another performance. He had no intentions of living up to any of the promises he had made and appreciated the dishonesty of the elected officials around him. Several envelopes full of cash from hopeful vendors found their way to his entourage at every gathering. Ladies discreetly slipped personal phone numbers into his pockets.

Clearing out the remaining stragglers, Gozan signaled the security to sweep the restrooms and adjoining public areas. No chance could be taken to have a mortal present considering Koal's demonstrated proclivity for morphing into his demonic persona at the first possible moment.

The Fallen Angel detested his mortal form and was frustrated with the mundane, inconsequential questions continually volleyed from all angles. When Gozan signaled, Koal transformed. Swirling as he stood, a misty haze encompassed his face as two blood-red eyes began to bulge. The stench of oozing slime filled the room. He stood up, stretching to his full potential, his wings completely extended, their constriction finished for the day.

"I did it again," he said to Gozan and the security demons.

"Had the crowd in the palm of my hand. Lambs to the slaughter, the simple-minded fools. Dangle a little power, and they all fall in line."

The security detail and other children of The Darkness, those who had crossed over, agreed with Koal's self-assessment. Almost as if in a euphoric cloud, Koal folded his wings and sat, relishing the moment.

But it was only a moment.

Gozan, standing in the far corner of the room, felt the shift as Koal stumbled to his feet. Sounding as though it was coming from a loudspeaker, and growing in intensity, were the sounds of hundreds of voices shrieking in pain, crying for help that was not arriving. Koal shook with rage and despair. He weakened and staggered, trying not to fall.

Gozan leaped into action, signaling the security forces to form a wall around Koal. As that shield positioned, the team morphed into their demonic personas and spread their wings, completely encircling Koal, who became short of breath and nearly passed out. Gozan moved inside the circle and supported Koal, whose eyes glazed over, a low moan escaping his throat.

After what seemed like an eternity but in reality was little more than thirty seconds, the incident was over. Silence reigned. The painful wailing of those dead and dying faded away as quickly as it came. It was clear to all present that the cacophony had been the anguished cries of demons meeting extinction in a battle somewhere, on this Earth, at this time. The sounds had to be hundreds, if not thousands, of dying, given the volume of noise. It went unsaid that these were troops under Koal's command, his men, his quadrant.

It was late afternoon. No battle of any significance should ever take place in the daylight hours. Demons from The Darkness were night fighters, engaging only in the absence of light.

Koal started to shake, stopped, and took a deep breath. Memories of previous encounters with Michael and his Dread Warriors flooded his mind, but this was different. He looked at Gozan.

"It's daylight. How could this happen? Losses like this have only come at night."

Hoping it was a rhetorical question, Gozan said nothing, being in shock himself.

"Arrow," said Koal with certainty, "this is his doing."

"Where is Arrow?"

Thoughts of battles lost came crashing in.

"Only Arrow or Michael could bring this much destruction," he cried out, vanishing instantly to transport himself back to his headquarters.

Arriving in his suite there was a message from his mole in Sonta's headquarters.

"Master, Sonta commanded Zorah to make an attack on a target this afternoon, in the daylight. We lost many."

53

JONES MOVED THROUGH THE WOODS
SILENTLY. HIS YEARS OF TRAINING IN THE
SKILL OF SILENT RUNNING WERE
A DEFINITE ASSET.

AS HE APPROACHED HIS TRUCK, HE NOTICED THERE were visitors sitting nearby. That was just a small part of it. Ephram and Arrow were on a downed tree having a quiet conversation, apparently oblivious to the outside world.

"That mass of demons was certainly more than I had expected," Arrow said. "They are stepping up the pace of the takeover, and although we haven't seen Sonta yet, he is nearby. To have picked a fight in broad daylight when their vulnerability is highest is a clear signal that the fight is escalating."

"There were more recruits in his force than I ever remember seeing," said Ephram. "It must have taken a while to gather that many.

"Some were watchers. The massacre would have been higher if they had stepped across the boundary."

"There is still hope for their redemption," said Arrow. "Even the evilest hearts can be reclaimed."

Ephram stood, acknowledging Jones' arrival, and then turned back to Arrow. "Our Warriors responded well to their mass attacks. Our flow as the battle shifted was swift and effective.

"Peace my brother," Ephram said as he walked toward Jones' truck.

54

---◆◆◆◆---

SONTA DID NOT REQUIRE
A REPORT FROM ZORAH.

HE HAD FELT THE ATMOSPHERE AROUND HIM SHIFT with the passing of souls; all headed to Hell. A significant number of Fallen were not coming back.

Mass confusion reigned in the Wondren as the recruits, still in training and not yet thoroughly demonized, scurried around, talking nervously among themselves.

As bad as the situation was on the ground, the anger of Koal and the high council far exceeded anything Sonta had ever experienced. His life was one step from extinction, which did not bode well for Zorah or any underling. Koal had sent a message that simply said, "Never again."

Sonta knew Koal was referring to daylight sorties. The type that got them all dead. What had he been thinking? He knew the power of the Angelic Warriors, and their presence here had been confirmed. Arrow had crossed over, and his field commander Ephram was nearby. They fought when asked, and the sheriff or someone had done just that.

Once again, Sonta had deviated from his blueprint. There could be no more loose actions taken on a whim.

55

◆◆◆◆

KOAL HAD NO SOONER ARRIVED AT HIS HEADQUARTERS WHEN A SUMMONS WAS DELIVERED TO REPORT ON THE SLAUGHTER.

HE IMMEDIATELY TRANSPORTED TO SECOND HEAVEN where all the top-ranking members of the high council, including Satan himself, had assembled. Satan personified as an angry lion, swiping his huge claws toward the Heavens, roaring and snarling as though to devour everyone in sight. His Supremeness was beyond angry. There would be no more tolerance for failure. That point was understood loud and clear by Koal, who chaffed at the dressing down he received from his equals on the council, not to mention the wrath of He Who Ruled.

"Did you approve this action?" asked Amon, one of the most senior council members whose thoughts carried significant weight, even by him who must be obeyed.

"I did not," replied Koal, his rage evidenced by the smoldering red eyes that protruded from their sockets.

"Sonta wanted revenge for the loss of several of his army in an earlier engagement at the homestead."

"He had to know the angels were guarding the property," said Amon.

"It was beyond foolish and will not happen again," said Satan, "or you will be called into account."

"Yes, Your Grace," replied Koal, understanding this was no time to mount an argument.

"The other High Commanders—Bel, Chemosh, and Kalwan—are all watching the execution of your plan. It cannot fail, or we will have to start from the ground up. Do I make myself clear? Starting over consumes time we cannot lose. We are staring down the book of Revelation, which spells out our fate quite clearly, wouldn't you agree?"

Satan now became a giant serpent, coiling, and hissing, his elongated fangs inches from Koal's neck. Writhing around Koal's lower body, he enveloped the Fallen Angel's entire body, the coils oozing into slime before once again becoming a Fallen whose eyes glowed red-hot as he spoke. All present remembered the Falling and the appearance of embers preceding their destination. It was Lucifer burning the night sky into Oblivion.

56

---◆◆◆◆◆---

JUSTIN BRYANT WAS
IN A FUNK, UNABLE TO PERFORM
EVEN ROUTINE CHORES.

H E FELT AN ENORMOUS WEIGHT THAT HE WAS
unable to shed. Pressure froze him with inaction. There
was no defense against this mysterious presence the likes of
which he had never encountered. The darkness was all around
him. He stopped to pray and refocus, but the shadows returned.

Evil was afoot. *Has there been a shift in Heaven's gate,* he
wondered? *What exactly is going on in this world?* His growing
lack of focus presented enormous problems, not only for him
but all true believers.

Suddenly, the weight lifted. Without the slightest hesitation,
Justin went to the stable and saddled the two horses Ellie and
her friend had previously taken. As he tightened the last cinch,
Ellie pulled up inside the shed.

Great timing, he thought.

"Justin," she said quietly, "Jones and I will need the horses
again. Sorry I didn't call ahead."

Justin looked at Ellie with a big smile. She was one of his
favorite people. He had come to admire her over the years and
never knew what to expect when she showed up. Justin and

Ellie were on the same wavelength. They served a risen Lord and made no bones about it.

Flashing a broad smile, Justin realized the coming of Ellie and her friend had coincided with the lifting of his burden.

"You're ready to go, Ellie," he said.

"Do you think I need to tell you they are ready to ride, or will you just accept the fact that I already knew."

Ellie took a deep breath and nodded her acceptance. These were dangerous times. She was about to close again on the darkness, going deeper in than any human would ever want to do.

"Jones is coming," she said. "He is meeting me here." There was an edge in her voice, as though something massive was going on.

Justin nodded and handed Ellie food and canteens just as Jones pulled into the shed.

"I wasn't expecting you so soon, Jones," she said.

"Neither was I," Jones shrugged as he walked toward Ellie. "I never drove above forty-five, but somehow, I got here much faster than I should have."

Jones looked at his watch and said, "It was like being transported."

"Transported?" Ellie asked.

"Yeah, like when the Lord caught Philip away in Acts, he ended up in Azotus without remembering ever taking a step to get there."

Jones grabbed his shotgun and started toward the stable. Reconsidering his decision, he retraced his steps and swapped it for a 30.06 deer rifle. A little more stopping power might be in order.

57

━◆◆◆◆◆━

THIRTY MINUTES PASSED
AS THEY RODE TOWARD
THE WONDREN, HELL'S GATE
ON EARTH, BUILT AND INHABITED
BY DEMONIC HOSTS.

JONES ASKED HIMSELF AS THE HORSES WENT DEEPER into the countryside if this trip was essential. He knew what the destination offered. Danger. He was putting Ellie's life at risk. He had not been able to save Kaz. There was no reason to believe he could alter events here, should things go badly. It was his M.O.

Jones reined in his mount and said, "Ellie, you need to go back. There is nothing here for you to witness except evil. Let's stop for a few minutes and give the horses a breather, and then you turn around."

"I'm not going anywhere but forward," said Ellie, pulling up and dismounting.

"I need to make sure you know what this is all about," said Jones. "The danger here is life-threatening. You don't have to do this."

"I do," said Ellie, "and I will, as long as I have the strength in my body to go with you."

Jones was unable to respond.

"Whatever happens is God's will," said Ellie. "I'm just following orders."

"You could die here," said Jones.

"Then I will," Ellie replied, "and it won't be your fault, so don't go there."

Jones shut up and got back on his horse.

"There is one important fact, Ellie, you should know. There was a battle on the sheriff's property of almost biblical proportion. This enemy we are marching into can take on human form, but they are most certainly not human."

Mounting up, Ellie said, "I get it," and spurred her horse forward.

"We are heading toward what I believe is their headquarters," Jones said.

"Yeah," Ellie said, and rode on.

Jones felt the apprehension in Ellie's voice. Maybe an intervention was in order.

"Ephram," Jones called out, "are you able to take a moment?"

Ephram appeared in the trail a few feet ahead, just like that.

"Ellie, I'd like you to meet one of the ones for us."

Slowly she pulled her horse to a halt and looked directly at the Lord's angel standing squarely in front of her. Ellie's eyes widened.

Ephram was a commanding figure, by any standard, standing nearly seven feet tall, muscular, and scarred from head to toe.

Ellie was on the record as saying she would never see an angel. That was now incorrect.

She zeroed in on his face, wrinkled and also scarred, and those eyes, so compassionate they must reflect his true self.

Ellie turned back to Jones, who had a wry smile on his face.

"Ellie, this is Ephram. Remember that flash of light in the restaurant? That was him. It was your first encounter with an angel. He and his fellow Warriors got us out of there. Ephram came with us on our first trip here too."

Ellie's shoulders slumped.

The angel Warrior approached her.

"It is always a privilege to meet a mortal who is committed to the fight against darkness, Ellie. You are making a difference in the battle for righteousness. Your community would be less without you."

As Ephram spoke, Ellie seemed to regroup. The air itself took on a new texture. With a deep sigh, Ellie received the grace of God into her heart. She would need it all.

After riding in silence for what seemed like only moments, Jones stopped again and pulled out the notes and diagrams he had made from the first visit.

"Ellie, I think we should find a way to enter the compound directly instead of scaling the bluff like last time. If my diagram is right, there's a ravine that will put us in the area of the garages on the west side. From there we will get a good look at the whole compound. The sun will be at our backs, which will help hide our approach."

Ephram appeared just ahead and looked directly at Ellie.

"Ellie, not all of the enemy are spirit beings. Many at this hideaway are still human. They have been deceived, programmed to believe the thoughts of the Corruptors. The guns you have will be able to stop them. My Warriors and I will deal with the Corruptors, the Fallen. Deadly weapons have some effect on them, but only to slow them momentarily."

Ellie looked at Jones and then back to Ephram, who had already vanished.

"Please tell me we aren't watching some movie, Jones," she stammered as she wrapped one leg around the saddle horn and turned toward him.

"This is more real, Ellie, than anything you have ever

experienced. Every war story, every battle you read about in your Bible is manifesting itself to us right now in this place. Like Esther, I feel we are here for such a time as this. I don't know how it will end for us today, but here we are, caught up in the middle of a colossal battle for the souls of men.

"These demonic hordes are here to take over our world. My whole town is on the verge of collapse. You and I are a part of the battle, a small part in halting the darkness."

Jones nudged his horse back into the creek and headed out. Ellie didn't move.

"Are you coming, Ellie?" Jones called out.

She turned toward him with an aura of peace in her eyes. "Sure."

When they reached the end of the trailhead, Ellie moved ahead of Jones, dismounted and led her horse through a brushy outcropping.

Clearing the obstruction, she remounted, and with Jones following, started west. It was tranquil now and vital for them to be at one with that silence. The danger must be very, very close. Suddenly, a flash of light erupted from beyond the hill in front of them.

Ellie saw it too and dismounted. Jones followed suit.

Ephram appeared. "Come this way," he said, pointing in the direction they should go.

Ellie took the lead. Moments later, they entered a thick cluster of trees and brush. Looking through the branches, she could see four guards from the compound moving away from their position.

Tying the horses to some small saplings, Ellie and Jones did weapons check and moved toward the Wondren.

Twenty yards in, Jones crouched down, signaling Ellie to do the same. From within the walls of this man-created canyon, the sounds of cars and trucks stopping and starting competed with angry conversations, shouting and groaning. Something wasn't right.

Jones watched as Ephram positioned himself halfway up a sheer cliff face, where he could observe the entire complex. No problem for an angel.

A small group of men were gathered at the corner of a warehouse some thirty yards ahead. Jones could see they were human, probably locals under the command of the demons.

"I'm going to slip into that crowd, Ellie," Jones whispered. "You wait here and cover me. Maybe I can listen in on some conversations, get an idea on what's going on." Before Ellie could respond, Jones left cover and moved toward the group.

As he approached, someone asked, "Does anyone have a clue about what's next?"

The answer stunned him momentarily. "I hear the bullseye is still Jackson County. More help is supposed to be on the way, but you know how it is around here. Nobody ever has a straight story. Kind of like that posh job they promised me if I sold them my gun store. I'm still waiting."

Jones recognized Ed Zalinski, the former owner of Shooter's Alley. Seeing him here explained his absence. At least he is still alive. Trying to blend in and not draw attention, Jones bent over, tied his boot, stood up, and strolled back toward Ellie just as Zorah limped to the balcony jutting out from Sonta's second-floor office in the Wondren. His chin was on his chest in mock defeat from the verbal bashing Sonta had administered. The massive, self-inflicted leg wound was painful but healing rapidly, as was the wont for a creature that had existed for millennia. It had bought him some time, a precious commodity at the moment. Survival would depend on something special affecting his standing in the eyes of Sonta, who stood glowering at his subordinate in disgust. If either of the field commanders had survived, Zorah would now be a memory, or perhaps being tortured for eternity.

As he considered his predicament, some bright object caught the sun's rays perfectly and reflected its brilliance into Zorah's line of sight. He growled, zeroing in on the source, which was a crucifix on which the holiest of holies was crucified for the benefit of all humankind. This crucifix hung from the neck of Ellie, who never took it off, and never knew what hit her.

Flapping his enormous wings, the Fallen Angel traversed the distance faster than the human eye could follow, and in an instant, before Ephram or any of his Angelic Warriors could close on the demon, Ellie was snatched, gone into the darkness. Jones, only a few feet behind her now, could only watch as his friend vanished from sight.

Sonta had decided that Zorah had outlived his usefulness. In the chain of command, someone always paid for failure. Sonta had a boss that no one wanted to cross. After staring for some time at his underling, his anger a consumptive furnace in his belly, his pores oozing with the stench of death, Sonta decided that the failure at Cable's house, not to mention the loss of hundreds of dark spirit warriors, was on him, not Zorah, and that was not acceptable. Anger at the sheriff's house debacle had sent him back, only to fail again. He was determined to be the first high commander to assimilate his territory. His peers were watching, charged by his extreme highness with similar tasks all across America. He would win, period, no matter the cost. There was not an alternative. Satan's overall strategy to slowly envelop all areas of American society, turning neighbor against neighbor, was well underway. Any delay could cause his removal from the hierarchy of leadership in Satan's domain, and the privileges he enjoyed.

His anger subsiding, Sonta's demonic voice summoned Zorah, who had disappeared from view, "We cannot ever let what happened today repeat itself, Zorah."

"Yes, Master," said Zorah, landing on the ledge and unfurling his massive wing to reveal a beautiful human hostage, "I have brought atonement."

From his roost on the canyon wall, Ephram could see the capture unfold. It was one of those rare moments when nearly equal powers collide, and in this instance, evil had a head start. Without action, Ellie was doomed. That was a given. Any rescue must be carefully thought out, for Sonta was present and accounted for, which equaled the playing field. Only secondary in power to Satan and his top commanders, Sonta was indeed an angel of death. In demonic form, not in changling status, there was no safe approach to such a creature.

Ephram and his Warriors, under Arrow's leadership, had met Sonta and his hordes, and others like them, in many previous battles. Death and severe wounds always ruled those days. Across the centuries, the powers of darkness had continually tried to take total dominion over the earthly realm. The outcome of those battles had, so far, swayed in the balance, with an edge going to the Angelic Warriors. Arrow and Ephram knew, however, the strength of the enemy must never be taken for granted. The Fallen now had a new battle plan aimed at humankind.

"Well now," said Sonta, seeing the woman emerge from the wing of his subordinate, "what have we here?" Ellie did not respond, yet she did not cower as expected, which is what Sonta wanted her to do.

Zorah said, "She was spying on us from the grassy ravine west of the balcony when I spotted her."

"Why would you be here?" Sonta asked, moving closer,

hooking his long talon-like nail inside the chain holding the cross that hung from her neck, cutting it free.

Zorah didn't dare make a move. His crisis may have lessened with the capture of the human, but danger was still present. He shifted his eyes from side to side, trying to determine what Sonta would do next. The only light in the room came from the wide-open balcony doors, and that light diminished as the darkness of Sonta began to shadow the room. The demon glowered at Ellie as he fingered the delicate necklace.

"You will tell us everything, my dear," he said, his face so close to hers the stench was unbearable.

"You will not be able to refuse," he leered. "Who is here with you?

"You certainly are not brave enough to be here alone."

Ellie responded, *"The Lord is my shepherd, I shall not want, He maketh me to lie down. ..."* A mighty roar escaped the beast, swinging vertically with his massive claw-like finger he cut Ellie from the chest down. Her body sagged as she fell, having given the last ounce of devotion to her God.

Zorah said nothing, knowing Sonta's anger had bettered his opportunity. There would be tomorrow after all. Sonta would have to deal with Koal, who would undoubtedly have welcomed the human for his bed. Zorah would fight the angels of light again, only not in their world. He was one of the few in the Wondren who possessed the battle experience necessary for the next encounter, but there could be no more mistakes, no more daylight battles. No matter the orders.

58

————◆◆◆◆◆————

FROM JONES' VANTAGE POINT RIGHT BEHIND ELLIE, HE SAW HER TAKEN BY THE MONSTROUS WINGED CREATURE.

IT WAS OVER BEFORE IT BEGAN. HE NEVER SAW HER AGAIN. *Where there is smoke there's fire*, thought Jones as he retreated backward, ready for the worst. Surely the demonic master would assume more humans were present. He had to leave, even though every ounce of him wanted to charge.

"Don't do it," said Ephram, appearing from nowhere. "This is not the time. Evil has acted. What's done is done. Something good will come of this; trust in the Lord your God, for he knows all things."

To Jones, Ephram's request only intensified a problematic situation for a man who had lost his wife and now a friend. Ellie was gone forever.

He pulled back into the dense foliage just as Zorah descended into the surveillance spot with two other accomplices. The Fallen scanned the terrain, but there were no ready victims. As the trio lifted off, returning to the Wondren, Jones agonized. It was his fault. He had talked her into coming.

As Jones left, the Wondren came to life. Shouted orders and activity cranked up. It appeared the occupants were preparing for action. Alarms boomed over the sound of starting trucks.

Jones hurried toward the horses, careful not to make his position known. As he neared the creek bed and headed to Justin's, Ephram appeared standing on a large boulder.

"Don't worry; there will not be any demons on your trail. They aren't following because I created a diversion, making Zorah think the compound was coming under attack."

Ephram relayed the day's events to Arrow, who was saddened by Ellie's loss but understood more than most that the fight they were in was a battle of attrition.

"Tell your people, Jones, she did not die in vain," Ephram relayed from Arrow. "We will have our day of retribution for God's Warriors, which will now include Ellie.

"On that great and glorious day, she will be lifted up to be with the Father."

Jones nodded, realizing more than ever before that this was a fight to the death.

59

-◆◆◆◆-

THE SCOPE
OF THE EVENTS THAT
HAD TRANSPIRED
AROUND HIS HOUSE
LEFT CABLE AT
A LOSS FOR WORDS.

"AMAZING," HE SAID AS THE REALIZATION CAME OF what could have happened. The Angelic Warriors had moved across time, into this dimension, to rescue his family and friends. Without their intervention, Cable's life would be much different.

After determining that Abby and his wife were both functioning normally, the sheriff took his leave and headed for town. His responsibility as sheriff was taking on new meaning. Now it was much more than maintaining law and order. He was smack dab in the middle of a battle between Heaven and Hell, between Fallen Angels and God's Angelic Warriors. Perhaps this was his destiny all along.

Stopping by The Kitchen, as was his ritual, Cable parked, as usual, in the no-parking zone and stepped inside.

Cindy greeted him, "Are you here for your black with two sugars?"

"That would be great," he replied. "Everything okay?"

"Yeah. Most everyone came back and paid the bills they ran out on. Strange, though, nobody has been able to explain what happened. Not that it matters, I guess."

"Cindy, it does matter, and it's not good. You might want to close early today and send your help home."

"Surely you jest," she said, throwing up her hands in mock horror. "My regulars will be looking for supper; pies are in the oven. Servers need their tips."

"We don't know that what happened earlier won't happen again. Could be worse next time," Cable said with concern in his voice.

"Maybe you're right, Sheriff. After all that ruckus this afternoon, closing early sounds like a good idea. Getting my help out of here before dark sounds prudent."

"I'll call WINI and have them broadcast a public service announcement that you've closed, but that you'll be open in the morning. I'll tell them you're having some electrical problems," Cable said.

Just then, the whole town went dark. It was still daylight.

"Keep everyone in the building," Cable said, switching on his Magna light and running for the door, pulling out his phone.

"John, pick up, John," he yelled into his cell, desperately trying to reach the WINI station chief.

John came online. "What do you. . ."

"Get the word out to everyone who is listening, stay indoors, hunker down. We are having an emergency.

"Tell everyone to pray."

The next sound Cable heard was an enormous swooshing as the skies darkened, lights went off without assistance, and screams filled the air. Giant winged creatures descended. Careful to pick only believers, four were snatched up, taken into the air. The event was over as soon as it began. Gone just like that. What did we see was the question on many lips. Before anyone could process their thoughts, an enormous light filled the western sky and extended eastward toward and past the town. The sky was so bright, where it had just been dark, that those people of faith, those who believed, not knowing exactly how it would happen, raised their arms to Heaven, sure it was the Rapture.

Not so much, although it was emanating from that divine source.

Somewhere in the distance, cries and screams filled the air as Angelic Warriors, responding to the prayers of the faithful, descended with all the fury of God's chosen on the Fallen who were taking their prizes back to the Wondren for whatever torture and cruelty could be imagined. The demons were successful only in killing their prisoners, who may have already been dead from shock, before being engaged.

Zorah decapitated the body he was carrying and dropped the rest as a bolt of light blew the Corruptor next to him into ash, which filled the air. Getting off several powerful streams of darkness, Zorah disabled an angel, forcing him to retire, before seeing Sonta engage and bellow as Arrow presented himself and lit the powerful demon up with a tremendous bolt of energy. Sonta was stunned, but he had been wounded before, and it would take all Arrow had to end his life.

In an instant, as if by unseen command, the Fallen Angels left the dimension, dropping their corpses, and were gone.

The quad, which had followed the power of prayer, assembled around Arrow as if commanded by an unseen force.

"They are gone for now," said Arrow, "but we will see them again shortly.

"As more of their plans are unsuccessful, desperation will grow. Be ready, men, for anything."

Having seen some of the battle from a distance, Cable was in awe. In the darkness, he made his way back to the courthouse.

"I've seen that light flash before, Sheriff, like the time that Merritt shot at Abby and missed," Elbert said, his voice a question mark.

"This wasn't that kind of light, buddy," said Cable, watching everything around him return to normalcy as though nothing even happened. He felt no need to call his counterparts. Trouble was everywhere. The pieces were starting to fit. He had just witnessed more than a skirmish. Battlefield tactics were fully operational on the part of The Darkness, and he understood there could also be retaliation coming from God's Warriors.

His phone rang. He picked up. It was Jones.

"Sheriff, it's Jones. What just happened? Everything out here lit up."

"I'll tell you all about it," said the sheriff, and he did.

Cable knew the entire citizenry needed to be informed. An attack was imminent and it could no longer be a surprise. The demons had moved on. After an aerial assault, it was time for everyone to face up to the fact that evil now surrounded their town.

60

JUDITH WAS HANDLING THE MASSIVE
INFLUX OF CALLS FLOODING JONES'
OFFICE WHEN CABLE CALLED TO INFORM
HER THAT THE ATTACK WAS OVER.

AS SHE HUNG UP FROM TALKING TO CABLE,
she began to have difficulty breathing. Something was
choking her. Not knowing what to do, she began to pray.
"Father, I don't understand, and I don't need to know. Wherever
Sheriff Cable and Jones O'Brian are, cover them with your
presence. Establish a protective boundary about them, hold
them close. Send Angelic Warriors to protect this place and
establish a protective border around all those working here.
Let your peace be felt throughout our town. Drive away the
evil that is threatening our lives. Let your peace move in like a
flood! In the mighty name of your Son Jesus, I pray."

Immediately she sensed a cooling shift in the air. The
oppressive smothering dissipated. The chokehold let loose of her
throat. She had never felt like this. She glanced out the window
and saw what appeared to be a small glowing light on the ledge.

Judith could hardly wait to spread the word, and she would,
beating Cable and Jones to the punch. Soon, the whole town
was in on the demonic dirty mess. It was time to fight evil with
prayer; at least that seemed to work for just about everyone.

61

~~◆◆◆◆~~

CABLE WAS WONDERING TO HIMSELF HOW ALL THIS WOULD PLAY OUT WHEN HIS PHONE LIT UP. IT WAS JONES.

"WE NEED TO MEET NOW," JONES SAID. IT WAS impossible to miss the urgency in his voice.

"I'm on the way."

"Elbert, I'm leaving, so hold down the fort and call me for any reason. Use the radio for contact." Without waiting for a response, he left through the Sally Port, checked for unwanted observers, and made a beeline for the lake.

The two arrived simultaneously. Before Cable could relate the demonic assault on the town, Jones started talking. "Ellie is gone, Sheriff, snatched from this life by an ancient-looking demon the likes of which I could not have imagined. I don't want to think about what happened, but deep down, I know it was a terrible end to a beautiful life, a beautiful woman, a soldier for her Lord and Savior. She went out of this world saved. The beast could not take that from her. I'm sure he wanted to deny her that right, but she had earned it. First Kaz and now her. Our Lord must have a plan so far above my understanding that I am of no consequence. I'm sure to go soon. We are just pawns in this game. How can something like that be God's will? I will never understand."

Jones looked forlorn and lost. If his time came like that, he wanted to be that person. The world had enough Doubting Thomases.

There would be no peace for him until Ellie's taking was avenged and these creatures burned in the Hell of their own choosing.

Cable put his arms around Jones and held him like a brother. None of this was going to be easy. Faith was under attack, their faith, and Cable did not want to be found wanting. He did realize such a possibility existed. It was unsettling.

As they walked over to the closest picnic table, Jones felt overwhelming tiredness settle within his being. He had not been sleeping, at least not the solid eight on which his foundation rested. The deprivation was catching up.

As Jones started to sit down, he saw Arrow and an entire phalanx of Warriors encamped near the edge of the lake.

"Do you see what I see," he asked Cable.

"Good God," exclaimed Cable, "I guess I do. Are those angels?"

"It's a moment, isn't it?" said Jones.

"Takes your breath away," said Cable.

"They usually reside in a dimension not normally understood or seen by mortals," said Jones. "Now you see who is on our side."

As a car came down the road and drew closer to the picnic area, Jones felt a cool breeze around him signal Arrow's departure. He was always amazed at how fast they disappeared.

No one spoke then as they looked over the water. The time for words was past. It was time to fight. Jones felt he might not be able to kill that monstrous beast, but he sure was going to try. Before he could muster another thought, Ephram appeared in the back of his truck. The angel hopped out of the bed and moved into Cable's plane of vision. There are no words to explain such an intimidating presence, at least not on this Earth. Cable hesitated, which made perfect sense, being faced down by a nearly seven-foot-tall, muscle-bound angel.

"You better help me here, Jones," he said.

"His name is Ephram," Jones said, "and he's an Angelic Warrior, assigned to me a few days ago."

Ephram spoke, "Sir, you probably understand that all the unexplained phenomenon taking place around us are mere distractions. The demons who live in darkness are preparing to make a move in another dimension. As these activities build, they will manifest here before you. What happened at your property will soon occur all over your world. Our conflict is growing into a global battle. The United States is the testing ground. Resistance is the part you play.

"The war against Satan and his minions has been progressing since this nation was established. We are his enemies, and we despise him. He opposes the creation. For centuries, the battle between Heaven and Hell has raged on unabated. Now, the demonic poison is about to spill over into your world. The darkness has invaded this time and place. The enemy needs to establish a presence, a stronghold, to continue to lead people astray.

"Because of her prosperity, America has become complacent. She has been lulled into accepting ungodly principles, shedding innocent blood, ignoring the weak and the cries for help from the widows and the orphans.

"We now know the intent behind the activity of the evil forces at work here. They have a hierarchy, and two of their top commanders are directing this invasion. Their names are Sonta and Koal. Their troops are called Corruptors or Fallen, and if they are successful this time, they will add your part of this world to their list of subjects. It will become another base for spreading false information, lies, and deceit.

"You also need to know that your friend Ellie is now with the Father."

Cable stood in stunned silence.

Ellie was gone. The truth had surfaced. Cable took another deep breath, and in the silence of the late afternoon, he heard birds singing, God's creation stirring. In the distance, a rainbow appeared as a reminder that God was still on His throne and that His plan for this place, for this time, was established.

As Ephram returned to the truck, he looked over his shoulder and said, "You have a phrase here on Earth. I believe it says no one ever promised that life would be easy."

"Right," Jones replied, "and I want you to know that I will kill that pig beast or die trying. You have my word on it. To kill that thing, I will have to ask an angel of Arrow's strength to assist. It is your obedience to the call that gives me hope."

"Maybe we begged for this punishment," said Cable. "Our nation today isn't what our founding fathers intended. We have strayed from the path of righteousness. We have gone to that place where a want becomes a need. Something sinister has entered our world, and they have succeeded in making money and power the gods of man."

Both men sat quietly for a time, each trying to process the enormity of the conflict. Things might get worse before they get better, but they both wanted to believe the situation would improve. Jones, for his part, believed that with all his heart. With the power of prayer as their ally, he and his friends were going to fight the Corruptors and their Supreme Master. Mortal men and women were going to call the holy Warriors from their dimension by asking, one at a time, for their intervention. When that happened, the God of the ages would tilt the balance of power toward the believers. He would swing His mighty sword, and they would be saved.

Jones and Cable discussed their future, praying that they would have one. They were ready to jump into action and were listening for the signal.

Jones understood being obedient to the call and knew that he must move forward. Standing still was the same as going backward. No time for that now.

"Sheriff," said Jones, "stay glued to your office. Ephram will be around if you need him. Just ask. Gear up and load up, be ready to move when I call."

Cable nodded and fired up the cruiser. The situation had clarified. Giving Jones the lead was the right decision.

Jones watched the sheriff pull away. He was opening the door to his truck when his cell phone rang. It was Abby.

"Hey there," he said, "what's up?"

"I'm home, but I think someone or something followed me."

"Go to your window and tell me what you see," said Jones.

After what seemed an eternity, she came back on the line, "They are out there, those men, like at the office."

"I'll have Arrow put a halt to your stalkers," he assured her.

"Arrow?" Abby said, sounding a little confused.

"Our guardian angel," said Jones.

After a few moments, he asked, "Are things clearing up outside?"

"One of those little glowing lights just appeared in my front yard. Well now, there goes the uninvited, running for their rides."

"Arrow is like Ephram, Abby, only higher up," Jones said.

"Sorry you haven't met him yet but you will. Make no mistake about that.

"Pack a bag and get to my house. I'm at the lake and headed there now."

"I don't believe this," Abby stammered. "With everything going on, you're at the lake! I thought you went to Jonesboro."

"Don't say anything else, Abby. Our phones are tapped. Get moving." Jones disconnected.

Abby moved around her house, getting this and that, stuffing the most wanted into her travel bag before starting toward the door. Conscious of what might face her outside, she shoved the .38 snub nose into her waistband and exited the premises. She had no intention of taking a knife to whatever this kind of fight was going to be.

Leaving, she noticed the faint glow light on the corner of her property.

Keeping a sharp eye out for possible tails, she moved forward into the next chapter in her life, which was about to unfold.

"

62

HEADING BACK TOWARD TOWN,
HIS MIND FLOODED WITH CONCERNS,
JONES REALIZED IT WAS TIME TO HAVE
A SOUL MEETING WITH ABBY.

H E LOVED HER, AND THEY BOTH KNEW IT WAS TIME
to confess. There had to be a time and place for him to move on from Kaz. Abby deserved it, and so did he. Kaz would have wanted it to be this way. It was time to deal with that longing in his heart. His feelings for Abby had shifted from friendship into love. Kaz was always the only one, but she was gone and wasn't coming back, not in this lifetime. It was time for him to move forward with Abby.

As Jones rounded the corner leading to his street, Ephram somehow fit himself into the passenger seat. "The perimeter has been expanded around your house, Jones. Your location is known. Abby arrived safely." Gone.

Reaching his block, Jones saw Abby's car in the driveway. He parked on the street, got out, and surveyed the neighborhood. The glow that started on the corners of his house now extended to every corner on the block. Just out of range sat the ever-present van. Jones picked up his gear and went inside.

The smell of fresh coffee came through the opened door. As Jones walked toward the kitchen, his nerves began to jangle as the reality of his situation struck him. He was alone with a woman in his own house, and she was here at his request.

"Jones, come over and sit at the table. Do you want me to fix you something to eat?"

When Jones didn't respond immediately, Abby asked again, "Jones?"

"Sorry, Ab. Thanks for fixing the coffee. That's enough for now. Maybe food later, okay?"

As Jones moved toward his seat at the table, Abby reached for the coffeepot. Their shoulders brushed together. They turned to face each other.

No words were spoken. None were needed. The silence screamed in Jones' heart. Tired, exhausted would be a better description, but full of feelings for Abby, Jones realized this feeling was here to stay.

Abby knew her past friendship with Kaz must be set aside, not forgotten, if she expected to move forward with Jones. She was here now in Jones' house, and he was standing in front of her. Telling herself it was time for action, she put her arms around his neck and looked up into his eyes. Jones wrapped his arms around her body. It was a moment that had been a long time coming. A new, deep, and bonding relationship had begun, for real, for the two of them. Time passed faster than angels fly as they stood beside the stove, holding each other. Neither of them was willing to let go.

Jones knew what to do, but he was immobilized, frozen in place. He had to do something; there had to be some resolution, some conclusion. *I haven't had a warm body like this so close in years*, he thought.

Maybe just a light kiss would be a starting point. Yes, that seems appropriate. Not so much for Abby, who took matters into her own hands, delivering a smoldering, fierce kiss right on the money. Jones did not disengage but squeezed her so tightly she gasped and got kissed back.

After a long moment, they both surfaced for oxygen.

"Sit," Abby said weakly, wondering if her legs were functioning.

"I'll pour your coffee, Jones."

Jones sat and attempted to do as told when he heard Abby gasp.

Warrior Angels had suddenly invaded the backyard, resting all around. No space was left unoccupied.

"Let's go outside, Ab. I want you to meet the team. These are part of the 'more for us' Elisha mentioned in the Bible."

As the couple walked down the back steps leading to the yard, Abby saw Arrow for the first time. She had never seen a more impressive countenance. Staring at this Warrior with scars on his face and arms, a weary look on his face, she knew without knowing that for an angel who fought beasts, Arrow radiated peace.

By his side were a half dozen angels, standing vigilantly near their commander, watching his every move. It was evident the chain of command flowed through him as, one by one, others approached, received permission with a nod, or a whisper in the ear, before leaving. They were working, always working. Even when resting the angels coupled activity with peace.

"Jones," Abby asked, "are these the Warriors from the battle at the sheriff's?"

"The same," answered Jones.

At that moment, Arrow said, "Answer your phone. Justin is calling you."

Without waiting for a ring, Jones activated his cell.

"Justin, what's up?"

"A man just walked through the woods onto the farm. He says he saw you close up on your visit to the Wondren earlier today. He needs to talk to you. Here he is."

"Jones, this is Ed Zalinsky. Noon tomorrow is D-Day. Get the word out. Tell my family I am okay."

Jones recalled Ed being in the small group of men by a warehouse when he and Ellie were at the Wondren.

"I don't know how you pulled this off, Ed, but I got it," Jones said.

Ed Zalinsky shook his head, not fully understanding how he had escaped. There was something special about being in a safe-haven.

Ed had been held inside the Wondren complex, just another pawn that had fallen for the demonic lies that formed the basis of the offer for his gun store. What he had gotten instead of an outrageous amount of cash was forced incarceration. After seeing Jones earlier, he'd drawn guard duty at the Wondren's entrance.

While on duty, something had snapped awake in Ed's heart. In a defining moment, he shed the darkness and came alive, recognizing where he was and what was transpiring around him.

He walked straight out of the shack and somehow, someone led him to a trail that took him to Justin's property.

"Hide him on your property, Justin," said Jones. "He will be protected there. Get Ellie's prayer group to your property, and whatever you do, keep them there. Let them know that the power of their prayers could easily be the margin between victory and defeat." Jones hung up. The proverbial was about to happen.

63

"I DON'T LIKE IT," SAID JONES, "BUT WE NEED TO KEEP A LID ON THE HIGHLIGHT REEL."

"PEOPLE AREN'T FOOLISH, ALTHOUGH THERE IS AN argument for that. Part of our obligation must be, for better or for worse, to inform everyone within reach of television or radio of the attack on humankind by these otherworldly demons. Some will panic, some will pray, some will just flat dig in. Our community knows, thanks to Judith, now the county and beyond have to know. The demons are here for everyone, whether we like it or not."

"I can see why you were so evasive," Abby said, realizing the seriousness of the situation.

"Yeah, when I was in the war," said Jones, "I saw up close and personal how people react when they are beyond fright. Can you imagine the response here in southern Illinois when your local TV anchorman lets you in on this dirty little secret? I want to keep people in the loop, but the results of transparency are not always favorable, no matter the clamor for inclusion. People are going to need more bath tissue, but the public has to know they are the prize, the end game of Satan's grand plan. I hate to think Ellie is gone, but we knew we were looking down the throat of evil."

"I can only imagine what happened to her," said Abby, "but all signs point to a terrible ending."

"There is that," said Jones. "But one outlier is the fact that she had no real information to give them because I hadn't said much to her about the war that was raging. I told her it was dangerous, but that wasn't enough. I had no business letting her go get slaughtered."

"She'd have gone anyway, Jones," said Abby. "Don't put it on yourself. She was one of the Lord's Warriors and had a faith for the ages."

"Yeah, okay," said Jones, sounding unconvinced.

"I am going to start getting this information out there. Call the radio station and get them on the line. I'll talk to them. Do the same with TV. I'll call Ed's wife and tell her to drag in the prayer group. She and the family have been living on the edge for too long not hearing from him. Their emotions need some relief."

Abby nodded her head. These intruders, The Darkness, were killers, plain and simple. They didn't care who or when. Knowing the power of prayer could stop them in their tracks, not to mention summoning the Angelic Warriors, gave Abby reason to hope. She understood why Jones had been so conflicted, even if she didn't like the message that sent. Her life had changed now, perhaps forever. She was going to hang with Jones, no matter what.

64

---◆◆◆◆---

JONES EXAMINED THE ASSEMBLY OF WARRIORS IN HIS BACKYARD AND RECOGNIZED SOME FAMILIAR FACES.

SEEING THEM ALL CROWDED TOGETHER WAS A ONCE in a lifetime moment. Why was his faith so shaken when this gathering of celestial beings indicated God's intent. It was a difficult question to answer and confirmed to Jones that he would never understand the mind of God. That was okay now.

Arrow spoke, "Don't forget, I'm here to assist you, Jones. I await your orders."

That kind of statement took a bit of processing, but Jones remembered the overriding rule: you have to ask. His mortal family was knee-deep in angels assigned by Michael, the most fierce of the Warrior Angels who sat at the right hand of God, to keep them alive and assist in the battle between Heaven and Hell.

"I never assume you aren't always one step ahead of me, Arrow," Jones said. "So, you may be aware that Ed Zalinsky, the gun store owner, who somehow escaped the Corrupters, has informed us the launch date for their offensive is tomorrow at noon."

"Yes," said Arrow. "We heard."

"Tomorrow at noon, then," said Jones, "we bring the battle to them, to a conclusion perhaps. The darkness controlling men's minds must be destroyed. In my time, the word of our Lord must triumph."

Arrow smiled, having received an assignment that fulfilled him beyond explanation. His cup runneth over.

Knowing the call would come soon, the angels left as silently as they came, crossing over to wait and rest. Jones watched his backyard clear in an instant but knew help was close. Moving between dimensions was the stuff of folklore; only what was happening here and now was not fiction.

Sensing Jones wanted to be alone, Abby went back to the kitchen.

"Tomorrow at noon." Jones' order had put a plan in motion. Now that plan needed clarification. Noon tomorrow would be a fight, unlike any earthly battle before. It would be an escalation in a conflict that has been growing more intense over time. Spiritual beings are closing ranks with The Darkness. Both sides would bring their best, with death the only retreat.

Jones bowed his head and took a deep breath. Quiet. Not a sound. He heard his heart beating. Somehow he needed to reach beyond himself—beyond his new feelings for Abby, his loss of Ellie, Ed and Justin's safety, past everything crashing in.

"Lord, you know my heart," Jones said. "I am trying to believe."

Prayer time was over.

Jones dialed the sheriff's private number and gave him a short rundown of current and future events.

"See you in five at your place," he said.

Jones walked around the house to get his truck on the street. As he passed by Abby's squad car, he saw the shotgun in the back seat and chuckled. Comfort comes in different packages. A 12 gauge is very distinctive packaging.

65

ZORAH'S AGONY WAS ALL-CONSUMING.
HE HAD ELIMINATED THREATS FOR EONS,
BUT THIS JONES MORTAL WAS PROVING
TROUBLESOME TO HIS LIVELIHOOD
AND CAREER.

AS HE STARED OUT THE WINDOW TRYING TO MAINTAIN his equilibrium, Zorah raged, reliving his cowardice that cost them hundreds of men and two seasoned commanders. He continually asked for updates on the preparations taking place and expressed his dissatisfaction at the incomplete reports. He needed information, and it was in short supply. Tomorrow, unless events altered, would bring D-Day. He fretted, knowing their planning was incomplete, which brought failure into play. That would fall on him, and he might well pay the ultimate price.

Zorah's thoughts were interrupted as Heqt, the new field commander, burst through the door without knocking.

"You need to know, Master. Someone walked away from the guard shack at the entry gate a short time ago. What should we do?"

Zorah's shout caused Heqt to cringe. "Nothing. We will silence the deserter tomorrow, with all the others. Organize your men; the battle is nearly on us. I have much to do."

66

JONES' ARRIVAL AT THE SHERIFF'S
OFFICE COINCIDED WITH THAT OF FOUR
CORRUPTORS WHO MADE AN ATTEMPT TO
INTERVENE IN THE PARKING LOT BUT WERE
TURNED AWAY BY THE INVISIBLE HAND OF
GOD, IN MOTION ALL AROUND THEM.

AFTER SEVERAL ATTEMPTS, THE DARK RED-EYED MEN gave up. Glaring at Jones, they turned back, arguing among themselves.

Jones just smiled and went into the courthouse.

Elbert was looking out the window as he entered the office. "Jones, I just saw what happened in the parking lot."

"It looked like those heavies had their plans changed, Elbert," Jones replied.

Elbert shrugged his shoulders. It was bound to happen, and it just did. He'd seen this play before. Jones walked into Cable's office and caught him up on the gun shop owner's escape and pronouncement of impending war.

With a pensive look on his face, Cable straightened himself in his chair. "Please tell me you've got a plan, Jones. Do I need to alert the National Guard?"

"No, they can't help us here. Tomorrow at 6 a.m., I want you to block all the roads leading south out of the county," Jones said adamantly. "The radio stations and TV networks are telling everyone tuned in to stay home and out of the way. Most will do that. We don't want anyone leaving or being forced to leave. The Wondren doesn't need more soldiers or more opportunity. They certainly don't need to be resupplied.

"Be sure your deputies are heavily armed, for all the good that will do. There will be resistance to the roadblocks. Possibly some of the transports will try to run through the blockade."

Jones took a breath and continued, "I'll be using Highway 127 to get to Justin's stable. Be sure whoever is assigned to that route knows we're coming because I'm not slowing down."

As Jones left, Cable began to unroll his county maps. Fortunately, only three roads led south. Besides Highway 127, there was US 51 and Route 3. Each had points that could be easily blocked and defended. Calling his deputies Cable said, "Every one of you, whether on or off duty, must be standing tall tomorrow at 4:30 a.m."

"What's going on, Sheriff?" was the first question on everyone's mind.

It was time to lay out the hard facts. Soldiers develop a premonition that can be a powerful tool in predicting incoming. No one needs to die for a lie.

"Men, we are in the presence of God's Angelic Warriors."

It was a moment of disbelief for some, but that was a fleeting emotion as Cable laid out the whole scenario, as he knew it to be. Even the most diehard among the deputies considered the possibilities and came around.

"The holy fighters are camped on our doorstep, and if they weren't, our chances of defeating this enemy would be nonexistent.

"It's going to be a long day, men," said Cable. For some, it could be their last day on Earth.

67

———◆◆◆◆◆———

IT HADN'T TAKEN LONG FOR THE GOOD NEWS TO SPREAD ABOUT ED'S SAFETY AND HIS UNEXPECTED RETURN.

AS HE APPROACHED ED'S HOUSE, JONES FOUND IT impossible to miss the mass of cars and trucks filling both sides of the street. All the lights were on, and the pizza man was walking out the door. It was a party.

As he pulled into the driveway, Elaine, Ed's wife, skipped down the porch steps and ran toward Jones. She hugged him fiercely and said, "Let's go in," pulling him by the hand toward the open door.

As Jones entered the house, he saw several familiar faces, including the men and women from Kaz's prayer group.

"Ed's coming home is truly an answer to our prayers," said Judith. "We've been pleading in the name of Jesus for his return."

Elaine had noticed a few weeks ago that Ed's focus was shifting. He had met with a group of these new businessmen, and before so much as discussing it with her, he had sold the store. Ed then proceeded to tell Elaine that he was taking a trip to the offices of the new owners and would be out of town for a while. In their lives together, Ed had never exhibited this kind of behavior. He was a thinker, a planner, a tortoise when it came to business dealings. All of a sudden, he went into hurry-up mode. Elaine was confused. Ed always told her everything until now.

"After Ed was gone two weeks we started praying," said Elaine. "We had no idea what was going on. We just knew it was not good.

"Turns out we were taking authority over the powers of darkness, who had Ed. It's so exciting to know he'll be home tomorrow."

Jones marveled at the mere thought of her words. That was a wow!

He could only imagine the return of the prodigal son and what that must have been like.

The crowd calmed when they saw Jones enter the living room. They had known Jones and Kaz for what seemed like an eternity. They all had been so supportive during her long illness. But today was different. Now, the power of prayer was needed to shield the participants. The Angelic Warriors, Jones, the Mountain Men, Lozen, the deputies, the people, would be lifted to the Lord. Every last person was important.

The battle for humankind was close at hand, and the group knew their prayers brought results. Ed coming back was proof enough. They had seen the Lord God Almighty at work, and this was not their first kneeling. Nor would it be the last.

Jones spoke then, "For several weeks now, I'm sure many of you have seen the darkness creeping into our town. The demons are here. The Fallen Angels control them, and their power is enormous. The forces of Satan are intent on turning our community and places like it all over our country into a haven for the demonic hordes.

"I'm sure you all know about the strange fires. Those

incidents were designed to distract all of us from the enemy's real plan, which was much more sinister. An enemy stronghold has been established south of here deep in the Shawnee National Forest. The darkness has drawn Ed and other members of our community into their camp.

"Tomorrow at noon a battle will take place. There will be no prisoners. Heaven and Hell will meet head-on, and there will be a loser. Lives are at stake. Our community and way of life are in danger. Destinies are at risk. Prayer for protection of our fighters is sorely needed.

"I believe in my heart that only one side can win this battle. I believe one side is more committed to the outcome than the other. I believe righteousness will prevail. It's the eternal promise to us, paid for by the blood of Jesus. There are many innocent people, some friends of ours, who have fallen under the demons' spell, trapped by the darkness, following after promises that will not be kept. They must be rescued."

Jones stopped then. Arms rose in unison, and the prayer chain lifted off.

After hugs all around, Jones headed for home. He was one tired puppy.

Anyone in their right mind would be terrified at the thought of staring down the wrath of a Fallen Angel. Only the Angelic Warriors could kill them. Humans were just along for the ride. Demons were another matter. Turned beings from other more human civilizations, including his own, did not possess the powers of the Fallen. Demons could be stopped, and Jones intended to participate. There were lives at stake, and defeat at the hands of The Darkness would put humankind in unacceptable jeopardy. All around, Jones could see the lights of the Warrior angels. Protection was close at hand.

As Jones walked toward his back door, Ephram materialized

and took a seat on the picnic table. No words were needed. Jones climbed the steps to the porch, opened the door, and went straight to bed.

68

SOMETHING NUDGED JONES, WHO
TRIED TO IGNORE THE GENTLE PUSHING.
FORCING HIS LEFT EYE OPEN, HE TAPPED
HIS ALARM CLOCK, WHICH HE FAILED TO
SET THE NIGHT BEFORE.

IT WAS 4 A.M.

Not feeling tired but not sure why, Jones looked in the mirror, only to see a dirty man looking back. There was also a smell present that only a thorough washing would cure.

Rushing around the house after his five-minute shower and shave, Jones realized the challenges that he would face on this day would be the biggest of his brief but unspectacular life.

Entering his study, he opened his Bible to 2 Corinthians 4:8:

"We are hard pressed on every side, but not crushed; perplexed, but not in despair, persecuted, but not abandoned, struck down, but not destroyed. We always carry around in our body the death of Jesus"—he went on reading, growing stronger with every word—*"therefore we do not lose heart."* Thus spoke Paul, not only to the Corinthians, but to all Christians forever after.

Getting himself together, Jones fired up his filthy dirty truck and soon found himself at The Kitchen. Pulling into the back lot, he saw several pairs of red eyes in the area, keeping their distance. He laughed to himself, understanding their learning curve. There would be no more messing with the glow lights. *Even a blind dog finds a bone occasionally*, Jones thought.

The restaurant was not yet officially open when Jones arrived, but the door was unlocked, so in he went. A couple of the regulars were already having coffee, and Cindy was in the back making biscuits. Jones took a seat and soon called out his order for two helpings of biscuits and gravy, bacon and eggs.

"You can't eat all that," Cindy yelled back.

"Abby's coming," said Jones.

That prophecy was fulfilled in short order as Abby, getting the same wake-up assistance as Jones, got it together in record time and scrambled to make their rendezvous happen. After yesterday's encounter in his kitchen, breakfast this morning had potential. She recalled how it felt when their shoulders touched, when they held each other. She was all in for more of that in her future. Today, however, was serious business with no time for distraction.

Cindy was bringing the food when Abby stepped through the door.

Jones stood up and kissed her before she could say a word. Not even a hello. *Guess that was a statement*, she thought. It did not go unnoticed.

"When we finish eating, we need to head for Jonesboro. When was the last time you were over there? Do you remember the stable at the edge of town?"

"Yeah," she said, "I remember."

She washed down the food in her mouth and said, "It's been a while since I've been over in that direction."

"Good. We're going to a stable there owned by Justin Bryant; he's one of us. Ed Zalinski is there with him. You're in the fight now, Ab, so be prepared for anything."

People came and went as they ate; most greeted them with a wave or hello. Relationships in the community weren't broken as much as the demons would have liked. Jones spent a few moments talking with each person while keeping an eye on the time, which was passing quickly.

Abby and Jones finished their meal, each deep within their minds, left money on the table, and departed through the rear entrance.

As Jones opened her car door, she felt his hand on her shoulder. She turned to look at him as he gently caressed her cheek.

"Take care today, Ab. Follow me close, but regardless of what happens, keep moving." They shared a tender kiss and moved into action.

Abby tailed Jones down Highway 127, a hilly and curvy two-lane road that eliminated high-speed driving. Eventually, the road would wind its way to Justin's stable. Three miles in, a long line of cars had traffic completely stopped. Without slowing down, Jones put his pursuit light on top of the truck and crossed over onto the shoulder of the oncoming lane. Abby followed him over, blue lights flashing.

As Jones closed on the roadblock, streams of angry people, apparently not having heard or bought into the recent announcements, had exited their vehicles. They were talking loudly and gesturing in the direction of the roadblock. It was the public in full regalia.

Deputies blocking the shoulder pulled over so Jones and Abby could pass, repositioning immediately. The two soldiers for God rolled forward toward the darkness.

69

---◆◆◆◆◆---

OUTSIDE THE READY ROOM, CABLE COULD HEAR SOME OF THE DEPUTIES DISCUSSING THE RECENT TV AND RADIO ANNOUNCEMENTS ABOUT THE NEW ARRIVALS.

"THIS IS GOING TO BE BAD," SAID A RECENTLY HIRED deputy, fresh from the poppy fields of Afghanistan.

"Yeah, this isn't exactly your daddy's rodeo," said another.

Cable decided he had heard enough and entered the room. There had been early mornings, but 4:30 a.m. was breaking new ground.

"Without a doubt," he said, "what you are about to experience has no precedent in our department's history. Today may be a one-off, it may not. In our little part of the world, there is a fierce battle underway. We are a part of that war you've heard about between Heaven and Hell." The statement was jaw-dropping and reflected upon the faces of those present.

"We have reliable intel that pinpoints noon as the launch for hostile activity. Be prepared to engage."

Cable then filled in the blanks, including the glow lights and Angelic Warriors, which wasn't a surprise.

"Jones needs help, and we are going to do our part," he said. Throughout the room, deputies signaled agreement. They respected Jones enough to join a fight that could not be assessed. Cable picked up a dry-erase marker and outlined each person's duties. Soon the whiteboard was covered with diagrams.

Each deputy received a written assignment sheet and filed out to the parking lot. Their main task was to maintain the roadblocks, and if asked, say the reason was a national emergency, no more no less. Their hope was most motorists not driving tanker trucks would turn around and go home. The tanker drivers were the enemy and would be treated as such.

70

-◆◆◆◆-

AT THE WONDREN, ZORAH WAS OVERWHELMED WITH GETTING SUPPLIES, MEN, AND TRUCKS POSITIONED FOR THE MOVE AT NOON.

HE ASKED HEQT FOR THE ARRIVAL LOG, ALARMED AT the lack of incoming tankers.

"I thought more help was on the way," he said, realizing at that moment what his assistants had understood for some time.

Almost as if on cue, Sonta called from his room and asked, "Have the special envoys from Chicago arrived?" Sounding more short-tempered than usual, he continued, "They should've been here some time ago."

Zorah had no answer. "I haven't seen them, but that doesn't mean they aren't here. I will find them, Master."

He called the main entry gate. After the fourth ring with no answer, his impatience got the best of him. Finally, someone answered. "Are you asleep out there?" he yelled into the phone.

"We're at our assigned posts. Don't you remember we had a walk-away yesterday? It was his job to be in the shack and answer the phone. No one was assigned to replace him, Sir."

Zorah recalled someone had gone missing. It had been a small nuisance buried in the avalanche of work piled up around him. He hadn't given it much thought. Rather than answering, he asked, "Have the envoys from up north passed through your gate?"

"No."

The one-word answer set Zorah on edge. It was nearly eight a.m.; noon was close at hand. The darkness needed those trucks. He needed them. Their passengers would be used to divert the Angelic Warriors' attention from the incoming Fallen Angels who had not arrived either. Zorah knew Sonta had to impress the King of Darkness with a victory. Other alternatives were undesirable.

Zorah rechecked the log. Something was dreadfully wrong. There had been no arrivals since 7 a.m. Whatever planning was in place had been interrupted. All visible proof pointed in a direction that unequivocally affirmed a disaster that awaited the confused and unplanned. Even if everything was in place, which it wasn't, no one ever wanted to fight in the daylight, especially with angelic angels. The demons had tried that strategy, and no one returned, except him, and he wasn't there. Sonta's anger had no explanation. This battle must be called off. Fearing for his very existence, Zorah penned a message conveying his feelings and summoned a messenger who delivered it to Sonta's quarters. At that point, he began looking for a place to hide.

71

-◆◆◆◆-

SONTA EXPLODED WITH VITRIOL
WHEN HE READ ZORAH'S MESSAGE.

THE UNLUCKY MESSENGER HAD THE PRIVILEGE OF watching a demonic changing, as Sonta, enraged, became his true self. That persona, frightful even to other demons, was hideous to behold. Blood, slime, and ooze dripping from every pore of his large frame, a reptilian skin-like substance overlaying fabric containing the structure, was more than equal to the most ferocious predator.

With a simple flick of his wrist, the budding demon flew backward through the open door at such velocity that every bone in his back, neck, and head shattered on impacting the hallway's stone wall.

Sonta called the front gate and received the same report that Zorah had forwarded. There was no excuse for inattention. Zorah was in charge of executing the plan. Deserters were his responsibility. Envoys report to him, and yet, if this report was accurate, they needed to delay this battle and fight another day. The timing was flawed, and fighting in the daylight had proven to be a bad idea. He did not have a good reason to repeat poor judgment. Sonta hated the Angelic Warriors beyond boundaries, but this battle had to be postponed. Zorah was right in his analysis and probably scared to death. Unaware of the roadblocks stopping the supply trucks, Sonta assumed the delay was all Koal's doing. Slowing down the vehicles and Fallen Angels would make Sonta look vulnerable. Everyone knew another defeat would ruin his chances of ever ascending to the high council. Worse still was the thought that Koal had lost confidence in his blueprint for global dominance.

Unable to find Zorah, Sonta checked every detail for the day. The schedule was holding and appeared to be on track, except for the Fallen Angels that had not materialized. The trucks carrying recruits were one thing. Though new to the cause, even though their demonization was not complete, their bodies filled out the ranks. There was never too much fodder. The full complement of Fallen Angels was another matter entirely. Only Koal could order them to fight, and Sonta could only admire the feint. There would be no ripple in the adjacent dimension to signal their arrival. The Angelic quads would be accounted for, no doubt in his mind. Arrow was surely close by the Wondren. Without hesitation, Sonta sent a courier to Koal explaining how poorly things were working out and suggesting they live to fight another day.

72

LOOKING OUT OVER LAKE MICHIGAN
FROM HIS PENTHOUSE HEADQUARTERS,
KOAL MUSED OVER THE REPORT WHEN
IT WAS BREATHLESSLY DELIVERED.

BEING OVERLORD OF THIS PART OF THE NATION CALLED
America, he continuously fielded updates from every
operation. Chicago was the largest city under his command,
which made it a logical operations center. There were myriad
highways and shipping lanes to facilitate his bidding.The
activities under Sonta's supervision were part of the grand
scheme blessed by Satan, or Lucifer, or one of many other
names for the Prince of Darkness, the King of the Fallen.
Sonta's blueprint had total approval, which was always subject
to change. The quarry was afoot today in southern Illinois.
Koal's lips separated in a cruel grin, or grimace. The end game
was close at hand and should result in a complete takeover of
all aspects of this rural society.

Koal was, if nothing else, a realist. Sonta had visited some time
back and offered reassuring promises for his grand plan. Koal had
his doubts then, but gave his blessing to the program, knowing full
well the terms for failure were his to execute. That might happen.

Koal had seen many peaks and valleys in Sonta's centuries-
long career. While successful in recruiting and turning humans,

his work on the battlefield against angelic hosts was marginal.

Deception was a powerful tool in the implementation of darkness. Koal maintained a full complement of spies who worked on all command projects run by subordinates. He had one carefully placed inside the Wondren, an exceptional demon whose last two reports had left no doubt in Koal's mind that his most extreme adversary was close at hand. Not only was he alarmed at Sonta's lack of attention, but he had also seen that pattern before. There was little doubt that Arrow had joined the fight. Nevertheless, the theory demanded certification.

Gozan, Koal's assistant, reminded him, "It is time, Master. If we are to observe the battle downstate, we need to be on our way."

Koal snarled, causing high anxiety among the other demons in the room.

Turning to look back over Lake Michigan, he said quietly, "We are going nowhere. No! No one goes! There was never going to be a battle. Arrow is there."

245 | Oblivion's Reach

73

JONES DROVE LIKE A MAN ON A MISSION, KEEPING CLOSE TABS ON HIS SHADOW FOLLOWING CLOSE BEHIND.

SOON ENOUGH, JUSTIN'S STABLE CAME INTO VIEW. The barn announced its message to all who passed by. Written in large, bold letters was the scripture:

The god who rules this world
has blinded the minds of unbelievers.
They cannot see the light, which is
the good news about our glorious Christ,
who shows what God is like.
2 CORINTHIANS 4:4

The truth of the scripture grabbed Jones deep inside. Ed had told Justin the darkness felt like a cloud settling on his mind. It was a useful tool used by the enemy.

Jones slowed down when he saw the glowing lights. Ephram was busy. He motioned Abby to follow and pulled off the highway into the stable area.

Reaching for his phone, he called Elaine Zalinsky, Ed's wife. Recognizing Jones' caller ID flash before her, she answered.

"I know you have a group there, Elaine," Jones said. "Have them pray into this verse: 2 Corinthians 4:4. Call as many others as you can. We need prayer warriors praying that what the enemy has done will be reversed by God. If Ed was freed from the influence of the enemy by your prayers, others could be, too."

Not waiting for a response, Jones hung up.

Elaine took a deep breath and relayed the instructions. The air virtually filled with ascending prayer. 2 Corinthians 4:4 was airborne.

There was no end to the request. The power of prayer, coming from true believers, had launched. One after another, the group interceded on behalf of the people whose lives had been captured by the evil residing in the Wondren.

74

-◆◆◆◆-

STANDING AT GROUND ZERO, SONTA SENSED A SUDDEN EXPLOSIVE SHIFT IN THE ATMOSPHERE.

THE INEXORABLE TRANSMISSIONS OF THE BELIEVERS, permeating the fabric of darkness, penetrated his consciousness. Anxiety crashed in on him as he remembered past unfavorable outcomes. The possibilities of the pending battle would unsettle the finest of Fallen Angels of which he considered himself one.

There was only one action that could save him. Before he could contact Master Koal, he was commanded to Chicago. "Transport and cross over," were Koal's instruction, and so he did, changing form and launching from the Wondren into the parallel dimension. There was no mistaking the fact that this could be his last flight.

Koal was waiting when Sonta materialized in his office penthouse. He looked dapper in his human flesh, smoking an Arturo Fuente 8-5-8 Maduro and appearing happier than Sonta could ever remember.

"Did you have a smooth ride?" he asked chuckling, if such a noise was possible.

"Yes, Master," Sonta replied, taken off guard by the unfamiliar demeanor of his superior.

"Relax then," said Koal, "you look stressed, to say the least.

"Everything is fine, Sonta. I brought you here to tell you that there will be no battle, but we are going to pretend anyway. The information we want is coming from the Angelic Warriors. They don't know we had no intention of fighting again in any semblance of daylight. I didn't tell you the whole operation was a sleight of hand because it served no purpose until completely necessary. As you probably know, and we have now confirmed, Arrow is here among us, as is his commander Ephram, with a full quad."

Sonta took the breezy monologue with a grain of salt. Koal didn't trust him. That was obvious. It was forward-thinking, though, to take a peek at the enemy unobserved.

"Carry on with your planning, only shift gears and, as quietly as possible, execute entry points for our angels at your place called the Little Grand Canyon. It will serve our purposes and encourage the enemy to cross over at the exact spot we will be waiting. Start the battle with demons and recruits. Engage the enemy until Arrow commits and shows himself and his force. Ephram's quad will already be wiping out the recruits and demons when The Fallen return the favor."

Hoping to capture the moment, Sonta said, "There might be an opportunity for us that is somewhat adjacent to our mark. Several so-called Mountain Men live around the Canyon. There is also a woman. I am advised she is prescient, so we should take her out before the battle. She might be able to reveal our entry points to Arrow or Ephram, or both."

"Make it so," said Koal. "Having her alive at the moment of entry could be disastrous."

"Yes, Master," said Sonta.

"Return now," said Koal, "as quickly as you came before your absence is noticed. Have a small skirmish and withdraw. We will know then."

75

SONTA TRANSPORTED
BACK TO THE WONDREN.
IN REAL TIME, HIS TRIP
HAD TAKEN LESS THAN
FIFTEEN MINUTES.

AS HE LOOKED OUT THE WINDOW OF HIS OFFICE, his changing finished and Earth body restored, Sonta could not miss the disarray among the recruits. The original battle plan would have been a disaster, he reasoned, one that had a predetermined outcome. The path now in front of them promised rich rewards. The time had come to execute. All must appear normal.

Zorah had naturally sought to protect himself from what he saw as a failed strategy, which it was. Sonta would have to be hard on the man but leave room for appeasement and reconciliation. Zorah was a valuable cog on the wheel. As a lesser Fallen Angel, his was not an enviable task. Zorah lived to serve and knew, without a doubt, he was dispensable. The first daytime raid was on Sonta, who fell victim to his anger. He should have known better. This second battle was a ruse, planned by Koal and forced onto Sonta, who handed off to Zorah, who had no idea it was never going to happen.

Sonta called the front gate.

"Have our visitors from up north arrived yet?" he snarled.

"No, Master Sonta, we haven't seen a truck in several hours."

"Why haven't I been made aware of this?" he asked.

"I apologize, Master. We were instructed to call Zorah."

"I should have known about the lack of coverage, the run-away," he said.

"The man just disappeared. We couldn't find him and have no idea where he went."

Sonta knew. Prayer was loosening their grip on the partially turned.

"Was a search made?" he asked,

"No, no search. We reported the incident to Zorah but never received a response."

Sonta slammed the receiver down, crushing the phone on impact. What a show.

76

❖❖❖❖

JONES AND ABBY PULLED INTO THE PARKING LOT AT THE STABLE.

ABBY TURNED HER CAR AROUND AND FACED THE road. She kept her engine running as Ed Zalinski came out of the house.

Jones intercepted him and put his hands on the man's shoulders.

"Ed, we planned to get you home to your family, but that is not going to happen. It's too risky now. Neither you nor Abby are ready for what I saw happen to Ellie. The demons are all around us, and none of them are sleeping. Stay right here in the safe zone."

Ed signaled his acceptance of this clear and present danger. Better alive than dead.

Abby turned off her engine. "What's my role, Jones?" she asked.

"Staying alive, working inside this perimeter, doing anything and everything you can to stop these monsters," said Jones.

Their eyes met. They felt their hearts touch and said no more.

Justin saddled the horses, and the two men rode off toward the darkness.

"We're praying for you," Ed shouted after Jones as the pair grew smaller in the distance.

"How many people do you think are praying back home at your house?" asked Abby.

"Hard to say," said Ed. "Everyone Elaine and her prayer warriors can locate, twenty-five or thirty at the house, all the churches in town, and more I don't know."

"Jones told me he called Elaine and told her to have everyone pray into the scripture on Ed's barn. That was the message that lifted you out of the Wondren," said Abby.

No sooner had Abby voiced those words than Jones, nearly a mile down the trail, felt a fresh breeze blow across his face. He turned to see Arrow and his company of warriors arrive on the other side of a small grassy knoll that fronted their path.

Justin gasped. "I've seen a Warrior Angel before, but never this many at one time."

"We've just neutralized the demon warriors at the roadblocks, Jones. The whole situation, though, has become puzzling. Not a single Fallen Angel has been spotted on the ground. A highly unlikely event if I do say so," reported Arrow.

"What does that mean?" asked Jones.

"It means we have a change in tactics. The Wondren has been alerted to my presence, which takes some doing. Sonta's commander, Koal, and Satan's Minions are standing ready. These are extremely capable battle-tested Fallen Angels who, like us, live in another dimension but can cross at will. Ephram and his quad can handle what we see before us at this time, but our time is upon us."

"What can we do?" asked Jones. "We are asking for God's help, your help, in this battle. Can we lose? Is that possible?"

"Evil cannot defeat good as long as good endures," said Arrow.

"We also have a trump card sitting at the right hand of God. I have been in battle once before with Michael because he was needed. You might tell your prayer group to alert Michael and his Dread Warriors to come if we have a major crossing of Fallen Angels. Now be about your business," said Arrow. "There is much for us to do.

"Regardless, we won't be far," he said, and just like that, they all disappeared.

Suddenly it was hushed.

"Wow," said Justin, "what was that?"

The two sat in silence to pause and think about Arrow's words. If he was thinking about Michael, Hell had opened its gates and spilled out pure venom. There had to be a reason for the escalation. The only reasonable possibility Jones could conceive was the biblical event known as The Rapture. Maybe the Fallen, whose future was ordained by God to be condemned to the fiery pit on that day, had decided to try a preemptive strike, worldwide. Kill the believers, and there would be no ascending souls. That had to be it. The Book of Revelation spoke of the end of days. Avoiding their demise would save Satan and his loyal Fallen one thousand years of misery. It was an avoidance worth great sacrifice.

As the battle for the souls of men began in this place in southern Illinois called Little Egypt, so called because of the many towns named after cities in ancient Egypt, Jones and those around him were integral parts of the coming conflict. Not sure what lay ahead, but knowing they were on the side of the Kingdom of God, they took action.

Each trip to the Wondren took less time. One hour into the ride brought them to their jumping-off point. They halted, dismounted, and left the horses tied under a bluff that provided cover and coolness. Checking their weapons, the two men walked toward the darkness. Halfway up the second hill, Jones saw ten men, all unarmed, moving cautiously in their direction. Remembering his instructions from Ephram, Jones stepped out, waved to the men, and in a calm voice said, "Over here, men. It's safe over here."

The group moved in his direction. The petition of the prayer warriors appeared to be working. Five minutes later, the total had swelled to nearly one hundred free men. The time was 11:45. Everywhere he looked, men were moving away from the Wondren. Jones sent them forward toward the stable with Justin in the lead.

77

◆◆◆◆

SONTA SUMMONED ZORAH, WHO EXPECTED THE WORST, ONLY TO FIND MORE THAN A REPRIEVE WAITING FOR HIS ARRIVAL.

"I OWE YOU AN APOLOGY," SAID SONTA. Zorah nearly passed out from exhilaration. Never would he have thought it possible for such a declaration. Of course, he didn't imagine or dream.

"I sent you and your field commanders into harm's way because I was angry and wanted to even the score. Instead, my actions caused the death of two competent officers and their entire force. That is on me as the earthlings like to say.

"We have postured a larger engagement here to draw out Ephram's quad, and the location of Arrow and his battle-tested Angelic Warriors. We are executing a false front, a sleight-of-hand if you will. Master Koal is behind this strategy, making it look to everyone as if we are going to be lambs for the slaughter once more. What we are going to do is sacrifice a few recruits and then withdraw once our intel is complete."

"I am relieved beyond words," said Zorah, "and await your commands."

"My first one will be for you to kill some of the recruits, which will draw out Ephram. The prayers of believers have lessened our power to control their minds. Do it now; the time has arrived."

It was noon.

Zorah relayed the order to Heqt, who assembled his company.

Streams of darkness flew from demonic hands. Mortals fell, wounded beyond repair. With no cover, no weapons to defend themselves, and unlike Angelic Warriors, with no supernatural protective shields, they were mere fodder.

Jones heard the screams and saw men he knew being wasted by the demonic hosts. The smell of burning flesh, cries of anguish, and instant carnage brought Jones forward.

Firing and pumping the 12 gauge furiously at the tightly compressed mass of demon bodies made aiming irrelevant. Jones loosed the double-ought buck at will. He took down demons with every shot, temporarily stopping the bloodbath and giving what few recruits remained a chance at escape.

He was not alone. At the first blast, Ephram and his quad made their move, entering the fray. Instantly, the demons began retreating, leaving the field as quickly as they came. There was no one left to fight. It was over in a flicker of time.

Jones tended to the wounded. Ephram left. Arrow never appeared. The Fallen stayed put. *This is one strange going-on*, thought Jones. The buildup had been all propaganda. There had to be a reason, and his feeling was the believers weren't going to like it.

78

——◆◆◆◆◆——

THE LITTLE GRAND CANYON, SO-CALLED BECAUSE OF A VERY SIMILAR, ALBEIT SMALLER, APPEARANCE TO ITS WESTERN BIG BROTHER, WAS A REMOTE, OUT-OF-THE-WAY BOX CANYON.

THE AREA WAS FREQUENTED REGULARLY BY HIKERS and outdoor enthusiasts able to navigate its steep trails, adverse weather conditions, isolation, and lack of communication. Located off Hickory Ridge Road, seven miles south of Murphysboro, the canyon was a regular destination for Jones and Kaz. They had found a great parking spot there with never an interruption.

The area was also home to three of the Mountain Men clan, except one wasn't a man. Dale Chambers and Mike Estle shared their wilderness retreat with all the critters who called it home and Lozen.

When the Indian woman had reached out to Jones, it

signaled trouble that was both unseen and unexpected.

"I told you before you knew that we were closing ranks with the other world. That world is evil and has come for us," Lozen said, standing in front of Dale Chambers' log cabin, which occupied a small clearing on the north rim. His view was astounding, a three-hundred-foot drop-off that ran vertical to the property and extended for nearly one mile.

"Where are they, Lozen?" asked Jones, anxiously rubbing Hunter's belly.

There had been precious little contact with the demonic intruders since the withdrawal at the Wondren. No unknowns at The Kitchen. Surveillance was nonexistent. The fires had stopped. Even the black vans had disappeared. Something was happening, and Jones needed information.

"The beasts are moving the Wondren," she said, "only at night when men sleep."

"Here?" asked Jones.

"Yes," said Lozen, sweeping her arm in a full circle. "I had felt their movement for some time now but had seen nothing until yesterday when Hunter led me to the south rim. Two acres of material, temporary structures, camouflaged tents and vehicles, and Sonta," she said.

No sooner had she uttered that name than Ephram appeared a short distance away. He walked straight to them and said, "Lozen, did you see recruits and demons or the Fallen?"

"No Fallen have arrived," said Lozen, "but I scout the Shawnee and the Canyon. It is my home and was the home of my people when they walked the Earth. My people are gone now, but they are still remembered. Their spirits remain. I sense movement all around. The Darkness is here, and their presence is growing. Their force is as yet unseen, but it has closed the distance between our worlds. Perhaps the Fallen are poised to take over the battle and are resting in the Second Heaven where Satan resides."

Jones was listening with rapt attention. So much so that he failed to see Arrow, standing a few feet behind Ephram, nod in agreement.

"Why would they move the Wondren?" asked Jones.

"It no longer serves their purpose," said Arrow, moving closer to Lozen.

"Soon we will collide," said Lozen, "and the fate of humankind will be sorely tested. I will walk the night paths with the demons. Their plan will be revealed. Stand ready."

Jones turned to speak to Ephram, but both angels had departed.

79

LOZEN LAY QUIETLY ON HER STRAW
MATTRESS IN HER CABIN AT THE
CANYON, TAKING IN THE SILENCE THAT
SURROUNDED HER SMALL ABODE.

HUNTER WAS STRETCHED OUT BETWEEN HER AND
the door, offering himself as the first line of defense.
Her love for him stemmed from that commitment and had
only grown stronger during their time together. As the light
from the morning sun broke through the branches of the old
forest growth, she stirred, receiving within her being that most
ancient of gifts, the knowing.

Somewhere in the Garden of the Gods, high up towards
Craggy Bluff, north of the little town of Herod, lived an ancient
Cherokee Seer named Dani. Her name was pronounced Dan-
yee. She was an old soul whose family ancestors had walked
the Trail of Tears, a forced migration of Cherokee, Chickasaw,
and Creek families from their lands east of the Mississippi to
Oklahoma in 1838 that resulted in more than 10,000 deaths.
The Cherokee had been forced to give up their homes by

the Jackson administration after the American government dishonored yet another treaty.

Dani was reaching out to a kindred spirit. The call was too important to dismiss. Lozen packed some supplies, mainly food and water, into her rucksack, summoned Hunter, and returned to Etherton Switch. They jumped into the old Chevy truck and took off up State Route 127 to Murphysboro. From there it was 45 miles to Harrisburg on Route 13 and 13 more miles on Route 34 to Herod, which sat at the base of the Garden.

Parking her truck at the post office, Lozen set off on foot up the 2-mile dirt and gravel road to Dani's cabin, which sat high on Craggy Bluff. The scenery was spectacular, but even in the best of conditions, it was a strenuous walk. As Lozen crested the ever-rising road, she spotted Dani moving slowly around a firepit that occupied a prominent position hard on the rock face of Craggy Bluff. Her hands were lifted towards the sky, as if calling out to some unseen yet genuine power for guidance and strength. Lozen knew to whom she called, the Lord God of the Heavens and his Son Jesus. For Dani, there was no other Lord. Like Lozen, she walked the walk. As the old Indian lady danced, Lozen noticed Awahili, a giant Bald Eagle and great sacred bird of the Cherokee, flying high overhead, gradually descending in a graceful series of concentric rings.

Out in the distance, Lozen could see Camel Rock, perhaps the most famous landmark in this pristine wilderness. As she fixed her attention on the camel's hump, the air around her began to quiver and dissipate. There was no mistaking that feeling, but before Lozen could so much as call upon her Lord, she saw Awahili dive at tremendous speed, shrieking the most haunting cry, straight for her position on the roadbed.

At that very instant, Zorah, having stayed vigilant in his hunt for the Prescient, and watching as she left Etherton Switch for the old Indian's home on Craggy Bluff, broke through the alternate dimension at warp speed, attempting to hook Lozen with his fully extended razor-sharp talons. He would have succeeded had not the giant bird, whose wingspread nearly matched those of the beast, crashed headlong into the Fallen Angel, propelling him off the ground onto his back, wings flailing as the beast sought to maintain balance. The eagle separated just as Dani implored her God to intervene. That happened in an instant.

A bolt of lightning emanated from the right hand of Soldier, who appeared from nowhere, striking Zorah's left wing. A foul curse filled the air as the demon shot back a powerful wave of dark matter that blew Soldier over the edge of Craggy Bluff. Dani asked for more. More came in the person of Arrow.

Zorah, shaken by the blow from Awahili, had suffered a significant strike from Soldier's bolt. Arrow's appearance cemented the deal. Realizing who just arrived, Zorah transported instantly, deciding life was preferable to death. He would live to fight another day.

Lozen rushed to Dani, embracing her tightly.

"Thank you for calling out," she said. No more words were necessary.

Soldier came into view, scaling the cliff edge and joining Arrow, who stood near Lozen and Dani, looking calm as always.

"Close call, Lozen," Arrow said. "You must be aware by now that they are trying to rid themselves of your prescience. They would have killed the old lady too, had Soldier not intervened."

"Yes, they would have," said Lozen.

"They would have had to kill Awahili," said Dani.

"I'm not so sure they could have," said Soldier, speaking for the first time. "The bird is sacred to your tribe; the Father might have reached out his hand."

"Are you able to proceed, Soldier?" asked Arrow.

"Yes, I will be fine," replied Soldier, flexing.

"We are at your request," said Arrow. They both left immediately.

Dani and Lozen sat down around the firepit. The old lady gave Hunter a gnaw bone, which he set upon with great vigor.

"The Darkness has come to Earth," said Dani.

"Yes, it follows the affairs of men," replied Lozen.

"Evil seeks to alter the course of human events before the clock ticks zero," said Dani.

"Your task is mighty, Lozen, and filled with peril. Keep the Lord close, and all things are possible. I wanted to inform you of my vision, but it is evident you have already had your own."

Lozen nodded her acceptance.

The two women hugged and exchanged small smiles. Tomorrow would be what it would become. For them, they would continue the walk.

80

————◆◆◆◆◆————

SONTA WAS A VERY
BUSY DEMONIC ANGEL

AFTER LISTENING CAREFULLY TO ZORAH'S RETELLING of the encounter at the Garden of the Gods, he got busy mapping out the Little Grand Canyon terrain to allow for the transportation of recruits and material. It proved to be quite a task given the road conditions. There was little traffic at night, which greatly facilitated the relocation. The south rim was closer to the Wondren and more accessible to supply than the northern side. Both were planned points of entry for the Fallen Angels to cross from their dimension.

"We will go after the Mountain Men first," said Sonta, grinning as though pleased with himself. "They are west of the north rim, far enough away to make detection difficult. If they get too close, we will eliminate them. The woman has a log cabin at Cedar Gorge, inside the south rim. The fight will be on top of her before she can react."

"The Angelic Warriors will never permit it," said Zorah.

"No, they won't," replied Sonta, "but there is no human army available to the locals, so when our recruits and fledgling demons appear Ephram will have to intervene. At that moment we will bring over our first wave, coming in behind Ephram and his quad, pinning them on the south rim. Arrow will back them up at the very moment we open our dimension and flood the battle scene with our most seasoned warriors, who will enter from the north. The first wave will turn on Arrow while our second wipes out the quad and proceeds to overpower Arrow. Our troops will have a numerical and strategic advantage. It will be a humbling defeat for the Angelic Warriors."

81

———◆◆◆◆◆———

ARROW SAUNTERED ALONG THE SHORELINE THAT FRONTED AREA 17. BREAKS IN THE ACTION WERE HARD TO MANUFACTURE.

EVIL SELDOM RESTED, AT LEAST NOT IN THIS PLACE. Opportunities to minister and encourage one another were few and far between. The incursions of darkness were becoming more frequent and intense, leaving the Angelic Warriors less time to recoup. Injuries were an accepted part of their immortal lives. They lived to serve. As the end-time had grown closer, the battles blurred into a seamless stream of conflict. Arrow recalled Matthew 24:6, which says: "And you will hear of wars and rumors of wars. See that you are not troubled, this must take place, but the end is not yet."

Arrow found a peaceful grassy knoll with a clear view of the water and began to organize mentally the myriad number of assignments he was managing. Foremost among those was Jones O'Brian. Jones had migrated during his watch from being a Doubting Thomas to a man who was fighting through his uncertainty. He wasn't there yet, but progress was moving in the right direction. Jones' discovery of his love for Abby had helped him get his mind refocused on positives. He was still unsure of God's intentions for mankind, but Arrow had confidence his questions would be answered in the affirmative.

Without warning, Arrow heard his Warriors shouting at the top of their lungs. Walking back toward the encampment, he saw the source of their excitement, a messenger named Andreas, who had traveled from the Heavenly Realm. Arrow and Andreas had met several times over the centuries, but their last encounter was distant in Arrow's mind.

"My friend Andreas, what brings you to our gathering?" asked Arrow, knowing full well that he was being summoned.

"Michael has called for you," said Andreas. "He has pushed all matters aside to spend time with you."

Instantly, the two angelic beings stepped into a portal. Passing through the Second Heaven, they arrived at the Heavenly Court, where the twenty-four elders resided alongside the four living creatures with six eyes.

Michael had been in continuous battle mode since the day Lucifer and one-third of the angels were cast out of Heaven. Standing near the heavenly choir as Arrow approached, Michael turned to look at Arrow, tears of joy falling from his eyes.

"I never tire of hearing the constant praise to our Creator," he said.

"Nor do I," responded Arrow.

"But to the point," Michael began. "I understand our enemy has employed new tactics recently, fighting in daylight."

"Merely a diversion, or at best an error in judgment," said Arrow.

"Perhaps it was desperation in action," said Michael, "but that has never been one of Koal's calling cards."

"All signs point to Sonta, one of Koal's second in command, bearing sole responsibility for this action," said Arrow.

"Knowing Commander Koal as we do, having faced him

many times in the past, I would be inclined to believe there is a bigger plan in the works. Watch him closely, as he gets great joy from the destruction he conceives. Now, tell me about this Jones O'Brian you are protecting. What is so special about him?"

"As I am sure you will recall," said Arrow, "you sent me to comfort him as his wife was succumbing to the attacks against her health and ministry for the unborn. He struggles even now with his loss. His faith in God wavers occasionally, but the man has a beautiful heart. He wants to help others."

"For the eyes of the Lord run to and fro throughout the whole Earth, to show Himself strong on behalf of those whose heart is loyal to him, so sayeth the word in Second Chronicles, chapter sixteen, verse nine," said Michael.

"Jones must realize humankind is under attack by The Darkness, although he can not possibly grasp the scope of the conflict," Michael observed

"I believe he does," said Arrow. "He has fought in a significant Earth war, in a place called Afghanistan. He killed people there, soldiers," said Arrow.

"Yes, I am aware," said Michael.

Taking a step back toward the Heavenly Choir, Michael paused and turned back to Arrow. "One more thing, I have heard that Koal is paying unusual attention to this conflict his demons have started in southern Illinois. It is just a field test. Be ready to face him once again on the battlefield. He is a mighty Fallen Angel, barely lessor to Satan himself, and he will not go quietly. My guess is this confrontation could be the precursor to a global war. The Fallen know there is no going back. Hell will open its gates for them at the Rapture's first moment. They can only have one strategy. Every believer must die or be turned; then there can be no Rapture. I see battles coming between the angels. It will be a dark time, but we must prevail. We must save every believer possible and all mortals who have no possibility of defending themselves against this evil. Even though our God will resurrect them and make them whole, losing them now is not our path forward. I have alerted our other commanders to provide you any support that might be required. All you need to do is ask. The Dread Warriors and I stand ready at your call."

Michael turned then to look once again upon the Heavenly Choir. Arrow nodded to Andreas, acknowledging his dismissal. Taking one step back, he reentered the portal and rejoined his Warriors.

82

——◆◆◆◆◆——

LOZEN WORKED HER WAY SLOWLY UNDERNEATH A ROCKY ESCARPMENT JUTTING OUT OVER THE SOUTH SIDE OF THE LITTLE GRAND CANYON.

HER CONSTANT COMPANION HUNTER FOLLOWED behind, continuously raising his nose to the Heavens, probing for any tell-tale scent of the beasts that were quietly moving above her position among the rocks.

For the past two days, the Mountain Men had surveilled the canyon rim with all the stealth learned from long-range recons in distant lands much more unfamiliar than the canyon terrain. What they saw was alarming. The demonic force had arrived. Their presence was growing daily on opposite ends of the canyon as men and material were transported by trucks to access points on Hickory Ridge Road that runs along the east side of the canyon, then reloaded and carried to assigned locations.

Located in the western part of the Shawnee National Forest, over 415 square miles of old-growth timber extending from the Ohio River on the east to the Mississippi on the west, the Little Grand Canyon sits on the east bank of the Big Muddy River with Turkey Bayou fronting its western boundary. The Canyon is an isolated area of 1,090 acres with a circumference of more than five miles and vertical drops exceeding three hundred feet. Traveling at night, as Lozen, Hunter, and the Mountain Men did, required expertise not easily acquired. It was highly unrecommended for all novices.

Lozen had left her home at Cedar Grove just before midnight, joining up with Mike and Dale near Swallow Rock, not too distant from their cabins on the north side of the rim. The trio had spread out with Lozen working her way back south while the other two men went north and west. They planned to meet up at daybreak near Lozen's cabin, compare notes, and pass on their intel to Jones. Phone calls were too risky; hand delivery was foolproof.

Just after midnight, as Lozen ascended a series of slippery sandstone steps, constructed during the Depression of 1933 by the Civilian Conservation Corp, Hunter growled menacingly. The Three Sisters Waterfall roared as its cargo descended to the canyon floor. Only the most acute hearing would have heard the displaced air caused by Zorah as he flew overhead, landing on the Bluff and surveying the area where Lozen and Hunter had frozen. There was no more exceptional night vision than that of the Fallen. The night was their refuge. After what seemed to be an eternity, the beast rose up and flew west, where men moving like ants dotted the western rim.

Lozen stayed crouched with her hand on Hunter's back when suddenly her senses overloaded. He was here. Before she could so much as move, something hit the rock face near her head with such force that centuries-old sandstone crumbled under the impact. Looking into the darkness, she saw the beast, standing in the air, throwing what seemed to be a mountain of pure darkness in her direction.

"Help me," the words barely came out of her mouth when a thunderous bolt of pure energy screamed by her head and struck the demon, shredding his right wing. Still yet, the creature, whose hideous appearance Lozen would never forget, began to fly toward her, crippled but not stopped. Another bolt of light hit the monster, who emitted a blood-curdling scream while unleashing his own wave of darkness, which found its mark.

Soldier grunted with pain as the force of the blow spun him around, knocking him to the ground, blowing part of his right ear entirely off. Before Zorah could do further damage, two members of the quad appeared, pounding lightning bolts at his location. Outnumbered, Zorah was forced once again to leave the girl for another day, even though she was a danger to them all and must be eliminated. Her prescient abilities could not be tolerated. He moved immediately into an alternate dimension.

Lozen and Hunter climbed up the slippery slope and soon stood face to face with Soldier.

Lozen was spellbound, seeing him once again. There were no words that could express what she was feeling.

"Thank you for saving Hunter and me," she said.

"All you had to do was ask," said Soldier, whose ear had already begun to regenerate.

"As Arrow told you before, it is clear the demons want to rid themselves of your presence. Use your gift to know when they approach. Call us silently. It will be good hunting. The next time we will all be here."

With that, he and his two companions vanished.

Lozen moved to her rendezvous point, and soon after Jones was made aware that the Wondren was moving. The attack plans had indeed changed.

83

-◆◆◆◆-

ZORAH BRIEFED
SONTA ON HIS ENCOUNTER
WITH THE APACHE WOMAN.

HAD HER READY TO SNATCH UP AND BRING TO YOU, Master. An angel intervened, and I was once again forced to abandon my quarry. She will not be so lucky next time."

"That means they are here with us," said Sonta, changing as he spoke.

"I must get this information of yours to Master Koal," he said, entering the alternate dimension and disappearing only to reappear in Chicago at Koal's command headquarters.

Since his presence had not been requested, Sonta couldn't transport directly to Koal's suite. Changing as he landed, he took the elevator, and after passing security was ushered into Koal's office.

"This must be special," Koal said, entering the room from behind Sonta, "to arrive without an invitation." At that point, he became himself. Sonta shuddered.

Looking at the oozing Fallen Angel, Sonta said, "Master, Zorah uncovered the Apache girl and perhaps others spying on our operations. We no longer have secrecy as an ally."

"It was bound to happen," said Koal, "and now it has. Do our plans proceed well?"

"Yes," said Sonta, "our portal is in place. The entry points are established."

"Good," Koal replied, "now let's set the trap and bait them into coming."

"And what would that be, Master?" Sonta asked.

"You will know soon enough," Koal replied. "I must take a trip of my own now to make sure our plans have the backing of the high council."

Sonta had never addressed Satan directly. He was not at that level, although he wished for it to happen, more than anything. Koal was his conduit without which all was lost. Satan was not easy to please. Koal, on the other hand, felt just as uneasy about addressing the council.

The trip to Second Heaven was uneventful. The council was waiting for him.

"State your case, Commander," Satan said, "but understand that we have been paying close attention to your progress, or lack of it, and are concerned. The end-times are coming and with them comes the Rapture. We have many souls to turn, or a fiery fate awaits us all. Do I make myself clear?"

"Yes, Your Grace," said Koal, "that is why I am here, to suggest a change in tactics that might encourage our side and produce tangible results."

"Go on," said Satan, looking left and right at the Council.

"If we must kill or turn all the believers before the Rapture, or be thrown into the pit, the stakes have to be raised. The believers attend their churches, even though unbelievers sit among them. I propose we kill them all. This action will throw humans into a panic. An overall coordinated attack will not only sow confusion but also eliminate hundreds of millions of believers. The slaughter has to be conducted on a random basis, or we will risk a plea for help like no other. We Fallen are only one-third of the angelic force and are outnumbered and outgunned. Stealth must be our weapon. Secrecy is absolute. Should this plan be revealed during the planning, well, I don't need to say more."

"We will need misdirection," said Satan. "To accomplish this massive initiative will require an appropriate cover."

The council nodded in affirmation.

"Destroy another church. Let's see how they react. The angels covered up our last one to stifle the public outcry before it started. I wonder how many they think they can cover up before the public loses faith, maybe stops going, maybe turns away from the Creator. Look what the terrorists have done. Killing and leaving the bodies for discovery will make bombings seem like child's play."

84

-◆◆◆◆◆-

IF SATAN HIMSELF GOES DISGUISED AS AN ANGEL OF LIGHT, THERE IS NO NEED TO BE SURPRISED WHEN HIS SERVANTS, TOO, DISGUISE THEMSELVES AS THE SERVANTS OF RIGHTEOUSNESS.

2 CORINTHIANS 11:14-15

JONES COULD SEE THE STAKES BEING ELEVATED AS he moved around his small town. People were edgy. Some of the captives were home again, worse for the wear. Sheriff Cable spent most days putting out fires, of the human sort. The prayer chains were in nonstop action, but things on the surface were relatively quiet, which made some of the believers wonder if the enemy was defeated.

They were not.

On a quiet Sunday evening, just before dusk, in a little town called Alto Pass, deep in southern Illinois, thirty-two General Missionary Worship Center attendees were gathered together to worship the Lord their God. Fundamentalists to the core, they were small in numbers but mighty in belief. They had no sooner occupied their pews than thirteen of the Fallen came through a portal of their alternative dimension and took no prisoners.

Streams of dark energy flew forward in such powerful bursts that the bodies of the faithful exploded like firecrackers on the Fourth of July. It was over so fast; there was no time to ask. Sonta, leading the dozen seasoned warriors, including Zorah, pulled the heart out of a chest that was no longer attached to its body. Holding it aloft he practically smiled with joy at the success of their latest foray. The heart was still beating when Sonta swallowed it whole.

Even though the town of Alto Pass was an out-of-the-way burg to a mere 398 residents, it was almost impossible for the folks who lived nearby not to notice the dark misty cloud that settled over the church in one moment and disappeared an instant later. A late arrival walked in a few minutes later and, seeing the carnage, threw up, recovered enough to pull out his mobile phone and text an SOS to 911. Two hours later, local, state, and federal officials increased the population by nearly 100. That number grew when national television hit the town.

Thirty-two dead people down where they fell or were blown. No poison, no weapons, no shell casings presented themselves for examination. There was no evidence except the death and dismemberment lying everywhere. There was no cause of death with which authorities had a working familiarity.

News of the massacre went viral. PBS sent Judy Woodruff and ran a special the very next evening. All the major news agencies had their version of events. The Governor of the great State of Illinois choppered in the day after to hold a press conference. Swearing to find those accountable for the tragedy gave him a day's reprieve from the scandals of his administration.

Koal was pleased that Sonta had been so efficient and told him to plan on a repeat performance.

Jones reeled under the weight of knowing who was responsible. It could only have been the Fallen. Demons and recruits could not have executed such a plan so efficiently.

"We have to inform the public of the escalation," he told Ephram. "But is anyone going to believe we are under an assault from Satan's Dark Minions?"

"Even if they do, we still cannot intervene unless asked," replied the angel. Securing a request of such magnitude, one at a time, presented a severe problem.

85

-◆◆◆◆-

JONES HUGGED ABBY
AND HELD HER LIKE A PRECIOUS
COMMODITY.

ABBY SQUEEZED HER ARMS AROUND HIM AS HARD
as possible and kissed him as if it would be her last. Coming
events could lead to that reality, and she knew it. Whenever
the conflict resumed in their part of the world, Jones would be
front and center, and these Fallen were the most dangerous of all
enemies. They could not be stopped by mortal men operating in
the absence of prayer. The prayer chain was a rogue wave over all
evil currents, a deterrent to the most powerful of the Fallen, Satan
himself. Prayer ruled; without it, there would be no solution.
How to achieve total coverage was the question that had to be
answered. As dangerous as the situation was for the believers, it
was equally, if not more so, for the nonbelievers. They had no
coverage and were absolutely in the crosshairs. To the Fallen, they
had no value.

"If I lose you, Ab," said Jones, "know that you are truly loved."

"That's not going to happen," Abby replied, kissing him again.

"I had to lose my faith to get it back," said Jones. "The water was so deep around me I told myself I would never love again, I believed the angels had their agenda, granting dispensation when we asked for what they had in mind."

"I am so glad you came around," said Abby.

"Maybe God allows humans to pray because it does them good, not because the prayers are going to be answered," he said.

"That's hypocrisy," said Abby.

"Yeah," said Jones, " I have seen the prayers of our friends stop evil personified, so I know it works, but I still think God decides when it works."

86

KOAL PACED BACK AND FORTH,
OCCASIONALLY STOPPING
TO LOOK OUT THE WINDOW
FRONTING LAKE MICHIGAN.

THE SCENE ON THE GROUND FAIRLY BUSTLED WITH pedestrians intent on achieving some destination known only to them, in as little time as possible. Life far below was in a constant state of hurry. It was Easter season, a sacred time to the Christians. There had to be something he could do to further their confusion and desperation at the life they were living. It needed to be tied to their faith. His mind was a blank slate. He had nothing.

His attention was diverted to a homeless man, pushing a grocery cart full of lost and found. A handmade sign rose above the junk, proudly announcing, "Kneel before the Cross of Jesus." Another sign, seeking equal billing, said, "Jesus Saves." That was all it took. Koal sent for Sonta, who arrived post-haste, transporting directly to his office.

"Sonta, that church congregation you destroyed, wasn't it in a little town called Alto Pass?"

"Yes, Master, I had a most delicious meal there." They both laughed.

"How would you like to schedule a return engagement tomorrow, Easter Sunday?"

"For what reason?" asked Sonta, worry crossing his brow. "Did I miss something, was my mission incomplete?"

"No," said Koal, "I just remembered seeing, when we were planning your church visit, a giant cross nearby. The faithful flock there every Easter by the thousands. It has a name." Sonta watched as Koal went to a pile of maps strewn across the conference table and pulled one out. "Bald Knob Cross. There is a sunrise worship service there tomorrow. We could drop the Fallen in on the faithful just before dawn, which would make that extraordinary day live in infamy."

Sonta was fully engaged. Such an opportunity seldom occurred at the right time. There was always a conflict of interest. Killing that many believers at one time would energize their flock, not the Christians. Their angels could use the same portal they opened for the church. It was another escalation that would prove to any believer that there was no real safety net.

Koal sought approval, which was immediately granted by the high council. There was no more profane time than the Rising, as it was known.

87

◆◆◆◆◆

THE PARALLEL DIMENSION SHUDDERED AND CONVULSED AS TIME FOLDED UPON ITSELF.

A LARGE NUMBER OF SATAN'S FALLEN ANGELS MOVED silently and with purpose from their home in Second Heaven. Comprising a portion of the one-third of all the heavenly host, these warriors were only slightly less potent than their angelic enemies. Over the eons, they won many battles and incapacitated Angelic Warriors beyond count. The dark wave was not insignificant. Reversals had increased when the philosophy of whatever it took became the celestial standard.

Lozen, standing in an open field filled with wildflowers, felt the disturbance caused by the Fallen as they transported on their way south. She and Hunter had left before dawn to check on the thriving bee colonies making a comeback from near extinction. Their numbers had decreased dramatically over the past decade due to the overuse of pesticides.

Without hesitation, she said, "Help, please come."

Before the words had scarcely left her lips, Soldier, one of Ephram's quad lieutenants, stood next to her. Hunter did not bark or growl.

"The Fallen just passed over," said Lozen, "going south. The church was south. Alto Pass is south."

"I will alert Ephram and Arrow," he said. "Are you able to tell how many? Was it a significant passing?"

"Yes, many," said Lozen.

Soldier took his leave and rendezvoused with Ephram.

"She said they went south."

"It could be anywhere," said Ephram, "maybe another church, a gathering for Easter."

The light went on, and Ephram summoned Arrow.

"I could be very wrong," said Ephram, "but isn't there a huge gathering at Bald Knob Cross to celebrate our Savior's victory over death this morning? It will be dawn soon."

"We have not been asked," said Arrow. "Even if you are right, we cannot intervene until someone asks."

"Let's move the quad and your Warriors just in case someone does," said Ephram.

Someone did, although the request was made with no inkling of what lay in store.

Bernice Hartman, an elderly lady who had attended every Easter sunrise service since the cross was constructed in 1963, insisted on walking from her nephew's apple and peach farm, located just off an abandoned dirt road near Hutchins Creek. The same spring that grew the luscious fruit was widely considered the purest water in that part of the state.

Bernice, after a thirty-minute hike up the steep road, while dodging the heavy traffic on their way to the cross, was getting short of breath and had more than one mile left on her pilgrimage. Out of her mouth came the words, "Lord, many of us on this journey today are older than we were. Look out for us, Lord, and hold us near that we may worship in your presence."

That got the job done.

In the near darkness, just before dawn, a full company of the Fallen slipped through the portal in the cover of darkness and surrounded nearly three thousand of the faithful whose plans did not include gruesome deaths. Before they could unleash so much as one dark wave, Ephram's quad hit their left flank, crumpling the Fallen like so much paper-mache. As the other Fallen wheeled to address the threat and protect their own, Arrow's Angelic Warriors descended on them from three sides, effectively cutting off their retreat. For what seemed like hours, but in reality was only minutes, the two enemies fought for their lives. The mortal worshippers were an afterthought.

Sonta watched as Arrow blew a hole through Zorah that ripped his torso entirely in two. Other old evil souls died that day.

More than one dozen Warriors were so severely wounded by the dark waves that crashed into their bodies that they might never fight again. Only an immortal could live through such injuries.

Without warning, the Fallen that still lived exited to an alternate dimension and left the battle. Mortals who had witnessed the lightning and darkness did their best to leave Bald Knob under self-propulsion. Most succeeded, some did not. No one would ever forget what happened on that early morning in rural Union County when Heaven and Hell collided.

The Fallen had lost nearly a third of their number at Bald Knob. Moving to an assembly area near the Little Grand Canyon, Sonta heard the sound before he saw the reinforcements. Koal, accompanied by thousands of Fallen, settled into resting positions just outside the portal. They were there to fight.

Ephram and Arrow, following the Fallen, ran directly into the massive army of Fallen Angels spewing from the portal. Before they could adjust, the whole south rim exploded into chaos. Several Angelic Warriors, seriously outmanned, were shredded by streaming darkness. The sky lost its light as evil commanded the battle. Arrow and his loyal troops fell back, fighting with every tool at their disposal. Lightning bolts blew away an uncountable number of Fallen, and still, they pressed forward.

Suddenly, the sound of a Shofar pierced the air. It was an unwelcome sound to all the Fallen, who immediately felt the strength and power of Michael, who had come to Arrow's aid with Dread Warriors by his side. The light from the very throne room of God preceded Michael's arrival and brought confusion into the Fallen's ranks.

Lightning streaming from his hands like no other before him, Michael tore into the center guard of the Fallen, separating them from one another, which meant certain death. The Dread Warriors, seasoned since the dawn of time, ripped into the Fallen with all their might, taking them apart, one at a time.

Thousands of the Fallen died that day all because of a prayer lifted to the Heavens by an elderly lady willing to walk farther than her body could take her. The power of prayer had overcome evil. Humanity was the winner.

Lozen and the two Mountain Men watched their part of the world take on a glow brighter than any sun. The clashing immortals filled the air with light and darkness the likes of which they had never seen. The battle for humankind was no longer imagined. The stakes had become more significant than life itself, and for the Fallen, there would be no holding back if they were to survive.

88

JONES AND ABBY
NEEDED EACH OTHER
AND COMMITTED
THEMSELVES
TO FINDING THEIR
WAY WITH LOVE.

THE LOCAL FOLKS DECIDED TO FOLLOW THE ADVICE of the angels. When in doubt, ask. The conflict was spreading. Even though there had been a victory of sorts at Bald Knob, the ensuing battle at the Little Grand Canyon had revealed the power of the Fallen Angels and what it took to stop them, momentarily. They were coming for the believers and anyone else who got in the way.

The Fallen were real to Jones and the small community of people who had lived to tell about it. It was up to them to get the word out as quickly as possible. Jones wanted to believe there would be a Rapture. He was sure if the Fallen had their way that would not be the case.